Titrate to Effect:

A NURSE'S STORY OF LIFE & LOVE IN THE PRESENCE OF LIFE & DEATH

Anna Fares

Cover Artwork by Alison Coté

Publisher's Note: This is a work of fiction. Names, characters, places, and incidents are a product of the author's imagination. Locales and public names are sometimes used for atmospheric purposes. Any resemblance to actual people, living or dead, or to businesses, companies, events, institutions, or locales is completely coincidental.

Titrate to Effect: A Nurse' Story of Life & Love in the Presence of Life & Death/ Anna Fares. -- 1st ed.
ISBN 978-1-350122-0-9

For Ali, Aaron, Matt, and Lilly. Thank you all for being the loves of my life and my biggest support. Megan, Kelly, Sidia, and Shauna, you will forever be my sisters from other misters. Thank you, Clayton Cowles for helping get me to the finish line. Thanks, Alison for giving my book such a lovely face. I love you guys.

*Author's note: the characters in this book are fictional and in no way representative of real people or situations the author has encountered in clinical practice.

CHAPTER ONE

The Ending

God knows I wanted to put a pillow over the back of the defibrillator to muffle the incessant *beep, beep, beep*. Or at the very least, lower the volume of the alarms, so the entire unit doesn't have to listen to *beep, beep, beep,* all night long. This was, after all, *my* patient, and this was *my* fresh heart, but Bernice was charging tonight, and far be it from me to ever dream of getting between Bernice and any patient on the unit, including my own. So, Bernice had her thumb on the button, and her gaze affixed to the monitor.

We ICU nurses are nothing at all if not territorial, so this posturing act of another nurse being in *my* room, guarding *my* patient like a lioness guards her kill, would otherwise grind my gears, were that lioness anyone but Ms. Bernice.

It's July, and a fresh crop of corn-fed, bouncing baby residents were just haphazardly flung out the gates of med school a handful of weeks prior, and they had now descended upon our sterile, mercurial little unit. These pawing, doe-eyed, vacant-minded children were *touching* our stuff. Worse yet, they were *touching* our fragile-as-spun-sugar patients, when they knew nothing, *nothing* of the intricacies or finesse of cardiovascular intensive care. Not at this point in their career anyway.

I wasn't always this possessive, this parochial. I was the farthest thing from the fretful, idiosyncratic, obsessive compulsive fretter this place had made me out to be. I was an ED nurse (Emergency Department for the uninitiated). I was, at one point in my career, the exact antithesis of this breed.

ED nurses are the pulsating, unwashed masses, the hooligans, the pillaging Vikings of the nursing world. Our lot is a veritable rag-tag Island of Misfit Toys. The discounted, discredited, forever-scapegoated, redheaded stepchildren of every floor, PCU, OR, and ICU within the hospital system. No one takes pity upon us or defends us or our asinine nurse-to-patient ratios, or the unending, undiagnosed, clamor of humanity tearing up our waiting room. And we wouldn't have it any other way. I'll explain why in a minute, but first this fucking *beeping*....

*

On July the second, Mr. Johnson was two hours S/P AVR/MVR/CABG x4, LIMA to LAD, RIMA to RCA, SVG to OM and diag (bear with me, I didn't know what any of that shit meant when I started either, just go with it).

For clarity's sake, I'll paraphrase: Mr. Johnson had the misfortune of being two hours post-op following major open heart surgery on July the second, the *day after* two newly minted cardiac surgery residents and an anesthesiology resident walked through the hospital doors for the very first time as full-fledged MDs.

Little do these optimistic gems of human ambition know, their first day on the job would include one very sick heart, and a generous handful of salt encrusted ICU nurses, standing poised and at the ready to dampen that enthusiasm down to an imperceptibly low murmur.

In the case of Mr. Johnson, the old adage goes, *no one dies in the OR*, which, though intrepid, is very misleading. Read, *no one is declared dead in the OR*. Mr. Johnson clearly died in the OR. He was just riding an epi wave until the resident could get back up to the room to phone his upper level and tell him *those epi and neo bumps on the trip upstairs are wearing off. He's too acidotic for his drips to even be effective.*

We'll either need to take him back down to the OR and reopen, or we'll have to start him on ECMO at the bedside.

So here I am, crunching q5 minute vitals, with hemodynamic numbers resembling the countdown to the Times Square ball drop, while Bernice lies in wait, her thick thumb hovering precariously over the *charge* button on the defib just *waiting* for Mr. Johnson to code, and, me again, furiously stripping clots from any number of Mr. J's five chest tubes, while this newborn resident, the alleged Dr. Omar, (but let's just call him Baby Doc for transparency), Baby Doc, dances around outside the door. It's a scene evocative of an Ovidian Renaissance fresco. Each player poised to do their God-ordained task, eyes maybe lifted ever so slightly heavenward, the fluorescent light emanating not from above, but from within, until…*skreeeeeeeee*….. Mr. J bought the big one.

"Shock him!" Baby Doc cries as I teeter up the stool to start CPR.

"You can't shock asystole," I spit through my tightened jaw as I tried to get high enough above the jammed side rail to adequately compress Mr. J's chest.

Crunch. Goes at least four of Mr. J's ribs.

At least he's got five chest tubes, 'cuz that's gonna be a flail segment before this is over, I think to myself.

"Push more Epi!" Baby Doc begs.

"We did that already. It isn't time. Plus, he's been maxed on his epi drip for hours now," snaps Ryan. Bro-Time Ryan. Always ready to take over compressions so he can flex his sinewy guns with maximum visibility. Bro-time Ryan came in the room about a minute before the red heart alarm sirened across the unit, along with about one other useful person, and seven slack-jawed gawkers.

Bernice put a fast ending to the shit show that was now churning outside my room, and kicked out all but myself, Bro-

Time, Baby, and Lincoln the respiratory therapist. In her staccato Jamaican accent, she sent the stragglers scattering with a thunderous, *if you don't need to be in here, leave. Now!* If there was any doubt, she gives a jarring flick of the seafoam green privacy curtain to emphasize that the show is definitely over.

At the two minute mark, Bro-Time Ryan swapped back in for me on CPR and began having a competition with the monitor to see how forcefully he could compress Mr. J's chest to give him a blood pressure with systolics closing in on the 200's. The crazy thing about running a code on a unit where every patient is lined to the hilt is that chest compressions become a Coney Island strong-man hammer slam, where the guys and newbies hump a chest to see who can get the highest blood pressure per compression. It's usually Ryan.

The remaining ribs and sternum I had left intact were now surely fragmented splinters floating around Mr. J's mutilated mediastinum.

Just as the chug of our well-oiled code machine is starting to gain momentum, Baby Doc's thin voice rises above the monitor squelch.

"Well, doesn't he have epicardial wires? Why haven't you guys paced him?" he says accusingly.

Silence.

I hold my breath as my eyes flit around the room over the faces of my tenured colleagues, stunned to near speechlessness by the stupidity of the statement. I didn't have the tact left in me to state the obvious in a professional enough tone, so dear Sister Bernice, fed up with the copious bullshit spilling from this resident's mouth, spun around on her pristine white clog heel and bellowed,

"If you can't shock asystole, you sure as shit can't pace it!"

Golf claps. I so longed for a crescendo of golf claps to encapsulate this moment. I needed a cacophony of golf claps to frame the exact instant Baby recognized his Ivy League medical degree didn't mean shit in this place.

There's a special place in heaven for Miss Bernice. Possibly nestled somewhere between the pendulous breasts of Mother Teresa, with her sore feet and calves being massaged tenderly by Saint Catherine, the Patron Saint of nurses.

This megalith of a woman has been a nurse for thirty-seven years. The majority of that time was spent on this unit, back when it was only a four bed corner of the SICU unobtrusively marked *Open Hearts*.

Ms. Bernice came to New York City an already seasoned nurse with eleven years of nursing experience earned back in Jamaica. She fled a physically abusive, drunk husband, and set her meager savings alight in hopes of making a better life for herself in America. While stateside, though she was happy to leave her bruises behind, her nursing career stayed behind while she bided her time taking minimum wage housekeeping positions, as she waited on her green card, and her authorization to take the NCLEX exam to obtain her U.S. nursing licensure.

In the eighteen months she waited while her paperwork languished on some pencil pusher's desk, she buffed floors and smoothed out her halting Patois sixteen hours a day, every day, between three jobs. At her lowest point, she abruptly lost her sponsor and found herself briefly homeless and haunting the streets of Flatbush, while she waited on immigration to reevaluate her visa. When she finally received approval from the board of nursing to take her NCLEX and become eligible to practice as a nurse again, she had put in more time, more grit, more blood sweat and tears, than this obstinate, entitled boy that stood before her could ever have the capacity to comprehend.

An extremely proud woman, Bernice would have never willfully told anyone of her adversity, but a few of our more senior nurses can recall a time when a much thinner version of Bernice used to collect laundry bags from our unit two decades prior. Just like the diamond never breathes word of its time spent as coal, Bernice would have never willingly given up a crumb of detail that would hint at her struggle. But let me tell you, this woman now shines.

Bernice has undoubtedly wiped up turds bigger than Baby Doc. She is not having any of his crap today. Miss Bernice's eyes flash and hold Baby's stunned attention, until the realization finally reaches it's full, exquisite potential, leading him to skulk away silently to make the agonizing call to his attending, and have them ready the OR.

Calling the attending is no joke. It is a shit sandwich with an extra side of shit. It means you fucked up. Hard. It means you couldn't come up with anything at all that could work to hold the dam until the attending could obtain his full eight hours of uninterrupted beauty sleep prior to the start of his shift. It's an admission of your own failing.

As much as I would genuinely love to relish in this small man's ultimate undoing, I sneak a glance over my shoulder, just long enough to catch him pressing his fist into his forehead with slightly too much loathing for his festering self-castigation to go unnoticed.

As an offering of a very small olive branch, I decide to call the OR for him. I slip out of the room and let the ICU train chug along seamlessly, as it does, and I reach over the desk for the receiver punching in the four digit extension I don't even have to look at to know I dialed.

"Hey Doc, you good?" I offer, as the phone rings away.

"Yes." *Clears throat.* "Yes, of course. Dr. Farouk is on his way in now, we should package him, and ready him to go to the OR."

"Already done," I say with a little flash of smile.

That's all I need. I may come off as a heartless bitch, and that may be an accurate description, but contrary to popular belief, some vestigial organ still pulsates behind the cage of my chest.

What I needed to hear Baby Doc, *ahem*, Dr. Omar, say, or at least recognize, is the notion that, *I'm scared. I don't have all the answers, and these people are real, and have lives, and families I don't want to take that from them*. That's it. Just some semblance of recognition that this shit is real as hell, and there is exactly zero margin for error. The goal is not brokenness. The goal is respect for what we do here. That's all.

As for my primary function in this little game of chess, I am here to save this patient's life, and to keep anyone from getting in the way of that goal. Despite what you may have come to believe, I'm not here to ruin anyone's day, or to suck every molecule of joy from the room, I'm here to make sure you are the best at what you do. That goes for every member of the team. From Lori, the cleaning lady, who makes sure the dust motes collecting on top of the light fixtures, never organize to the point of being able to float their way into a freshly opened fasciotomy when the doors swing open, to every last one of these nurses who live and breathe this shit day in and day out. We are here to make sure your dumbass doesn't mess up because you thought, for one split second, you could kick your feet up and have an easy shift for once.

This is hard. Its real fuckin' hard. It's an ever-turning, bloody grindstone of mass casualty that is never, ever satisfied. Despite all our shiny new technologies, our ECMOs, RVADs, LVADs, TAHs, or transplants…there is still some mystical force, omniscient, wilier than even our cleverest devices. And that…that is what this is all about.

CHAPTER TWO

The Beginning

So, who am I? Why should you care about some tired nurse bitching about her day? It seems somewhat self-indulgent to think that my story is deserving of a moment of your time. Unfortunately, I don't have a persuasive answer for you. I don't think I'm particularly interesting, or ambitious, despite being called *hero* on some rare occasion by a patient or family member, who wouldn't know a true hero if they slapped them across their face. I truly haven't done anything particularly heroic. Nothing more heroic than any of my peers that punch in and out three or more nights a week with me. I'm not anything special really, but I think what I do is pretty special. And I think the people around me are pretty special, and that our collective story might be of interest to you. If I haven't convinced you to put the book down already, I'd like to tell you about them.

First me. My name is Daniela, Dani for short, but only in rare circumstances. I am first generation born and raised here in New York City by my Dominican mother and father, who came here before I was born. Carrying all the weight and burden of my parent's hopes and dreams, and the hopes and dreams of every *abuelita, tia,* and *primo* we left behind in D.R., I was expected to succeed even before my birth.

I say I'm Catholic when asked, and the nuns at Nuestra Señora de Guadalupe would attest to the fact that I have met all the rites of being a good Catholic. From baptism, to Sunday School, first communion, to confirmation, to choking down the grit of the holy wafers, and washing them down with watered down wine every Sunday, to confessing the wrung-out version of my perceived sins to Padre Dominic every Saturday. I checked all the boxes. Unless I was at Jenni's two bedroom on Horatio St. while her parents were at work. Then I was decidedly un-Catholic. Rummaging around in her pants for that auspicious opening between her legs where I felt sane, and deliciously worshiped. That part didn't make it to the confessional. Instead, I spoke in a code that only God could understand. *Forgive me Father for I have sinned. It has been seven days since my last confession, and these are my sins. I have felt lust in my heart* (for Jenni)*, and I have disobeyed my mother* (by being with Jenni). *I have had impure thoughts* (about Jenni)*, and I have coveted* (Jenni). *Amen.* Regardless of my indulgence, or my supposed wickedness, my "punishment" was always the same. *For your penance my child, you will pray ten Hail Mary's and five Our Fathers.* I would plead for mercy, hop on my yellow hand-me-down Huffy with the tattered banana seat, and pray the Hail Mary's as I pedaled my way to Jenni's sixth story walk up, only to drink deeply of my sin once again, until my head spun and my thighs quaked. Hail Mary's were a small price to pay for a moment in the sanctuary of Jenni's heavenly eminence.

So, there it is. That's the deep dark secret, the nexus of all my muddled thoughts, suicidal ideations, anxiety, and churning inner turmoil.

My mother, Magdalena Lupe Gomez de Martinez, would die if she knew about what I did when I said I was playing soccer with Leslie, or going shopping with Molly, or staying after school with Britney to work on math. I'm not just being dramatic, I think she would actually die.

I think somewhere deep in her heart, she knew. *Lesbiana.* But throughout the years I have learned to soften my half-truths. I oil them and spoon them to her like honey. Knowing that the poison of my reality would steal all of her joy. It would take whatever light she has in her eyes for me and snuff it out forever. She would hate me. Like, actually hate me.

My Mami had worked in practically every Mexican and Dominican restaurant in the city washing dishes, bussing tables, and eventually waitressing once her English got her to the point where she could parrot out the day's specials without the patron's looking helplessly confused. She worked endlessly on three, four hours of sleep tops. Sun up to nearly sun up. She had a breakfast spot, Bailey's on 14th where she manned the drink station, pulling glass after six dollar glass of fresh squeezed orange juice. Then she ran to her lunch job on 32nd where she wrapped massive burritos for *gringos* that ate the bland, refried bean-laden monstrosities by the kilo. Finally, at dinner, she caught the A train up to Washington Heights to El Mofongo where she skated from table to table, furiously scribbling orders and running plates until one or two in the morning, only to be up at five to do it all again. She did this every day, except Sunday morning. Sundays were for us.

It was the only time I would see her in her housecoat, standing in the filtered sunlight of one of our only two windows, in front of our doll house sized gas oven cooking *mangu* and *queso frito.* She looked lovely in that kitchen. Her chestnut hair still steaming away in her heated curlers. She always cared about how she looked. I would catch her sometimes doing old Jane Fonda moves in the living room, breathing out sharply with each twist and knee lift.

She told me one day between huffing breaths, "Daniela, one day you will get a man, and no matter how much he says he loves you, he will never love that thick waist of yours."

This "man" she was always talking to me about sounds like an asshole. I was told he would never love my flat feet, or my clenched eyebrows, or my kinky hair. I was told throughout my life, that all of my efforts were to eventually allure this elusive man into my trap made of compression wear, false eyelashes, and relaxer.

"Get a good education because a man doesn't like a stupid girl." "Get a good job because a man doesn't like a broke girl." "If you can't be smart, you better be sexy, that's the only way to get a man."

Before I ever had any inkling that I may one day desire a man, I already hated him. He represented the theft of everything I ever wanted for myself. That job, that education? That was mine. These lips, these flat feet, this kinky hair you loathe so much? Also, mine. This thick waist you say will deter you? I love its protuberance. These thighs that are getting too thick for you? Well, they're not for you.

I think that was why I became so hopelessly enraptured with Jenni. She didn't ever make me feel like I owed her anything, or like I existed to give her what I had earned for myself. I felt like we enhanced each other. Like, everything she radiated reflected brightly off me. It was a deeply symbiotic relationship. I was the reflective moon to her the brilliant sun. I would turn myself toward her and let her light magnify off my surface. I was fully convinced that her radiance controlled the pushing and pulling of tides, the drawing out one's most carnal instincts, calling the creatures of the sea to and from shore to mate and drop their eggs, and that my eclipsing, waxing, and waning were based solely on my proximity to her.

I met Jenni when we were just in high school. We were typical, oblivious girls. Completely engrossed in sports, and popular music, and the latest sneaker craze. In that flow of change driven by the tidal wave of hormones that had washed our child bodies downstream, we almost failed to notice that we had turned into women in front of each other. Soon, those changes became too much to hide under a hand-me-down faded pink Jem sweatshirt. Breasts swelled and ripened beneath the pilled fabric. The mystery of bras and practical, unadorned, modestly cut underwear, became a new reality forced upon us by our mothers who were anxiously plotting and anticipating "the change." Forcing torturously underwired bras, deodorant, and inexplicably thick, uncomfortable maxi pads on us with only a veiled explanation of what it all means.

The cultural differences between us magnified in the explanations we received. I am Latina. *Dominicana*, which is its own special breed. Femininity is revered, celebrated, put on display. All that booty and rapturous glow of femaleness is heightened, exacerbated, pulled and stretched with pushup bras, potions, lotions, sky high heels, everything and anything to reach peak estrogen-oozing womanhood as lushly and vibrantly as possible. Our words, our passions, our mannerisms, movements, dances, walks, smiles, turns, everything is done in a way that sets our femininity in its best light. For me, being not exactly a tomboy, but not exactly peak *Dominicana* was a netherworld of not-quite-rightness. It was like shrinking. I was clinging to the last foothold on the ledge of innocence that I could grasp by my fingertips, before entering a careening free fall, only to be snatched up and set on an elevated turning pedestal in a frothy pink *quinceañera* dress to herald to the world that, *this one's ripe!* It was a wholly mortifying and deeply traumatizing experience.

Jenni had an entirely different set of flaming hoops to traverse than I had to endure in my noisy clamor to womanhood. For starters, just so we're clear, Jenni was her "white name." To her kinsman, and for those times when she and I were breathing the same humid breaths, melding together in our most sacred and cherished encounters, she was Jaanvi.

In Hindi Jaanvi means *as precious as your life*, and I can think of no more accurate or fitting moniker. For those times when we were untangled from one another, when aunties, and walls had eyes and ears that were fixed upon us, she was just Jenni, and no more mine than the gawking panhandler catcalling her on 7th Avenue. For her, puberty was a much more reverent and restrained time. In her house, it was a time of nervous anticipation, but overall, it was a quietly and privately welcomed blossoming of potential energy.

Jenni was your typical Desi girl on the outside. Born in America to quasi-successful Indian parents, who came to the States to give their lotus-born perfect baby girl the life of opportunity they could only dream for her back home in Maharashtra.

She was expected to be in this Western world, but not of it, and she walked the

tightrope of that ether with exquisite balance. Her complexity, her intricacy, was a tapestry woven from silks, and spices, and colors, and patterns that were wholly separate, sacrosanct, and intermingled with thousands of eons more history, mysticism, and magic than my Western profundity could contain. She was an enigma, a cipher, an oracle to me.

There were times when I would reach for her and she would inexplicably vaporize, like mist passing through my fingers. Although I watched her process of becoming a woman from the corner, there were parts of its metamorphosis that remained in shadow to me. As close as I would draw to her, as much as I tried to absorb her into myself, she simply would not go to the depth that I sought to drown her. It was as if she had this invisible, semipermeable membrane surrounding her being, and bits and pieces of herself would pass through me until I could taste them on my tongue, but never fully break them down and metabolize them within myself to incorporate them into my being.

Jenni and I had a cosmic story of our meeting (she would say it was karmic). We have the same birthday. Literally down to the day, the hour, the minute, maybe even the same second. I like to believe so anyway. They don't often document seconds in a birth record, but I imagine it to be so.

We were both born at St. Vincent's Hospital in Greenwich Village, nine years before it closed its doors for good. Our mothers labored feverishly in the L&D ward just a few doors down from each other. Once we were both smacked on the ass, confirmed to have ten fingers and toes, and scrubbed down of our afterbirth, we were set side by side on display in our plexiglass bassinettes in the fishbowl of the newborn unit. Two brown roly poly bundles of joy, consummated in a foreign land, by two couples born worlds apart. The fruits of their loins cooing and squirming away in tiny, white burrito swaddling, just inches away from one another.

From outside the glass window, a distinguished, slender Indian gentleman beamed down at his prize silently, taking in the thick crop of glossy, vernixed hair that covered her head, and shoulders and back, and her nearly translucent supple skin, and those grasping, hungry fists.

Arbad Vadabhaat was the proprietor of a small silk-screening business located in the Meatpacking District. His office hand screened hundreds of canvas tote bags, S, M, and L cotton T-shirts, and anything else a buyer requested to have ink laid to cloth upon. His business turned a modest profit with the last seven years landing them solidly in the black. No small feat for a freshly naturalized, new American, arriving here with little more than the savings he had squirreled away after two and a half decades working under his father back home in India, and the substantial-to-him inheritance left by his father's estate when he ultimately succumbed to a torturous battle with lung cancer. The family business stayed with his brother Vijay a world away, and Arbad took his portion of the inheritance, and his new bride, and headed West, to an exciting and terrifying life in The Big Apple. The storefront he ultimately willed into being was located not far from our own crowded little 15th Street apartment.

When my parents arrived from D.R. with my two older sisters in tow, my father spoke minimal English, and though he had training as a mechanic back home, he quickly realized his life's work was rendered meaningless without a formal education from a mechanics school that is accredited to grant licensure. Just the trip over had nearly wiped out my parent's meager savings. To delay a paycheck by even another two weeks would mean certain doom for our little family.

My father was a proud man, and the grating reality of his lack of marketable skill was no doubt a slap in the face, but his impending failure, and ultimate return trip back home empty handed was a fate he refused to accept. So, my father did what any hardworking expat in this country does, he applied for work anywhere and everywhere, accepting any meager recompense anyone was able to extend to him. It was Arbad Vadabhaat that had the pleasure of lowballing my Papi with an offer of three dollars and thirty-five cents per hour. *"Absolutely no overtime, no benefits."* My dad ravenously accepted and had been there ever since.

My father, Ignacio Martinez instantly spotted Arbad, *El Jeffe,* as he rounded the corner on his way to the newborn unit. As Ignacio strode closer, his excited greeting startled Mr. Vadabhaat, and abruptly broke the spell of his enchantment. The out of context meeting caused him to fail to recognize my father as he fervently interjected his hand into Arbad's belly in an eager offering of an overzealous handshake.

"Sir is me! Ignacio! From de shop! Why you here? What you doing?" Papi stammered in his patchwork of English.

"Ah, yes, of course, Ignasio," he prematurely offered as the synapses slowly connected to make the association, "I'm here checking on my daughter, Jaanvi. She was just born this morning. She's right there," He said in his precisely annunciated, rolling Indian accent.

Almost as if on cue, the nurse, dressed in baby pink scrubs, picked up little Jaanvi in one arm, and scooped me up in the other as my father looked at me for the first time.

"¡Aye Padre Dios! ¡Aye Padre Dios! ¡Gracias Dios para esta niña saludable!" My Papi exclaimed, giving glory to God that I had survived the strangulating journey of birth into this world.

In Spanish, the word for birth is *dar a luz*, which translated literally means *to give light*, and in the moment of our birth, both of us were born of light in the same instant, completely unspoiled and whole in every sense.

"That's me! That's my girl!" He pointed out to his boss and slapped his sweaty Yankees ball cap against his thigh for emphasis.

In that moment, the boundaries of caste and station had dissolved, and here were just two men, similar in age and gratitude, arriving at the same serendipitous juncture in life, at the exact moment.

Like I said. Cosmic/Karmic.

CHAPTER THREE

The Y Chromosome: Ignasio

Ignacio. His name sounds like a stranger's to me now. The joy that bubbled through him upon my arrival on this earth fizzled out by my third birthday. What filled in behind it was black, and toxic, and acrid, and threatened to permeate every square inch of our now haunted home. The space that was once filled with dancing and flurried merengue clamor, was now lifeless, and that evil pestilence crept through the vacuum of the silence left in its wake.

Drugs. *Drogas,* Mami whispered harshly as she made the sign of the cross about her forehead and chest.

We didn't know it at the time. We didn't know what we were looking at when we saw the change in him. To me, the memories of him that I have now are only extrapolations of grainy photographs. I had to imagine how his voice sounded when he was happy, or how he would have smelled fresh out of the shower with a clean shave, based only on the casualness with which he held me in that photo taken outside the *gelateria* on West 4th.

I picture his walk, and how his mustachioed upper lip would feel kissing my forehead, and I consciously will myself to envision him a happy man. One who had the surety of grasp to toss me high up in the air and to catch me solidly as I careened back into his arms. I imagine a loving father, a chivalrous and doting husband. The type to come home with a bouquet of carnations and a spray of baby's breath for his cherished wife just because he loved her. I need this. I need him to be this man, and I need all the evil in him to be the twisting of the drugs that envenomated his mind, and not a latent and inherent characteristic of his being.

My breath catches in my throat when I think of the possibility of any of his actions having been of his own free will. I must believe him possessed by some roving demon that snatched up his body and strode around in his skin suit. No one would do the things my Mami accused him of if they had any love for themselves or their family. It had to be the devil himself, or perhaps some wicked and powerful *mal ojo* that had run rampant and unopposed, and possessed, and infected him to his very core.

What I've been able to piece together from the hushed tones of my mother and older sisters as they allude to some darkened history from before my father's abrupt ejection from our family, is that it started out with alcohol. Late nights, foolishness, vomit on the carpet, falling asleep on the stoop. Mami would pace the length of the apartment with hurried, pounding steps as her *chanclas* slapped the floorboards. It was a span she could cross in ten strides or less, her momentum being halted when she reached the wall just as she was getting up to speed. She would flail her arms in the air as she flung them out to God, and Mary, and Joseph, and any Saint who happened to be awake at this forsaken hour to hear her lamentations.

Glasses breaking. A china doll's head crushed upon the floor. Blood in Marisol's underpants. Mami says he raped her.

In his fucked up inebriated state, Papi hadn't been home in three days. Mami had taken me and my seven-year-old sister Valentina to the clinic to get our throats checked for strep, again. I was a month from my fourth birthday. Marisol had finished out her school day and was waiting at home for us at the apartment when Papi came home ravenous, murder in his black eyes. Not the passionate murder of anger, or blind rage. This was far more sinister. Far more steeped in evil, worse than death itself. The type of evil that doesn't recognize life. Doesn't see a beautiful daughter, eight years old, cloistered in innocence and fear. Doesn't see the joyful light in her eyes at seeing him walk through the door, collapse into cowering terror. Doesn't feel the warm piss run down her legs as the horror flushes out of her system. Doesn't feel her vomit down his back as he thrusts into her tiny body, destroying her. Ruining her.

When Mami found her still frozen to her little trundle bed, eyes flicking around the room wildly at an unseen specter, ruffled My Little Pony panties hanging from her thin ankle, covered in urine and vomit and the foul odor of guttural fear that stenches from an animal gulping for its last breath of air.

Mami screamed. The scream of a mother whose child had been torn from her arms and cast into a wolf's jaw. Papi had slid down the wall into a pile on the floor once he had finished, still covered in her fluids and his own sickening ones. Mami dropped me and I hit my head on the doorframe, and I started to cry from pain, or confusion, or just as the only possible response to the wave of panic that had engulfed us all.

Mrs. Lopez, our next-door neighbor, ran to the door and took in the horrific scene and waved Valentina to come inside and she pulled me up by the arm and yanked me into her apartment to call the police.

We heard sirens, and muffled yelling, followed by more sirens, more yelling.

I remember spending that first night with Mrs. Lopez and not seeing Mami for three days. The rest is blurry, like a pitch-black hole that warns me away anytime I go back to retrieve a memory from anything in a four-year radius of that time frame.

What I do know of that early hell I learned from sorting through endless slides of microfiche at the old brick public library on 6th Avenue.

Mami killed Papi.

According to the *New York Post* dated December 10, 1995, "*the Medical Examiner's report concluded that Mr. Martinez was killed with a kitchen knife, alleged to be wielded by Mrs. Martinez, the victim's wife, in self-defense, and in defense of their eight year old daughter, whose name is not being released at this time. According to court documents filed late last week, the child was brutally raped by her father, Ignacio Martinez, 42. Mrs. Magdalena Martinez, 37, a resident of Chelsea, on the Lower West Side of Manhattan, has no prior criminal record. Court documents state that Mrs. Martinez came upon the horrific scene after returning home with their other two young daughters, whose names are also not being released to protect their identities. Mr. Martinez suffered a total of twenty-seven stab wounds to his head, neck, and torso in the attack. The Medical Examiner's toxicology report shows that Mr. Martinez had a combination of crack/cocaine and four times the legal limit of alcohol in his system at the time of his death. Mrs. Martinez also suffered multiple defensive wounds, including a broken hand and other broken facial bones, as well as multiple bruises and abrasions. Today, circuit court Judge, Jonathan Phiffer, ruled in favor of Mrs. Martinez, declaring her not guilty of all charges, including manslaughter.*"

And that is all I'll say about Ignacio.

CHAPTER FOUR

Safe Haven

I'm not sure exactly where my story began to sort out after the edges of the black hole began to slowly abate and lessen its omniscience on our lives. Maybe somewhere around ninth or tenth grade? More than likely, the darkness receded where her light began.

I formally met Jenni at an after-school drama club in the West Village. Despite our clandestine encounter on the Labor and Delivery Unit at St. V's, we wouldn't officially be introduced until long after the dust of our lives, well, mine at least, had settled into some semblance of normalcy. Through some inadvertent ripple in the space-time continuum, we somehow, inexplicably, both ended up spending our Saturdays at The Street Level Theater on the Lower West Side.

They held a youth outreach program where we put on ultra-low budget theater productions for our parents and whatever locals happened to wander in accidentally during off-off peak hours. It was never anything earthshattering, but it always felt a little bit like a séance when we were performing. What we spoke into being on those afternoons was nearest to a conjuring. When the lights went down, what undulated from that stage was an overwhelming sense that anything could happen. It was quite magical, for lack of a better word.

Jenni had been performing there since its grand re-re-reopening in 1997, at which time it had been rebranded, and was grandly bequeathed *a true community theater for aspiring local actors, and a platform for native playwrights to see their works breathed to life on the small stage.*

After several iterations dating back to the 1800's the tiny playhouse had masqueraded as everything from a tobacco processing plant, to an Irish whisky distillery called *The Usquebaugh Cork*, to a factory that made nothing but Panama hats, but what was housed within its walls today was no doubt its truest form.

The excitement of the professional mentors who put on the real shows for paying audience members, trickled down to us in the glow of the kick lights, and filled us with a wonderment that any one of us of could potentially be *the next big thing in theater*. It was a sprinkling of fairy dust that made us feel like we held something divine within ourselves.

If anyone was to be the barer of that *IT girl* mantle, it would have definitely been Jenni. As the most seasoned youth performer, Jenni meandered the stage with this air of calm and belonging that rested easily upon the fleshy apples of her cheeks. There was a polish and a smoothness that made her always appear unbothered, nearly regal, near to divine. She always knew where she was going when the lights were turned down. As I stumbled and felt for the heavy velvet curtains with my arms outstretched before me, like a blind man that hadn't yet adapted to his darkness, Jenni would glide through it like a cat. The curtains practically parted for her when she went to step through. She had an ease like that about her with everything, which lent itself well to her acting. You could hand her a sword and she was suddenly Joan of Arc, or you could set her atop a plaster horse and she would be Lady Godiva, or you could give her a bow and quiver and she would be Robin Hood. Her fluidity and comfort level with every circumstance and situation made her enigmatic, inhabiting every role.

I would wait in the wings watching her run lines during rehearsal, and an enchantment would befall me. It was as if all the world faded away but her. She absolutely commanded your attention when she was performing.

One day, after we'd been at this cat and mouse game for a little over a year, I stood like a sentry at my post, safely enveloped in the shadows hanging over stage left, while she sashayed an abbreviated waltz for a part she played with Robert, my second period English Teacher's son. They were supposed to be lovers, and the scene was coming up where they were scripted to exchange a kiss. Something about that shared moment slapped my face, and I nearly raised my hand to my cheek to dull the sting. There was something titillating and infuriating at the same time about how she parted her lips for him, that brief surrender where she appeared to belong to him, despite how awkwardly he put his hand behind her head. Something about that motion with his hand incensed me to no end. I wanted to shout, *no, asshole, you're doing it wrong!*

At the absolute boiling point of my irritation, I hadn't noticed that Randall, one of the resident actors, had been silently watching from the darkness beside me. He put his hand on my shoulder and it startled me so bad I nearly stumbled on stage.

"Easy girl! Sorry! I didn't mean to scare you!" He hissed loudly in a feigned attempt at a whisper.

I tried to push my hair back jauntily and blow it off with a, *nah, you didn't scare*

me. But I think the fact that the blood still had not returned to my face had been my tell.

"Baby girl, you look like you could use some air." He said as he gently guided me by the hand, out the side door and into the alley. The crisp September chill filled my lungs and jolted me back to reality. Now I was awake.

"Honey," Randall said as he appraised me, looking me up and down with his hip kicked out to the side and his neck askew. "Honey, all this time you been coming around here, I didn't realize you were *family,*" he said as he pointedly arched his brow in my direction.

"What do you mean *family*? I ain't your family, man. Do I look like family to you?" I spit back at him in my best thug voice.

Randall laughed at my baby-tough-girl display as he demurely covered his mouth with his long thin hand.

"No girl, not family," he said as he held his pasty forearm against my *café con leche* flesh, "*family,"* he said as he let the full weight of his surprisingly heavy hands rest on my shoulders as he swished them side to side, nearly knocking me off balance.

Searching my eyes for some recognition of the term left him unsatisfied. Finally, he pushed me back, and sat down on an overturned empty paint can. He exaggeratedly crossed his waif thin legs and lit a cigarette. He pulled a can beside him and motioned for me to sit down. I plopped down reluctantly, still trying to work out what this ridiculous man wanted from me.

He offered me a drag. I was sixteen, soon-to-be seventeen at that time. I had never smoked before. Mami didn't even smoke. She would slap the mouth off my face if she was lurking in some recess of this meager courtyard, unbeknownst to me. I knew I shouldn't, but something about that moment felt conspiratorial, like an initiation into some brother or sisterhood I knew nothing about yet. Very cloak and dagger.

I took it, inhaled greedily, and coughed until I felt my diaphragm spasm and my throat try to slam closed.

Randall swatted my back until my sputtering subsided. He plucked the cigarette from my peace fingers.

"Enough of that for you," he said. As he looked me over while I fitfully caught my jagged breath, I felt a peacefulness rest upon me. I felt almost…I don't know, cool somehow, as foolish and immature as that sounds.

"So. Daniela. What a great name that is. Daniela. So glamorous…Anyway, Daniela, my love, I've been watching you. You, darling, are a strong and talented actress. You are," he reiterated, staring downward at me, eyes intense and sparkling. "You have that *je ne sais quoi* we're all searching for. You have that thing. In spades. But what you don't have, is a full realization of who you truly are. Sweetheart, I'm here to tell you, your acting will always be pretending if you don't really know who you are underneath the character you're playing." He narrowed his gaze on me. "Honey," Randall paused for dramatic effect. A technique he taught me last summer, and it felt contrived knowing that he was using his tricks against me. Like a magician trying to convince his assistant he had made real magic. "Honey, do you even *know* who you are?" The intensity of his laser-focused gaze on my face could have melted the overturned paint can I sat upon.

I stared back blankly at this wisp of a man. So thin, I thought this unseasonably crisp breeze could blow him away like dandelion fluff, yet his fortitude held me captive, commanding my attention. Randall's intensity defied his frailty.

The catalytic nature of the conversation finally caused me to ignite, and I sprung to my feet, knocking over my paint can.

"Does anybody!?" I dodged, finally forcing some sound to resonate from my vocal cords.

"Yes honey," he retorted, unmoved by my flailing. "Yes, some of us know *damn* well who we are. And I think you do too, you just haven't admitted it to yourself yet." My expression remained dumbstruck, only now the blankness I had at the start of our conversation was flushed with throbbing redness. Randal quickly tired of my obliviousness, and finally blurted it out.

"You're gay honey," he said bluntly as he snuffed out his cigarette on the concrete, averting his eyes to allow the weight of his accusation settle in my ears while he inspected his cuticles.

"Gay? What?? Gay?! I'm not gay!!" I said as my mezzo alto voice crescendoed to a creaking falsetto.

"Baby, calm down, it's not an insult," Randall said calmly. "It's not a bad thing. It's just another way of being. It's the glasses you look out at the world through," he said. I was panicked. Shocked. Trapped. The illusion that I had so meticulously crafted was falling in blubbery chunks around me.

"I can't be gay," I interjected, but my voice sounded like it had passed through a sieve.

"Why not? Why can't you?" Randall curtly countered, sounding mildly irritated.

"Because it's wrong! I'll go to hell for it!" Suddenly, I was struck with a primal fear, like an arrow through my heart.

My deepest unspoken fear. *The curse.* Was I too, a sinner? Was I a roving pestilence? An abomination? A wave of nausea crashed over me. Was I somehow in some twisted way a deviant like my father? *Was I cursed*?

As my thoughts scrambled and disassembled into wilder accusations of myself, Randall caught me in his arms. I hadn't realized I was falling.

"Baby, the world is wrong," he murmured into my hair. "Love isn't perverted. And there is no hell. Hell is what men create when they can't face the truth. They say you are going to hell because it's easier than believing all parts of this life are good. It obliterates all of their notions of good and evil, because in the end, love is always good." He pushed me back from himself and again searched my dark eyes with his languid honey-in-sunlight shimmering ones. This time I searched back, probing desperately to see if this was an intricately laid trap, lying in wait for me to confess to something that would ultimately bring about my undoing.

"Darling, think back for me for one moment. Have you ever bought into that lie that you were only put here on this earth to make dinners and babies for some *man*? Do you really believe in that fairytale horse shit?"

"No." I whispered, now averting my eyes as my search of his ill intentions came up empty handed.

"Ok. That's a good start. I'm not trying to force a confession out of you, and I'm not trying to embarrass you. I just wish someone had taken me out into a strange alley and shook me up at your age, and just given me permission to be myself. It would have saved me a lot of pain." In that moment, Randall pulled up his sleeve revealing a meshwork of a thousand silvery scars on the inside of his left arm that I had never noticed before.

"I just want you to live a happy life," Randall said as he hugged me tight, "that's all," and I hugged back.

Just as the tears had begun to sting in the inner canthus of my eyes, the rusty metal and faded graffiti side door flung open abruptly, forcing me to jump back a step. Out from behind it stepped Jenni. In all her smirking glory.

"Am I interrupting?" she said breezily, knowing full well that she had.

"No baby, we were just having some lite girl talk. We just finished. I think I hear Deter calling my name anyway," he said as he unfurled his graceful arms from around me and dissolved back into the shadows of the theater.

"Hey," Jenni said, now acutely aware that her arrival had lifted the veil of whatever spell had been cast in that alleyway.

"Hey," I said as I swallowed hard against the ball in my throat and tried to sniff back the tears that had threatened to betray me.

"That looked…intense. What were you guys talking about?" She asked coolly, with a Mona Lisa half-smile pulling up the corners of her perfect lips.

"Nothing really. Life. I don't know, choices maybe?" I said.

"Enlighten me," she pushed back.

I wanted to run, or capsize, or spontaneously combust. I didn't know which.

I gave a little nervous laugh. God, how was this girl so wise, so practiced, so many light years ahead of me? She was an old soul to be sure. Ancient. She was an expert at a game I had been given no instructions to, and didn't even know I was playing in.

"I don't know. Like, Randall's gay. Did you know that?" I said in a half disgusted, half accusatory way.

"Daniela, everyone's a little gay. Randall's just a little more-gay than most." Her answer shocked me. Though we had come a long way from the backlash of the '80's and the Stonewall riots, we weren't that far ahead. Hatred and bigotry surrounded us at all times, even here in the Gay Mecca of the West Village. Her statement was almost futuristic. Ahead of its time, and certainly ahead of her years.

"Well, not everyone's gay Jenni," I said. "You're not gay."

"Says who?" She retorted, with a plotting smirk.

I was stunned silent, in awe of this girl. This fucking woman-child, whatever she was. She stepped closer to me. Soon she was standing inches away from my face. I could feel the heat from her powdery breath hit my upper lip in contrast to this autumn chill.

"You should try it some time," she said as she leaned in and slowly docked her lips into the harbor of mine.

Lightning bolts. Fireworks. Fucking cannons. I had no earthly metaphorical reference for what she did to me in that alley, but, rest assured, it was the first kiss to end all first kisses.

CHAPTER FIVE

Growing Pains

Though Randall had dragged me out of the proverbial closet at a tender young age, it would be years before I fully accepted my given form. The demand for conformity at all costs from my family, my community, my classmates, and just the world at large, was a sweeping tidal wave of persistent reminders that I "wasn't quite right," I was less than, or more than I needed to be. I was never that steaming bowl of *just right* porridge Goldilocks so desired.

Jenni helped to ease my insecurities. And she also created new ones I never knew I had.

I don't know how many more adjectives I could use to describe the type of being Jenni was. She was a lesser deity, a halfling suspended somewhere between flesh and light. And, as is the ways of creatures not of this realm, she never belonged to me. Much as she let me breathe her in and exhale her in whatever tidal volume I had capacity for, she always removed all of herself on that parting exhalation. She was never diminished by giving herself to me. But I always was. I would leave parts of myself behind in her bed, on her floor, behind the equipment shed at school, and more times than I can count back in the fateful alleyway beside the theater. I had scattered myself far and wide and I had nothing left to gather back to myself at some point.

When you become enthralled with another human to that extent, it becomes very isolating. No one else can compare. That person is so eclipsing that the idea of communing with another soul that vibrates at a more attenuated frequency feels filtered, diluted, faded. It's just not the substance of interaction that you're accustomed to engaging in. Conversations feel superficial, and beneath you to an extent. It's disorienting. You forget how to be reserved, demure, how to disengage. It makes finding friends difficult, and it makes the burden to maintain that level of intensity feel unbearably weighted.

Like the twilight of every first love, you feel gutted, emptied, inadequate, and you are helplessly convinced that love will never feel that freeing, that unadulterated, and any confabulation of the real thing seems intolerable. You convince yourself you will never love again.

In that fallow time, I decided that I had to get out of the city. I had to get away from the haze of gypsy cab exhaust, and being jarred from sleep at odd hours by police sirens, and fist shaking neighbors' shouts reverberating from rusted fire escapes. I needed peace, and space, and stars, and sky. I needed to rid myself of the deafening void I had been left in. I needed to breathe, I needed a space Jenni did not occupy, because for me, she occupied the whole of New York City. Manhattan was her playground, and she had laid claim to every corner, every song that I had soothed myself to, every meal, and smell smacked of her essence. In the din of the most mundane detail, she had already laid her claim, and I could no longer stand having nothing of my own. I saw her fingerprints upon everything, subway lines, coffee shops, specific arrangements of plants and park benches. *Fuck this place.* New York was no longer my home.

*

We were in our senior year of high school when the floor dropped out on our story. I felt her withdrawal. I noticed her keeping more of herself when we would lie in each other's arms. She was mist again, and gather as I would, she would not recollect for me.

Our lovemaking felt less lovely. She acted like she didn't understand my body, and she had so neglected the parts of me that when touched, caused me to spring to life, to the point where I would find myself touching them in her absence. Chest aching wishing that my fingers stroking the side of my face and my sternum were her own. There was more friction, more resistance, more effort required to achieve that meteoric rise, if it happened at all. When I would kiss her lips, they no longer kissed me back.

I begged her to tell me what was wrong. I searched her to see if I could triangulate where she had retracted to, but she was already far away from me, despite how she insisted she was sitting right in front of me.

In reality, our two years together could really only be distilled down to a handful of good months. The last one was a feeble ghost of the people we were in each other's arms back when we were playing at being fairies, or pirates, or sisters, back on stage all those Saturday mornings. I think both of us recognized that we looked better under the stage lights than we did in the harsh angle of the noontime sunshine.

For all of Jenni's self-assurance, clarity, and desire, she definitely didn't take the lead on our ending. She handed me the loaded gun, but it was my line to take the safety off, chamber the bullet, and pull the trigger.

It started with me pushing her away. It was that hurt game of, *fine, if you don't talk to me, I won't talk to you*, until the silence became too deafening, until the convulsions of detoxing from her became too severe. Finally, I would cave, and crawl back to her feebly and start the process of losing her all over again. My shock and denial would sour to anger. Accusations of cheating, of *straightness*, of fraud began to be thrown carelessly about, all of which were met with that tepid, unmoved face of hers, that challenge of *darling, do you truly believe that?* The lack of outrage on her behalf sent me back into a deeper, more anguished exile, leaving me questioning my own sanity. I bargained, I was depressed, I tested, I cycled through all the stages of grief at least twice. Until, finally,

finally, I knocked upon the door of acceptance, and walked straight-backed through it, and out of Jenni's life forever.

*

When Mami tired of my lovesickness, she unapologetically heaved my now thin and bedraggled corpse from the sea of blankets I buried myself in my bed with. I peeled open my eyes against the glare of the eleven a.m. Sunday morning sunshine now streaming through my window. I didn't even know how long it had been since I noticed the walls around me. I had expected to find endless void, a world riven from any sort of light or love. I weakly swung my legs over the side of my bed, head spinning, my world temporarily fading to black, then slowly shifting back into focus. I looked around and saw my bedroom, unchanged in all the years I had inhabited it, except for the Ani DiFranco poster I recently hung on the wall directly in front of me, that I had jauntily carried home from Rebel Rebel one hopeful day before everything went sideways. I traced the curve of the tribal tattoo gracing Ani's collar bones and imagined the power she stomped her Doc Marten boots with. It was like that imagined stop snapped me to attention. Like she had leaned out from her rectangular forcefield and said, *time to get up you sad bitch.* Looking around, I saw my same childhood life, but, to my surprise, when I turned the knob on my door and stumbled through it, I found myself in nursing school.

*

I don't know how, or why, but when my guidance counselor Ms. Culotti sat me down on Monday morning in her dimly lit office that faintly reeked of divorce, Newport ultra-light menthols, and cat dander, and asked me that fully-loaded question of, *what do you want to be when you grow up?* I hesitated. I had this moment of shock, like she had tossed ice water in my face.

I blinked. Had I arrived here already? Was it time to provide an answer to that ineluctable question? I suddenly felt like I had a mouth full of peanut butter. Then without any prior consideration or premeditation, I blurted,

"I want to be a nurse."

Satisfied, and nodding emphatically, she said in her distinct Long Island diphthong, "Very good answer. I like your… decisiveness. That's a very realistic goal. Your grades are good, not too good," she paused and pointed her long Lee Press-On at me to emphasize the fact. She continued, "your SAT isn't phenomenal, but you shouldn't have any problem getting into a nursing program."

Before I could even begin to comprehend the egg that I had just laid on Ms. Culotti's desk, I was leafing through brochure after brochure of local nursing schools. There had to be a hundred schools around New York State for me to choose from.

None of the CUNY schools around the city sounded good to me, and they were all just a train ride away from our apartment, which I felt was definitely too close for comfort. As the baby of the family, and the last one to fly the coop, I had to give our little apartment a chance to air out.

We had never really dealt with our mess. We were all shell-socked survivors of a massive, reverberating trauma, and life just carried on as usual after the bomb that my father had detonated had torn us each apart.

Marisol had fared far better than anyone expected. We all watched her like she was made of blown glass, like the slightest errant draft could shatter her. She went through adolescence hermetically sealed. Mami was convinced that she was one disappointment away from going completely postal and burning our entire building down.

Despite her fears for everyone's sanity but her own, Mami took it the hardest. She went through a phase where she was convinced that the apartment was haunted, or cursed, or both. She had the priest come in, and a shaman, and when all else failed to meet her inexplicable standard for spiritual purity, she looked to voodoo practitioners. She was constantly lighting candles, and frantically reciting prayers, and smudging smoldering sage in the ceiling corners, walking block after block in search of onyx, or quartz crystals to squirrel away in propitious locations around the apartment, to radiate some good light into our dark pit of a home.

But Marisol persisted. It was in there. Deep. She had some abyss that she had locked that monster into, and eventually we all just accepted that if Marisol wanted to starve that beast to death in some recess of her psyche, she was the only one in possession of the key to its cage, so it was up to her to keep it in its prison.

Despite the tragic circumstances of her early childhood, she was remarkably "normal." To whatever extent a wild human can be considered as such. But, befitting the mold of society's expectation, Marisol was nearly thriving, for all intents and purposes, despite our skepticism. She loved softball, and she sang in the school choir. She got really good grades, better than mine in every subject. Science was her favorite, and she was a voracious reader. She especially loved books with a theme of any sort of travel. She loved the thought that the world was alike, and different at the same time. She loved telling Mami how long a flight it would be to some far-off land. She would end every statistic with, *and they fly there out of JFK. We could just buy a ticket and go*. Mami would always pull her back out of the clouds and remind her the cost of such a flight of fancy, and she would wait a few days before reciting another obscure travel factoid.

Marisol had a few close friends. Not popular, but not isolated either. Her best friend Lola was the one she confided in the deepest. To my knowledge, she was the only soul Marisol had ever disclosed any detail of her darkness to. Without missing a beat, Lola bared her own scars, and they exchanged a knowing glance and nod, and went about their business, as if to say, shit happens. *Let's get some pizza and walk down to Soho*, as if their early trauma was simply a shared tragic rite of passage.

As much as we all accepted her insistent reassurance that she was "completely fine," we all reserved the right to believe she secretly possessed the capacity to rip the head off a kitten, or destroy a priceless work of art. But to our knowledge, she never did.

Marisol had left home six years before me, leaving me with a significant portion of my adolescence without the guidance of my older sister. As much as Mami called her daily, pleading for a visit, she remained unmoved. She had crossed the GW for the last time, and found herself at Cornell, where she was studying veterinary medicine. Even though I missed her dearly, and despite my lack of confidence in her kitten husbandry, I was happy for her. She seemed completely on track to have a genuinely fulfilling life.

I could always count on her calling me on my birthday, and I looked forward to that fleeting connection all year. She would occasionally surprise us and send a note and a few pictures of herself standing in front of a waterfall from her hikes through Ithaca's gorges. I always wondered who held the camera on these excursions, and if they knew the version of Marisol we had lost track of better than we did. Apart from her brief Sunday morning phone call to Mami, Marisol had gone about her business without us, and didn't appear to show any evident untoward effect of her past trauma. She moved on with her life and never looked back.

Valentina was our wild child. Drugs, boys, booze, you name it, she'd tried it, twice, just to be sure. Valentina worked at The Argyle, a gritty bar/greasy spoon in Hell's Kitchen. She eventually got her own place above the restaurant so she could simply roll out of bed, and fall into her scant bartender's uniform comprised of a tattered Slayer t-shirt, ripped fishnet stockings, button front black corduroy miniskirt, combat boots, and a thick slash of kohl across her lids. She would just be waking at four o'clock in the afternoon to go into work at four thirty, where she served and shared drinks until last call.

Mami was furious. To her, Valentina's bartending career was indecent, immoral, it was blasphemy. She was convinced Val had followed in her father's dirty footprints and was destined to be a blip on the police blotter as a nameless overdose. She begged, plied her with guilt and tears to go to rehab, but despite Mami's pleadings, Val knew her limits. She was a self-declared "functional alcoholic," amongst her other vices. Her largesse and magnetism are what got her all the good tips, and boys, and the longing glances from the Guatemalan kitchen staff. The debauchery somehow suited her. The noise and swirling chaos complimented her inner fire, and somehow made her seem calm and collected in the eye of the storm, more so than she did outside of it.

Though Mami forbade herself from offering any sort of approval of Val's life choices, she never thought of her as a lost cause. She lit a candle for her wayward child every Sunday before mass.

Despite Mami's disapproval, I was in awe of her. Val knew all kinds of bottle flipping tricks, and recipes for hundreds of concoctions and tonics and tinctures that could send anyone to the moon. There was a ballet to it, and she moved about at a hover that was truly mesmerizing to watch. Her true gift, when her waking hours coincided with enough time between shifts to remember herself, was that she was a secret artist. Secret because she never told anyone, and we had been unaware of her proclivity for art her entire life, despite our close quarters. She worked long crazy hours, hiking her bosom up and placing it prominently on display, to maximize her earnings and ultimately keep her in paint and canvas. The liquor, the coke, and I would learn later, a very deep yet brief love affair with heroin, were what she insisted fueled her art. It threw gasoline on the fire and gave locomotion to her incendiary abstract expressionism. Evidently, what was bad for her heart, was good for her art.

Watching her creative process, if you should be so lucky, gave you a shrinking feeling, as if nothing you have ever done in your life has been so impassioned and so bold. I fell asleep at her flat one time when she had me over for a sleepover my senior year of high school. I was awakened on her thrift store futon by a harried shuffling sound. When I blinked, and attempted to reorient, Val was in her underwear and a moth-eaten tank top two sizes too small. Her hair and eyes were wild as she furiously filled the void of a five-foot by three-foot canvas with crimson impasto. It was like watching a pagan ritual. It felt like if I did anything more than take shallow sips of air it would disrupt the incantation.

I sat in wonderment, eyes transfixed upon her, awestruck by the simple fact that I didn't know she could even draw, let alone paint like this sorceress that writhed before me. It was a shocking and deeply unsettling display, primarily because of the jarring realization that, even when you live with someone your entire life, you will eventually arrive some pivotal moment when you discover that you never truly knew them at all. It would probably be similar to how she would feel if I told her my secrets, but two of us pulling off our masks in front of each other before nine a.m. was probably a bit heavy for a Saturday morning.

When she finally spun around and saw me watching her, she disappeared into the little studio kitchenette to wash the paint from her forearms and brew some coffee. We sipped it black, and she poured me a bowl of Froot Loops, while she pulled drags off a cigarette for breakfast. We didn't utter a word to each other about the five by three-foot red elephant in the room. Instead, she asked me about boys, and school, and if I was excited for my senior trip to D.C.

As Val and Marisol left to find their own paths in life, I was the only one home to mop up Mami's tears as she cried standing over me while I began packing my bags and preparing my supply list to head Upstate to college.

I had found a community college that had a nursing program just outside the city of Rochester, New York, in the Finger Lakes region, not overly far from where Marisol was attending vet school. On paper, it sounded perfect for me. I was fully convinced this school "the one" based solely on the lake vistas and smiling Gap ad looking teenagers pictured in the glossy brochure. I took a deep breath, filled out my application, and prayed a hasty supplication to Saint Jude.

*

I'll never forget the pained look on Mami's face, wringing her hands on the stoop as I strode down 15th into the subway station at the end of our block to board a train destined for JFK, armed only with a one way ticket to a place I had never been, nearly jumping from my hot little hand.

My only prior venture outside of the City was for a field trip to Hoboken when we went with our fourth-grade social studies class for an immersive lesson on the Underground Railroad. This was another experience entirely. I wanted to be sad. I wanted to know that I would miss this place, that I would miss Mami and Valentina, and our too familiar block. But if I was being honest with myself, I just wanted to get the leaving over with. I was ready to be like

Marisol and soar from the nest without hesitation, looking ever forward and never back.

When we landed, I could instantly tell that I was not in Manhattan anymore. It was August, but not the suffocating August depleted of oxygen that I was used to. This was hazily overcast, more still, despite the rustling subdued bustle of the airport. It felt placid. I yawned three or four times in succession to try and clear my ears before I had to just accept that it was, in fact, that quiet and my ears weren't just full from our decent from altitude.

I found the baggage claim downstairs, but when I headed to the transportation area, I was shocked to see that there wasn't a train platform. I backtracked and asked the gentleman at the information desk where I should go to catch the train to Canandaigua. He smiled widely and shook his finger in my face lightheartedly and said,

"You're not from around here are you?" I told him no, and he almost apologetically explained that there was no direct line of public transportation to Canandaigua. It was at least a forty-five minute highway drive to get there. I was too young and too broke to rent a car, and a taxi would be expensive.

I thought about calling Mami. Just turning around and calling the whole thing off, but I dug my heels in and decided this little podunk town was not going to defeat me.

"How much for the taxi?"

*

It took nearly all of my cash on hand to pay for the cab, but the relief that washed over me was absolute once I surrendered myself to trust the driver to get me to where I needed to go. I fell asleep in the backseat as soon as we made it onto the main drag, if you could call it that.

I woke a while later, startled from sleep by the driver rudely pushing my knee off the seatback, causing my foot to hit the floor with a thud.

"This your stop?" He asked.

I blinked the sleep from my eyes and looked around. A squat concrete structure loomed before me, nestled amongst what looked like a thick forest.

I cleared my throat.

"Um, yeah. Yes. Ok, thank you." I paid the man and he drove off without glancing back to see if I had even stepped back from the curb.

Once in, my eyes had to adjust to the dim light. The atrium smelled like dust, and stagnant air only moved about by the frenetic transit of students in and out of its doors. I had the feeling I get when I first step inside a library or a museum. Like, that sturdy wonderment that *knowledge lives here.*

I checked in with the girl at the Student Life desk along with about five other wobbly recruits. They looked too young to be here. I began to wonder if I had been drifting on a different timeline. Like I had aged in City years, and everyone else had been aging in Upstate years, one of theirs for each of my two.

We went by the Registrar's office to pick up a copy of our schedules and we followed this girl Rachel's glossy ponytail like ducklings over to the bookstore to pick up our overpriced textbooks. After a brief guided tour of the few campus highlights, we circled back around to the entrance. Rachael intended to leave us with the parting words, "ok guys, the dorms are down the street, just pull your cars around and bear left when you hit Lakeshore and you can't miss them. Good luck!"

Wait. Drive? I don't have a car. I don't know how to drive. That wasn't in the student handbook!

"Hey, Rachael, so uh, about that car thing, so like, I don't drive."

She looked dumbfounded, and then her face filled with an expression that was most likely pity. She explained the shuttle system to me briefly, and left me with a perfunctory,

"You're gonna need to get a car sweetie," before turning crisply and walking away.

I waited in the front for the shuttle, which I learned after pacing and kicking rocks and slowly losing my sanity, that literally everything here is slow. The people, the cars, the time spent going through a checkout line, time in general was just really fucking slow.

When the shuttle finally mozied up to get me, I was irate. I was hungry, and exhausted, and disoriented. I walked back and collapsed in an empty seat and waited, until I felt a focused pair of eyes fixed upon me. I looked over the seat in front of me and I saw the driver smiling back in the mirror directly at me.

"Hi sweetheart!" she sang. "Where are we going?"

Oh, bloody hell. You have to tell them where to go? They don't just have a route? God, why does everything require so much explanation around here?

"Uh, Lakers Landing? I guess?" I said.

"Yes ma'am," she replied cheerily.

Ma'am. Shit maybe I am old. I'd never been called ma'am in my life. I felt like I had landed in Mayberry.

"Ok hun, you have a good day now!" She called to me as I vacated the bus in a pouf of exasperation.

*

I found my room number right away, 505. Fives had always been lucky for me, I'm not sure why, but I had a good feeling about this.

I was almost surprised when my key fit in the door. I half expected it not to, only for me to return to campus to discover the inexplicably bad news that there had been some quirk of a bookkeeping error that had mistakenly allowed me entry, and that I was not actually matriculated, as I had been lead to believe, and I would need to vacate the premises, and return home immediately.

But, alas, open it did. Much to the sheer terror of my roommate, Bethany, who I scared half to death when I shoved the door open as she was teetering on a chair in front of the doorframe hanging a bundle of eucalyptus above the lintel.

"Jesus," I said.

I waited for her to climb down and open the door for me.

"Hi!! Sorry! Wow you must be Daniela! Hi! I'm Bethany!" I offered my hand for a shake, but she pulled me in to hug it out as I stiffened.

I was already annoyed. Daniela. Like, Dan-yella. Just the aggressively Caucasian way she said it bristled me. This was not going to be a good fit for me. I could feel it.

The room was pretty much as-advertised. Bed, bed, desk, desk, chair, chair. Nothing out of the ordinary. I was accustomed to not having any personal space so it wasn't the proximity that concerned me, it was the fact that Bethany had put a line of blue masking tape down the middle of the room and up both sides of the adjoining walls all the way to the ceiling. I'm not even joking. Honestly, I could probably deal with the tape. It was what she had already managed to vomit onto the walls on her side of the tape that I found most obnoxious. Ballet posters, ribbons, pictures, even a tutu had been stapled to the wall above her bed. I was no stranger to performers, but this level of extremism, this overt obsession was way outside of my capacity to deal with.

"I'm a dancer," Bethany said, as she beamed and set up her feet in first position as if I hadn't noticed.

"Ok." I said and headed to the door to get some air.

I walked.

I fuckin' walked, man.

This was all too much for me.

The space, and the fresh fuckin' air, and these loud ass birds chirping. And Bethany and her goddamn tutu had gotten on my last fuckin' nerve.

I shoved my fists in the pockets of my hoodie and I took off. I had no place to go. Evidently, if I wanted to go somewhere, I would need a fucking car. I definitely should have noticed that before I applied to this God forsaken school. But what the *fuck!* This is their fault for not putting it front and center on the goddamn brochure!

I was furious. Suddenly everything that I thought I was seeking in this place, fresh air, trees, sky, was threatening to pull me apart. Like an astronaut foolishly venturing into outer space without a space suit on, that lack of confinement, that lack of pressure will tear you apart in all directions at once. That's what it felt like was happening to me. Suddenly I needed the confines of the city. I needed to be hemmed in on all sides to keep me from dissolving into thin air. I abruptly dropped to my knees on the side of the road. I felt like I was suffocating. Just then, I heard the crunch of gravel under tires as a car pulled up slowly behind me. The driver rolled down his window.

When I heard the buzz and whine of his automatic windows, I directed my eyes his way just enough to lash a scowl at him. I was used to having people all around me, but in this environment, for some reason, I was startled, and incandescently irritated to have to engage with another human being while in the throes of completely losing my shit.

"Hey there! You ok?"

I turned and looked back at this boy that had the audacity to interrupt my percolating meltdown.

If I could adequately describe a nondescript white guy, I would essentially be describing William, sitting in his blue Ford Focus.

"Yeah," I said into the dirt. "Tripped."

"Oh ok, well, hey, if you're interested, we were going to go hit up Wegmans for some food and then go see what's good down by the lake if you'd like to come with."

The plural of William was Justin. They looked exactly alike, but as I would come to find out, to my amazement, they were not actually related.

Before I could restrain myself, I managed to cluck out a "K," inexplicably abandoning any notion of ingrained premonition of "stranger danger." I slowly ratcheted myself up to a standing position and brushed the dirt from my hands and knees.

It was completely out of character for me, nearly akin to an out of body experience, walking over to this random car, and getting in, no questions asked, but here I am. It would be the first of many inexplicable firsts I imagined.

We exchanged nods all around as we muttered our cursory introductions.

If I had learned anything growing up in Manhattan, it was firstly, never get on an empty subway car at rush hour, and secondly, never trust an unassuming white guy. Mami had adamantly led me to believe that all serial killers were white males, and therefore, every kind gesture should automatically be highly suspect, up to, and including the potential for murder, rape, and pillaging. If I had truly held my level of suspicion to that preconditioned extent, I wouldn't be sitting in this Ford Focus that smelled ever so faintly of Abercrombie and Fitch cologne punctuated by an occasional waft of marijuana.

Evidently, the way to lead me into temptation is through the promise of food and finding out what's good by the lake.

Although William/Justin couldn't have appeared more impotent, more non-threatening, my guard was still up. I was a stranger in a strange place. The rules I had lived by all eighteen years of my life did not apply in this context. I could breeze through turnstiles, get up, down, and crosstown without arousing even the slightest sideways glance, but in this place, I felt conspicuous in every way. I suddenly didn't know what to do with my hands.

My alienation stemmed from the fact that, in New York City, I had never once been made to feel like a minority. Nationally, I had heard tell that Hispanics were categorically defined as having minority status, but to me, the brown tapestry I had been woven into made this notion seem impossible. Since my arrival Upstate, every single face that I had seen was nearly homogenous in every way. Completely whitewashed. To my untrained eye, there only appeared to be about three permutations of what people looked like here. Maybe one person wore a plaid shirt and one wore a red one, but the cut of the cloth was nearly always the same. From as far as I had seen thus far, this was not the place for non-conformity.

"The Twins," William and Justin were nice enough, and though I hadn't completely dispelled my fear of their homicidal tendencies, I was much more relaxed by their hospitality once we reached our destination.

I had heard tell of a structure referred to colloquially as a "supermarket," but this seemed impossible. We pulled up and I saw the sign, but I couldn't comprehend this place as anything but some massive warehouse.

"So this is just like a grocery store? Why the hell do you need so much food?" I asked.

The Twins laughed.

"What, you guys don't eat in the City?" William asked.

"Not like this," I said.

We had grocery stores in Manhattan, obviously, but Western Beef was a poor approximation for comparison.

This place was immense. And who knew so much food existed? Or that you even wanted it? Did I come here craving coconut flour crepes and Nutella? No. But do I want it now? Fuck yes I do.

Exquisite, unblemished produce for miles, specialty, and ethnic foods, organic, vegan, and every food-allergy-friendly delicacy you could imagine was there. I didn't even have a food allergy, but gluten-free peanut butter and chocolate puff cereal sounded like the breakfast of champions to me all of a sudden.

And the prices? Holy shit! Maybe I did have money for a car after all. In Manhattan, a gallon of milk would run you somewhere in the neighborhood of seven dollars. If you were at some fancy-schmancy specialty store, you're talking at least eleven dollars for the organic, hormone free stuff. Here, that same gallon was about two dollars and eighty-five cents, give or take. Literally everything I looked at gave me sticker shock. The good kind.

Once The Twins helped me satiate my hypoglycemic crisis (I hadn't eaten since the night before because I had gotten up at two o'clock in the morning to make the train ride to JFK from 15th Street for my six a.m. flight) I was shockingly congenial. Happy even. Like, bubbly happy, which was by no means an adjective that would have ever been used to describe me. Once I was adequately fed, patted on the head, and turned toward the exit, we got back in the Focus and rolled out for the second leg of our journey.

*

The Lake. Canandigua Lake. One of the eleven Finger Lakes located in Upstate New York, the Finger Lakes were formed by receding glaciers clawing at the surface of the earth as the Ice Age lost its grip on the Northern Hemisphere thousands of years ago.

Named Canandaigua by the Native American people of the Seneca Nation, the entitle means "The Chosen Spot," in the Iroquoian tongue. It is a perfectly befitting appellation, and easy to see why.

Though Manhattan is an island, and thereby surrounded by water, I should have had some vague frame of reference for what I was standing before. But this water was something else entirely. Jones and Riis Beach were great in the summer. I always felt a kinship to the sea. Maybe having roots in the island nation of the Dominican Republic entranced me in the siren song of the waves, but oceans and lakes are two entirely different entities, I would discover.

The beaches within the immediate vicinity of The City, by way of public transportation, are in no way pristine. They tend to be vastly overcrowded, as is to be expected. And invariably, there is always some dipshit out there who thoughtlessly leaves a churning torrent of trash in his wake, without concern for the patrons, the sand, the water, or any living thing for that matter. Not that that was a deterrent. Fourth of July on the beach in Far Rockaway was pretty much the zenith of summer bliss but being here felt entirely different than my usual beachside escapades.

For starters, it was nearly silent. The moment I burst out of the dorms following my ill-fated introduction to Dancing Bethany, the silence here felt like a vacuum. This was just a tranquility had never actually experienced before.

Crystal-clear navy blue waters, shallow, gentle waves lapping at the rocks, weeping willows listing in the breeze on the rocky shoreline. It was a profoundly restorative following the whirlwind of events I had endured since this morning, and in that moment, I feel like I found what I had been seeking standing in the smog clogged crosswalk back in the City.

My moment was jarringly halted when Justin announced:

"Well, this is lame, you guys ready to go?" I wasn't, and the disorienting thrust back to reality nearly knocked the wind out of me.

I captured one more longing glance at the pristine water before making my way over to William's vehicle, and heading back to the dorm.

When we arrived back at Lakers Landing, we did the obligatory number exchange, and promised to look for each other at orientation the following morning.

*

Now that I had a full belly, some fresh air, and a clear head, I steeled myself against the awkwardness of a second meeting with Dancing Bethany as I fumbled with my key against the closed door. I practiced my fake smile and whispered "hi" in a variety of inflections to see which one felt the least threatening, before thrusting my key in the hole.

When I walked across the threshold it became abundantly clear that my rehearsal had been in vain. The room was dark, and unless she was hiding in the closet to jump out at me, Bethany wasn't there.

I flapped my hand blindly against the wall in search of the light before it hit square in my palm. I was instantly startled once again by the cloying pink mess on the walls on Bethany's side of the room. Apart from my distain, I didn't have the energy to devote another moment's concern to it. I flopped down on the bare mattress and shoved my books, and all of my belongings to the foot of the twin bed and used the vacant half to curl up into a fetal position, and drift off into a state of motionless, dreamless, paralyzing sleep.

I awoke at four thirty in the morning, overhead light still blaring, fully clothed on a naked mattress, and I was momentarily disoriented to my surroundings. I had a brief moment of terror cross my mind that perhaps one of the Twins roofied me on the way back from the lake. To get my bearings, I reached across the bed for my purse, and rifled through my scant belongings in search of my phone, slowly connecting dots, and placing myself back into context. I looked over and noticed Bethany was still MIA.

As my eyes adjusted to the harsh illumination of my cell phone, I realized the ungodly hour I had found myself rudely awakened into, and I saw no less than forty-seven panicked messages from Mami.

"Dammit," I whispered to myself as I squeezed my phone so hard my grip threatened to crush its glass. As I pushed its cool face against my forehead, I realized Mami would be up in exactly thirty minutes. She was not a woman to dawdle. Her jarring old-fashioned brass bell alarm clock had no snooze button, but even if it had, she wouldn't have used it. She was no-nonsense, and hit the ground running every morning at five a.m., no exceptions. While we rolled over and moaned, and had to have the blankets ripped from our sleep-warmed bodies to set us in motion, Mami seemed to have a hot poker that sent her careening out of bed at the start of her day.

Not wanting to deprive her of any less sleep than she was already getting, I decided to wait for her to wake on her own terms before answering her rapid fire questioning for my dereliction of duty in letting her know I had arrived at my destination safely, and that I was not in fact clinging to life in a country road ditch somewhere.

While I waited for the appointed hour, I decided now was as good a time as any to unpack my few belongings, away from Bethany's watchful, unblinking gaze.

As I unfolded and refolded my little collection of shirts and sweaters and set my number two pencils and three ring binders in a corner of my desk, I was hit with a hollow loneliness. It was the edges of a burgeoning existential crisis that it was way too fuckin' early in the morning for, so I pulled my attention from it, and quickened my pace, carelessly shoving my sweaters in the closet, and attuned my focus to the meditation of bed making.

When I turned my phone on and pre-programmed the number to Mami's landline, I had to sit with it in my hand, thumb hovering precariously over the "call" button, for three anguished minutes, waiting for the hour to roll over.

Just exactly as I had fully anticipated, Mami picked up her receiver before the first ring had even finished.

"Buenos dias, Mami," I said sheepishly.

"*¡Coño! ¡Ay Dios mio Daniela!* My God, are you trying to kill me? My heart can't take this stress! I thought you were dead in a ditch somewhere! How dare you treat me like this!"

"Mami, I already know. I am so, so sorry Mami! I was so exhausted yesterday, and…" She cut me off in a maelstrom of Spanish curse words and descriptions of how I had taken years off her life, and explanations of the various maladies I had just stricken her with. Slowly though, her rage began to abate, and she began softening her line of questioning to include her usual mom-like concerns. Did you eat? Have you showered? Do you know how to get to all your classes? Who is your roommate? I decided to postpone asking for money to buy a car until I knew that she had not booked the next flight Upstate to beat me senseless and take me home.

Once Mami's panic had quieted, I said my *te amo's,* and laid myself back in my now-made bed, appraising the ceiling before accepting that the twelve and a half hours of sleep I had gotten would have to do for today.

I crept down the hallway to the showers, where I had believed I would have the entire communal shower all to myself at this pre-dawn hour. I was mistaken.

Entirely nude, in full sight of God and everybody, wet and slippery as an eel, stood the most exquisite, lithe creature I had ever seen in my life. Jenni, obviously had ruined me on women. She had glutted me with her sweetness to the point of diabetes, but this was another being entirely. The woman that stood lathered before me was without a doubt a stone-cold athlete. Her tanned face was plain as could be, mousy brown hair, sparse eyelashes and eyebrows, and an upturned thin top lip. Though her features were not by themselves alluring, they were endearing, and comforting somehow. She wasn't ugly by any means, just, non-threatening I suppose, but that body was a scandal all by itself.

My God, I was in it. I was decidedly back in the game. The glorious sight of her, against the stark contrast of the doughy composition of my own form caused me to retreat into one of the private stalls and take a dark, lukewarm, hasty rinse, despite my being in dire need of a shave.

When I emerged from my dank cave of a shower stall, she was gone. Vanished. As I stood shivering as the air hit my tepid skin, I collected my few toiletries and dressed as hurriedly as tugging tight jeans up damp legs would allow.

When I got back up to the dorm, I was shocked to find Bethany there, and I hadn't remembered to rehearse my "hi's" adequately before opening the door, so what issued forth was something to the effect of *hijo de puta.* Bethany appeared unmoved, sitting cross-legged on the bed, sipping her latte.

"Hi," she said, stealing my line.

I kind of adjusted my sails and pushed in, mirroring her lead, I slunk down on the bed across from her. We sat silently for a moment, taking each other in from a safer distance than our first meeting allowed for. Just as I opened my mouth to break the stalemate, Bethany interjected.

"So, you didn't stick around long yesterday. I had meant to ask where you were from. You kind of have that 'not from around here thing' going on."

"Yeah, no. I'm from the City. I'm from New York." It sounded odd. Having never been anywhere outside of Manhattan, I've never had to explain my origins to anyone. Real recognizes real, and when you are born and raised in Manhattan there is no need to establish that you're local, it's just a mutual recognition.

Bethany nodded, considering, and sipped her latte, cupping it in both hands, as if it was some sort of magic potion, or more likely, as if she was drawing its residual warmth into her no doubt cool hands, being that she appeared to be completely lacking in any evident natural insulation.

"I grew up here. Just down the street. My dad lives in Gorham, just a few miles from the school," she offered, though I didn't ask. As if sensing my confusion, she continued. "My dad's really overprotective. I got a dance scholarship to Butler, but he wouldn't let me go that far. He wanted me to start here and then I guess we'll talk about it."

I blinked. Although I hadn't asked for Bethany's life story, I was now engrossed. That seemed so heartless. Dance was *clearly* Bethany's obsession, why hold her back? Mami is overprotective, sure, but she would never keep me from a genuine opportunity. I suddenly softened towards her, uncrossing my arms and opening my chest in her direction.

"Well that seems like bullshit. No offense," I falter. "That just seems real harsh. I mean, obviously dance is your thing."

"I started when I was four. I went to Hochstein. It's my passion, but we'll see…" She trailed off.

"Well, I'm starting nursing. I don't know why I picked it. I guess I'm still looking for my passion," I say. "You're lucky you found it so young."

Bethany nearly smiled back, her lips terse, and nodded.

"You going to orientation?" I asked.

"Yes. We should probably get going actually. Are you driving?"

I kind of chuckled and pushed my knotted bun further back toward the crown of my head.

"Funny story, that. I didn't know you drive so much here. I've hardly ever been in a car, well one that's not a taxi, but I've definitely never driven one."

Bethany blinked and kind of leaned across the room as she stretched her long neck my way.

"You've never driven? Like, you don't even have your permit?"

I put my hands up as if to surrender.

"Well, we'll have to work on that. Come on, we can ride in together."

Bethany grabbed her keys and we headed down to her car.

Hardly the Ford Focus I was in earlier, Bethany had a glossy pearlescent winter white BMW. It looked starkly out of place amongst the rusted-out beaters that littered the parking lot.

I tried not to look as astonished as I was. I suddenly wondered if my jeans were clean enough to slide into her pale leather seat.

After a moment of playing it cool, my envy could no longer be restrained.

"Damn girl! You rollin'!" Initially not wanting to appear easily impressed, I abruptly abandoned my stoicism and fawned over every trim detail.

So enamored with the vehicle, I barely noticed that we had casually swung into a parking spot in front of the school.

"Shit, Bethany, I didn't know it was like that! Man, what a ride! Where did you get that?"

Bethany continued her gliding walk toward the school, eyes fixed in front of her.

"It was my consolation prize."

I stopped walking and grabbed her elbow before she blew by me. I put my hands out and shrugged my shoulders for her to elaborate.

"My mom had an accident at work. She died. We got a settlement, and that's where I spent my money. I wanted something that was beautiful, and mine, that I could ride away in if my father ever let me go. Now he's all messed up, and afraid to let me leave or do anything. Ok? Happy now?"

I felt the air get sucked from my lungs. I could barely hinge a breath to croak a proper apology.

"I'm sorry," was all I could muster as I dropped back a step behind her and slunk into the lecture hall. It felt like I had robbed her. Like I had pulled something away from her she wasn't ready to give up. I was an asshole. I just never expected all of that. On the surface, Bethany looked like this princess. Like the world bowed to her whim. Who knew that pretty Russian doll face could hide so much pain.

I puddled in my seat beside her, hoping the burlap-like fabric would somehow absorb me into itself.

The dimly lit, cavernous room felt vaguely sepulchral. The practically miniature fold down stadium seats barely accommodated my hips. I was womanly, but not large by any means. I wasn't sure how these claustrophobic accommodations would make my larger peers feel.

The murmuration of hopeful, wide-eyed students shuffled by in a trickle, then a flood, then back to a trickle again. I was surprised by the spectrum of ages of the students that pushed through the heavy double doors. The age range had to cover the gamut of the age spectrum from seventeen years to sixty five? Maybe seventy? I had arrived thinking we would be a washed and pressed, homogenous lot. Instead I found, more often than not, I would soon feel like a minority in an entirely different way each day. I never realized how sheltered I was, flowing through high school in neat little rows of ninth, tenth, eleventh, and twelfth graders. Always knowing where I fit in. I had always felt separate from those who had more years under their heels than me. I guess there was a piece of me that still naively thought that once you were of a certain age you had nothing left to learn, that you had "arrived," immaculately. To be forced into this comingled situation where we were learning alongside each other felt unsettling, intimidating.

The simmering chatter settled into stillness, as the groans from the seats being unwillingly lowered tapered off, and the Dean of Students addressed our incoming class.

Now, I would love to tell you that he gave some rousing speech that inspired us and sent us off into a churning sea of knowledge, but I have no recollection of what was actually said. Overwhelmed by my early wakeup, my delayed introduction to my roommate, and subsequent humiliation, I just couldn't focus, and I was quickly bouncing my knee and looking around the room for a clock.

We all spilled out into the hallways and went our separate ways. Even Bethany, who I swore was right behind me was nowhere to be found when the sea of students parted, and everyone settled into their respective assigned locations. After two wrong turns, I hunted around and eventually found my way to the cafeteria.

Thank the good Lord for the meal plan. I never truly realized how helpless I was until I was faced with the realization that three square meals didn't just magically appear before me at regularly scheduled intervals, as I had come to expect.

I visited every food station with my now crowded tray and hoisted my haul back to a far corner near the back of the room. As I sat to devour my enormous meal in peace, William sat down at the table next to mine.

"Hey! Daniela, right?" He said, as if he hadn't just met me twelve hours prior. "Still hungry I see," he chuckled.

“Yeah, hey William, what’s up?” I said, heavily annoyed at the implication.

“Not much, not much. Same as you, I guess. Great minds,” he said with a hearty smile and a nod in my tray’s direction.

“Great minds,” I said waving my bagel at him.

“So, hey, I never did ask you, what’s your major?”

“Nursing.” I said decisively.

“Oh yeah? Cool, cool, cool. Me too actually!”

I suddenly turned and gave him my full attention, realizing too late that I hadn’t fully chewed my somewhat stale bagel, I had to force it down with a hard swallow and a glug of milk before I could formulate a response.

“Are you shitting me?”

“Scout’s honor,” he responded raising his right hand.

“No way, what’s your first period?”

“English 101,” he responded.

“Oh, I don’t need that, I did AP,” I said. “What else you got?”

After comparing notes, we had two of our five classes together, Psychology, and Microbiology.

We chatted briefly between bites, and parted ways. It felt good to know that I would have someone in my classes that at least I had met before. I was slowly connecting dots, finding my way through this thing.

*

The next day when I awoke, again dazed, disoriented, processing, Bethany was already gone. I had never realized, the very definition of being a ballerina is that you are light on your feet, but I swear this girl didn't leave footprints when she walked. She maneuvered in this realm of total silence. You couldn't even hear her breathing when you were standing shoulder to shoulder with her. It was bizarre. I wondered fleetingly if she was really a vampire or something.

I pulled on my same hoodie and black jeans from yesterday and made my way down to the showers, hoping beyond hope to see the lithe and nubile Aphrodite I had spotted the other day. Alas, my gaze was instead accosted by fleshy, hairy, female anatomy that it was just way too early in the fucking morning to deal with graciously. Worse yet, the private stalls were all taken, and I had to cow beneath a lukewarm, sputtering shared showerhead. I quickly lathered, rinsed, and did not repeat, as fast as I could. Still no shave for me.

I opted not to crowd onto the shuttle, and instead made the half mile or so walk down to the school. The air was already growing crisp in the mornings. It felt refreshing to have the breeze rustle through my hair and rush past my ears.

I found my first class with relative ease and took the first seat I walked up to.

"Everyone here for Western Civ?" The Professor asked. One boy got up and walked out. "Anyone else?" Another boy scraped his seat against the linoleum and made a hasty exit. "Good? Ok then." He turned and wrote his name and cell phone number on the whiteboard.

The professor was a chubby, bearded, strawberry blond man with hipster horn-rimmed glasses, a neatly trimmed ginger beard, and a surprisingly witty sense of humor.

"So, hey guys, and welcome. I'm Jim. I'm going to be your Sherpa on this wild, wonderful journey called Western Civ," he opened. "Here's my cellphone number if you need to reach me. Text don't call me. Ever. And don't expect a response after nine p.m. I'm thirty-six. When you get there you'll understand." He turned jauntily for comedic effect. The class responded with a murmur of muted, polite chuckles.

I had no interest in Western Civ, but suddenly I didn't mind being there at eight thirty in the morning quite as much as I expected to.

I had a break before going to Micro and spent it sitting outside the Conservation Department's offices, where dozens of unfortunate taxidermied woodland creatures lay forever in state in their glass sarcophagi.

William had beaten me to Micro, so I had to work my way into the middle of the room to take the seat behind him.

"Hi," we whispered to each other.

After class, William said he had to leave and go to work at the Walmart across the street.

It really hadn't ever occurred to me to get a job. I suppose I had just always thought my obligation in life was being fulfilled by simply existing and showing up to class.

I had never before realized so acutely how sheltered I really was. Not sheltered, privileged. Entitled. *Spoiled.*

Mami worked three jobs back home, sunup to sundown and beyond. Never complained. Never kicked my ass out of bed and told me to pay my portion of the rent. I was just expected to study hard, be a good daughter and sister, and not make too much of a mess before she got home.

I was suddenly homesick. I called Mami when I got back to the dorm just to hear her voice on the voicemail.

"Hi Mami," I squeaked. "I just wanted to call and tell you I love and miss you tons. Love you Mami. Bye."

After I ended the call, I shut off my phone screen and stared at my face in the black. I felt my chest cave in. It felt like a portal closing, and I was back in my lonely darkness.

I was unprepared for how much less actual work college was than high school. I know that sounds backwards, but High School was non-stop, seven fifteen to two forty- five, Monday through Friday. And I felt like I always had homework in every subject. It was eleven o'clock and I was already done for the day. I could do homework, but I didn't have class again until Thursday. I had only been sitting in the dorm for a half an hour and I already felt restless.

I decided to investigate my job options. It would at least give me some spending money instead of having to pester Mami for it.

I spotted a corkboard covered in job postings outside of the Student Life Center when I went down to the cafeteria to get some food. Having never had a job before, they all looked promising. One particular flier caught my eye. Maybe just because it was on top, or because the font was bigger, but for whatever reason, I ripped a phone number from the tasseled bottom and stuffed it deep in my pocket.

When I got back to the dorm, I called the place as soon as I walked in. It was a little seafood restaurant called Schooners that did a locally famous fish fry on Fridays and had the "catch of the day" artfully scrawled on the chalkboard when you walked in. Fortuitously, it also happened to be within walking distance of the dorm.

After tripping over myself cold calling them on a whim in the middle of the lunch rush, the manager invited me to stop down for an interview the next morning between classes.

I laid back into my twin mattress a little deeper that night, feeling incredibly satisfied with myself for making such a grown-up decision all on my own.

The next morning, I walked the mile or so down the road to Schooners. It seemed an easy feat in September's brisk air, but I knew this walk was going to be hell come January when the winds change, and no matter what you have on, that cold cuts through you like a knife.

I wore my black pants and the only button-down shirt I owned. The collar threatened to choke me as I waited for the manager to come out to meet me.

If he hadn't directed his outstretched hand at me and introduced himself, I would have mistaken him for a displaced student. He looked maybe five years older than me, if that.

"Hi, I'm Kyle, the manager here. Daniela, right? We spoke on the phone yesterday."

"Right, Daniela," I said annunciating in way that showed the flatness with which he had pronounced it. "Nice to meet you," I said as I firmly shook his hand.

"Likewise. So, let's take a seat and get started, shall we?"

Kyle walked me over to an empty table and we sat, and he asked me a series of questions he had typed out in front of him on a sheet of paper.

"Where do you see yourself in five years?" That was his opener.

I hesitated. Why is there this sudden expectation to have a five-year plan? Five years ago, I was thirteen, playing with Barbies. How should I know? Feeling the second hand on my watch tick by gratingly, I responded the only way I could. With bullshit.

"Well, currently, I'm enrolled in classes over at the college here. I'm in my first semester. I'm majoring in nursing. My goal is to get through school, and see where my nursing career takes me, but in the interim, I'm looking for a job that can occupy my free time. I'm from New York City, and my family and friends are all back home, leaving me with a fair amount of available time to focus on something besides my classes. I've never personally worked in the restaurant business before, but my mother has been a waitress her whole life, so I've learned a lot about the inner workings of the industry secondhand, so I think I come into this role with realistic goals, and I think it is a natural progression for me to find my way into the field, until my education takes me elsewhere. I'm a hard worker and a quick study, and I like helping people, so I think I would be a good fit." I inhaled deeply, noticing for the first time since I started rambling that all of that was said on a single breath.

I saw Kyle blink several times and glance through the rest of his questions on his paper in front of him. He looked up from his paper and back at me and said, "Ok, well, when might you be able to start?"

I told him I was free after four o'clock. He passed me an apron and explained the dress code, and I headed back to my dorm with a newfound fullness in my chest. I felt in control of my life for the first time since arriving here.

That afternoon, when I returned, Kyle again met me at the door and took me around the restaurant explaining table numbers and introducing me to the crew. We pushed through the back and into the staff locker room. One of the waitresses was crouched down placing her navy and white Adidas sneakers into a bottom locker. Before she looked up, Kyle introduced her to me as Robin, the person who would be training me for the next week or two to get me up to speed.

When Robin rose to stand and face me, my stomach dropped to the floor where she had been squatting.

Showergirl. The sleek, wet, jungle cat-like creature I had seen naked in the communal washroom a few days prior. I thought my panties would drop to the floor beside my stomach.

She reached for my hand and gave it a firm handshake. Her eyes simmered as they met mine and she flashed a raucous little smile.

All I could think with her hand in mine was, *I am in so much fucking trouble.*

*

Bethany had been giving me driving lessons regularly for the past four weeks. She had driven me down to the DMV and gotten me the learners permit study guide, and I took the written exam, and passed after a cursory look over the material. After I was handed my temporary permit, Bethany inexplicably let me drive home to the dorm on the country back roads.

Bethany said she enjoyed being chauffeured, but as far as her motive for doing me such a tremendous kindness, I think she saw me as a project, her little urban revival. I was willing to overlook the implication. Ultimately, it was damn decent of her not only to have given up her time to help me with something that had set up to be a major stumbling block for me, but to have faith in my ability to not crash her cherished car.

She taught me parallel parking in a near empty stretch of side street by the railroad tracks on Saltonstall. She taught me how to pump gas. I used my tip money from the restaurant to keep her tank full, as a small debt of gratitude for her time and tutelage. Bethany insisted I was road test worthy, but there was a three-month waiting period before I was eligible, so it would have to wait at least until the end of the semester.

School was going well that first semester. I actually found myself excited to go to class in the morning, and I enjoyed the peace and quiet, studying in the low light of my desk lamp on the nights Bethany slept at her dad's. She paid the exorbitant room and board fees only to utilize the dorm as a reprieve from her father's constant need for reassurance and companionship, but when guilt got the better of her if he was having a bad day, she drove home to be with him.

William called me up that evening. He needed some help with Micro, so I stayed after with him and went over notes and assignments before work. There were a handful of us doing our prereqs together, and we were starting to mete out and identify each other as nursing students. We exchanged nervous and hopeful glances amongst each other when we realized our paths would all converge next semester in Anatomy and Physiology when shit got real and we all started taking our core nursing classes.

My job at the restaurant was going well. I made a killing on Fridays when everyone filed in from the VA and local assisted living facilities for the fish fry. I always made good tips those days. I was saving up a small nest egg for a car, and I was hoping maybe I would be able to afford one by the end of next semester.

Then there was Robin. *Fuck.* I followed her around like a puppy when I first got there. Mainly because I was required to while she was training me, then later because I would do anything to be in close enough proximity to watch her every movement.

She played soccer. Of course she did. You don't get a body like that shuffling back and forth to class, eating a steady diet of cafeteria food and kitchen excess at the end of the night like me. She was an education major and was hoping to get into Elmira next year after she graduated. She wanted to teach math. That was as far as I had gotten with her. I was walking to work one afternoon, and she saw me trudging in the misty freezing rain and pulled over and offered me a ride. We talked a bit on the short drive in. I told her as much about myself as I could before we pulled behind the building into the staff parking area, and our friendly banter quickly dissolved in the rain. Things were pretty much all business between us up to that point, until William's party.

First off, let me just say this, dating as a homosexual woman is difficult. There is no sitting back, waiting for someone to ask you out. The pool is shallow and rife with miscommunication. People talk about having a "gaydar," and being able to tell when another person is gay just by looking at them, but looks can be incredibly deceiving, and outside of the West Village it's not a safe assumption to make that someone might be "family," as Randall once asked me years ago. Here, in conservative Upstate, there was no secret language, no nod and wink, no special handshake, no nudge nudge. A flannel shirt and Tims are standard issue apple picking attire, not code for, "I am of the lady-loving persuasion." To be certain, you had to commit. You have to track movements, look at fingernails, and earring preferences, and scrutinize pop culture references, and musical tastes. It was an investment. A lesbian is not made by playing softball alone. Just because she has every Tegan and Sara album, and had seen them live four times in Delaware, or because she goes to beach volleyball tournaments every weekend, does not necessarily guarantee that she is on the taco-eating team.

I didn't have the *cajones* to just come out with it and save myself some pining by simply asking her point blank if she was into girls. The sum-total of my sexual experience had been with one very direct, very bold, and self-assured woman. She took the lead in every way, I just followed along like a hungry ghost. I had no clue how to initiate anything. For all the courage it took to get me here, I was an absolute coward when it came to expressing my romantic interest in someone. It wasn't as simple as just asking. Showing too much interest outed you. You risked seriously offending someone, and then having their shame and disgust potentially deflected back on you. These were dangerous waters, and I didn't necessarily want to risk anyone at work knowing I was gay, and I especially didn't want anything getting back to my classmates at school.

To be crystal clear, I was not ashamed of myself, or whom I chose to love. It has nothing to do with that. I no longer carried that burden of shame with me at this point in my life. That being said, having your sexuality be a topic of discussion at work amongst your peers is a disconcerting thing. It colors every interaction. Every straight female thinks they're being hit on, and every male feels instantly either threatened, turned on, or entitled to treating you like "one of the boys," or wanting to be the one that "turns you" to the other team. It's not a matter of shame, or being in a proverbial closet, it's just easier to not have to explain an inherent defining characteristic of yourself as if it were a subject that was up for debate.

With Robin, after several weeks of playing at the *is she or isn't she* game, I finally mustered the gumption to ask her if she would like to meet me at William's party.

William's grandmother had a charming little cottage on East Lake Road. It was three bedrooms and a screened in upstairs porch with a couch that pulled out into a bed. I had been there a few other times to study when we were struggling through new material, and twice before midterms. We always started out with the best of intentions. I would bring a smorgasbord of snacks and coffee to keep us going for a marathon session, but when the breeze called us out to the water, we all abandoned our books and clothes on shore and ran off the end of the dock into the cold blue expanse.

At first, I was nervous. Mami had taken us for swimming lessons at the Y when we were little determined that, *none of her babies would die in some damn water*. But swimming in the shallow end of an indoor swimming pool encircled by helping hands and watchful eyes was nothing compared to the gripping thalassophobia that seizes you as you plunge feet first into an unknown depth. Apart from that, there are swimming things, and creeping things, and things gliding about unseen, brushing against your legs. It is terrifying, and thrilling, until you just surrender to it, stop thrashing about uncontrollably, and commune with your inner mermaid. I grew to love it. All of it.

When I invited Robin, I was inviting her into my happy place, my Shangri-la. It was where I felt as if I was in my most evolved form, the most comfortable I ever was in my own skin. I waited with bated breath as dusk fell, cars began pulling into the gravel driveway, people from the college and William's high school started milling about, and the bonfire sparked to a roar. Beer bottles began clinking. Labbatt's Blue. Awful stuff. The majority of us were under-age, but the fear of being caught was blunted by the percolating buzz we were all wadding through.

Night fell, and crickets and frogs were singing away in a cacophony that sounded like an encore of summer, though it was solidly fall. The unseasonable warmth of that evening brought everyone a sense of heated anticipation to savor every drop of this moment, because it was all about to burnish red and yellow as autumn steadied its foothold.

I had been swaying to R.E.M.'s haunting lamentations for the last hour, feeling just fine, when I felt a hand on my shoulder. Robin. She turned me around and gave me an enveloping embrace in her thick arms. I hugged back deeply and inhaled her. I passed her a beer and she sucked down the neck of it in a single, thirsty glug. She smiled. Her best feature, hinting at years spent in braces to capitalize on her one beauty. I smiled back. Dizzy, effervescent, finally game for some witty raillery.

We sat down on one of the tree stumps surrounding the fire pit and talked for hours about school and work and soccer and the City. There was an ease to the cadence of our conversation that I had never felt around her at work, or the few times I passed by her making small talk between classes. There was never this level of engagement. I had wondered if there was anything substantive to her besides her soccer, and the way she could carry four entrees from the kitchen to the table without sending peas toppling from the edge of a single misaligned plate. I was pleasantly surprised by her depth, and how easy she was to exchange with. Just as I would conclude a thought, she would rally, and stood at the ready with a follow up to keep the ball in play. I loved it. It felt good to feel interesting, and like I had something worth saying, and someone charming and clever to say it to.

After far too many slightly punk, sweating beers, we made our way up to that screened porch under the guise of warming up, as night fall had brought with it a chill that quieted the frogs, and the dying embers of the bonfire could no longer keep the cool at bay. We provided faulty support to each other up the narrow, sighing staircase. I had the clarity of mind to pull the bed from the couch before tucking into our spots, and risk interrupting whatever was rapidly unfolding between us.

It wasn't until she put her tongue in my mouth when I went in to kiss her that I could truly rest assured that she was gay. I felt like I had won the lesbian lottery, finding the one girl I believed on campus may actually be into me.

We undressed each other hurriedly, ravenously, taking each other with an aggression and passion I had never fallen into with Jenni. She was always calculated, always in control, and she never surrendered to me completely. I had no choice but to follow the pace of her maddeningly protracted cadence, and any misstep on my end would unravel the moment. It would just evaporate in my hands and she would retreat and redress herself before I knew what had happened. I spent more time in longing and anticipation and bewilderment than I ever did feeling any semblance of mutual satisfaction.

With Robin, exploration happened organically. Desire was met in equal proportion with desire. This was fast, messy, completely present. It was hotter, wetter, completely uninhibited, and unedited. It wasn't pretty, but goddamn it was real. It felt so fucking good to just be wanted, touched, desired.

When we had both climaxed for each other we lay there breathless in each other's arms. I felt protected, emptied, yet my heart was so full. We didn't slide back into our clothes right away. I ran my fingers across her rippled belly, she pawed at my hips and ass. It was the intimacy that followed that left me feeling so contented, even more so than the sex. There was no pointed dash to the restroom to wash her face, no spraying perfume around the room to mask the scent of lust and a lack of self-control. There were just two women close to each other, wanting to be closer. The waves gently lapped at the rocks on the shore and the wind gave a soft whistle through the screens. You could make out Cassiopeia, Perseus, and Orion. Robin pointed out Draco the snake, and the waning Summer Triangle. On a night like that, I swore I could see heaven.

*

The close of my first year went by relatively unceremoniously. I celebrated my birthday alone in my dorm while Robin was spending the weekend back at her parent's house in Buffalo. Mami had called me at five a.m. to be the first to wish me *feliz cumpleaños*. I got a voicemail from Marisol when I was at class. I tried to call her back, but she didn't answer. In her message she mentioned driving up to see me one of these days, but didn't indicate any sort of timeframe, so I wasn't holding my breath.

As I sat on my bed alone in my dorm, I ate a cupcake that I had picked up the day before on my walk into work. It didn't feel as lonely as it sounds, but there was a decided realization that gone were the days of syrupy sweet birthday parties, and off-key renditions of *Happy Birthday*. My childhood was definitely over, but in a way that I had made peace with. It was an ending of a chapter, not the closing of a book.

William, another girl Avery, and I began having panicked study sessions between classes, nervously sorting through characteristics of bacterium. *Is this Serratia marcescens or pseudomonas aeruginosa? Serratia cultures out pink, and pseudomonas cultures blue-green, but they're both gram-negative rods.*

Anatomy and Physiology was a bear. Trace the path of blood through the heart naming all the valves and ventricles along the way? Pick up any random wrist bone and determine if it was a hamate or a capitate? Getting through that class with a mandatory B was the greatest testament to our sheer force of will and determination than anything I had ever accomplished academically. Any time I'd find myself frustrated and overwhelmed by the material, it was William who would say, *eyes on the prize girl*, and snap me out of my pity party.

Work let me go on a student release at the end of the semester so I could get back home before summer session started. Mami met me at the baggage claim at JFK and we took the A train home. She held my hand the entire ride to 15th Street.

Though I'd only been gone for six months, Mami looked older and thinner somehow. I thought it was my imagination at first. Her face was slightly hollow where her cheeks had once blossomed, and there were darkened little troughs welled out beneath her eyes. I pictured them as the perfect vessels for the tears she cried in private, allowing them to settle and dry there, before their trenches were overwhelmed, and they spilled out onto her empty cheeks. I asked her if she was eating and she looked at me with distain, as if I had asked her if she was still Catholic.

During my visit home, Mami did something I never expected her to do, nor did I have any recollection of her ever doing in the past. She took a vacation. Not just any vacation, she took two weeks off work for the first time in her entire life.

We sat in coffee shops and went to the movies. We went to the awesomely wacky Serendipity 2 and got frozen hot chocolates. We walked through Bryant Park and went to the Museum of Natural History. We ate pastrami sandwiches with brown mustard and pickles at Katz. We went down to Battery Park and strained to see the Statue of Liberty through the greying mist. She was a tourist for the first time in her own city. Taking in sights she had been too busy to notice in all her years there. It was the first time I ever saw her look up. Seeing her awestruck for the first time in two decades was movingly endearing. I found a deepening love for her in every step. As the days ticked by, she grew more relaxed. I stopped hearing the clangour of her alarm clock by day three as she let her routine fall by the wayside for the first time I could ever recall. Mornings of her cooking a hurried, practical breakfast in our cramped kitchen were replaced by crepes and coffee on Broadway, and lunch in Queens. It was a stark departure from our frugal life of restriction and going without that we had grown to accept as a lifestyle. We both needed that release from this life of fasting and wanting, but never partaking. And it was over entirely too soon.

I expected her to cry and linger after me on the platform as I left to go back to my dorm. Instead, she put her hands on my shoulders and kissed me on the forehead. Her eyes were glossy with tears, but they never dropped into those little hollows as I had expected. She squeezed me and said,

"Estoy tan orgulloso de ti," I am so proud of you.

It was the first time she had ever said it. Ever in my entire life. And now I was on the platform balling.

*

Robin and I were good. Real good. I went to all of her home games that fall. She was a beast on the field and the acclaimed team MVP without question. It was rousing to watch. I don't know why, but there's just something about soccer that gets me all fired up. We were not a sports family growing up by any means, but knowing that's your girl out there bombing the ball into the net like an absolute unit is the hottest, most intense sense of pride you can feel toward your partner.

Despite her triumph on the field, Robin didn't get into Elmira like she thought. It was a devastating blow for her because she had essentially planned on it since high school. She had to scramble last minute to get an application into SUNY Binghamton about three hours south of Rochester. It was a tearing, gut wrenching realization that the following year, once I started in clinicals, I would be left with no time or ability to see her. As I felt our intimacy sifting through my fingers, it was ultimately the reprieve I needed to focus on myself and get through my classes. I had invested a good portion of free time that I didn't have in following Robin to her weekend games and making room in my already overbooked schedule for Skype dates, which cut deeply into my study time. The pull of being there for Robin was starting to test the tensile strength of my ability to hold my grades together.

I have a nasty habit of going all in from the jump of a relationship. Not wading in and testing the waters as a responsible individual should. You want my heart, my mind, my body? Take it, it's yours, no questions asked. You would think Jenni would have taught me a lesson in self-preservation, but you would be wrong.

I wanted to be searched, known, accepted. The only way to plunge to that depth with another person is to leave no door locked to them. Or so I thought. But my romantic shortcomings aside, Robin taking off for Binghamton that fall is probably what got me through nursing school. By allowing me to focus less on white horses and picket fences, and more on pharmacology, clinical assessment, and statistics, I made it through my first year of core nursing studies.

*

Clinicals were weird. You'd be put in these bizarre situations that, in any other context, would be strangely intimate. Or horrifying.

My first-ever patient contact was with an emaciated, elderly African American gentleman named Clarence. At nearly six foot four, even after his vertebrae had settled into a kyphotic hunch, Clarence looked imposing, despite his severely deconditioned state.

A heavily decorated World War II Navy veteran, Clarence had swum back into the ruined hull of his ill-fated ship after it was struck by hostile fire from a German sub four times before it sunk beyond his reach. Clarence ended up rescuing three of his fellow sailors, and freed two more from debris to save themselves. The feat would be hard to believe looking at this time addled man, were it not for a faded sepia photo of a distinguished soldier, in full uniform, yellowing in a dusty frame at his bedside. Next to it sat a pair of bulky hearing aids, an old wedding picture of Clarence in his pressed white service dress beside a broadly smiling bride, and what appeared to be a new glossy picture of two chunky great, or great-great grandchildren.

I was told by the nursing assistant that Clarence was "a real handful when he was feeling ambitious, and he's prone to anything from throwing blows, to spitting, to biting," and to "be on guard, even if he looks peaceful, he's been known to play possum until he can get a hand around your wrist or your throat." Appreciative of the warning, I approached Clarence like one would approach a sleeping bear.

When I entered his room, my patient was lying in his bed in nothing but an adult diaper, with loose stool bubbling up from the leg holes like a tar pit. I knocked and approached the siderail of his bed nervously.

I introduced myself as I had been instructed. His smell slapped me across the face, and suddenly I felt that being born with a nose and a sense of smell put me at an incredible disadvantage in this line of work.

Clarence had abandoned, milky eyes, and gave no indication that he heard me or was aware of my presence. He lay in the bed unmoving, eyes fixed upon a water stained ceiling tile. I reached a nitrile-gloved hand up to his shoulder and saw no flicker of acknowledgement. I looked back at his nightstand and slowly, cautiously, as if I was pulling the pin on a hand grenade, hooked his whining hearing aides around his auricle.

Clarence blinked. In a low, honeyed voice, I nearly whispered, "good morning Clarence, my name is Daniela. I'm your student nurse for today. If it's ok, I wanted to get you washed up so we can get you to breakfast." Clarence's right eye and the corner of his mouth twitched, maybe in acknowledgement, or maybe it was just gas.

I turned to the sink and filled a soapy bucket with warm water. The faint perfume of the body wash provided some barely perceptible relief from the stench that was now stuffing my sinuses with an efflux so permeating, I could almost taste it. I carefully wiped his cachectic frame with the washcloth I had tucked into a mitten like we practiced in lab. Wipe as I would, the stool kept coming, and Clarence gave no glimmer of insight that he cared one way or another that he was actively shitting into my hand.

It was not my finest hour, to be sure. After nearly thirty minutes of wiping and shitting, Bitsy, the nurse's aide, again darkened Clarence's doorframe and put her hand on her wide hip and admonished me, "chile, you're still wiping that poor man's ass?" I looked at her pleadingly.

"It won't stop," I said, begging with my eyes for any form of assistance she could possibly offer.

"Girl, don't you know the more you stimulate that butthole, the more it's gonna shit. You gotta get in there and get out and send him on his merry way," she clucked.

Bitsy donned some gloves, grabbed a full towel, and tossed my mountain of filthy washcloths on the floor. In one fluid, swooshing movement she wiped his entire back like she was sqweegeeing a skyscraper window. With a swift shove, she tucked the soiled linens, putrid diaper, and anything else that happened to be lying in the bed halfway under him brutishly, and stretched a fresh sheet, bed pad, and diaper beside him, and sent me to the other side of the bed to pull the mess out from under him. As I pulled, Bitsy hiked up his balls, tucked his diaper and slid his pants halfway up his thighs. Within about thirty seconds, she had accomplished what would have likely taken me another twenty-five minutes. I had never beheld such efficiency in my life.

Once we had him spun onto the side of the bed, Bitsy slid a shirt over him, dropped his Navy Veteran ball cap on his head, and what looked like a corpse five minutes earlier, now looked like a respectable gentleman off to buy a Sunday paper. It was a Weekend and Bernie's level transformation.

*

My pediatric rotation was another story. I was assigned to a day school for developmentally delayed and disabled children. We helped the staff with med passes and tube feeds primarily. I actually loved it, and it gave me a profound sense of awe of the parents that have to care for these kids the other sixteen hours a day that they aren't in school.

It's a tremendous amount of work, and I can't imagine the thanklessness of providing a total level of care day in and day out knowing that your child will never be able to say "I love you," never go to prom, never graduate, never hold a spoon. Whatever hopes and dreams they once carried on their tiny shoulders were replaced by adjusted expectations of maintaining eye contact for three seconds, or being able to eat a few bites of pureed baby food in addition to their tube feed, or maybe one day throwing a ball.

Just when I was feeling absolutely fulfilled as a nurse and human being, and genuinely considering the possibility of specializing in peds after graduation, I had this one patient…

This boy, Jonathan. Twelve years old, developmentally eighteen months, cerebral palsy, gastroschisis, spina bifida, and Hirschprung's disease, wheelchair bound, and completely non-verbal. He was about eighth in line for a tube feeding and I went to lift his shirt to unsnap his Mickey Button to connect the tube feed, as I had done for the other kids that had wheeled or toddled over before him, and then *crack*! He fucking head butted me so hard I fell backward on my heels, landing hard on my butt, and legitimately saw stars. I was completely stunned. The nurse I was with began checking me for a concussion. When my vision cleared and the room stopped spinning, I looked back at Jonathan for any acknowledgment of what he had just done to me and saw absolutely no recognition or remorse flutter across his face whatsoever. The nurse helped me to my feet and said, "Welcome to my world. Can't take your eyes off the little buggers for a second."

After that, I determined, peds was gonna be a hard pass for me.

*

After peds, was Maternity and Women's Health. As a feminist, and avid lover of the female anatomy, I felt like I had a leg up on the competition.

Maternity was, well, it was really something else entirely.

I had always prided myself on being an expert on the female form. A connoisseur if you will. This was another beast entirely. That was not the lovely folded oyster I was used to beholding. Hormones, increased blood volume, and connective tissue laxity do wild and mysterious things to a vagina.

When it came time to watch a live birth, I was struck, not so much by the miracle of life, but by the horrific bulging of a perineum being stretched to the point of tearing. It was like a total pussy explosion. And not the fun kind. This was horrifying. Like, legitimately horrifying.

Following my live birth experience, I further determined rather quickly that I like my *vagine* like I like my coffee. Without a baby in it.

*

Nursing school was like that. Sweeping generalizations that caused you to paint the whole picture based on a singular experience. What I soon realized was that no two cases were ever exactly the same, even with all factors being equal, it was never like you expected it to be. Human beings under stress, whether physical or psychological, never behave as expected. There is a whole spectrum of possible outcomes that we have no way of predicting with any semblance of accuracy. That's what I loved about it. That's what all of us loved. People talk about nurses as being altruistic, and as being in it for the love of helping our fellow man. And, yeah, that's a thing, but for the most part, it is our collective, unbridled curiosity and need to know. It's also for the love of each other.

Nurses are a special breed. Foul-mouthed, witty, questioning, always skeptical, humor so vanta black that if anyone outside of our inner circle knew what we were smirking at they'd probably have us committed. We stick together. We have each other's backs. When it works, it's like being in the trenches, in battle with brothers and sisters who would take a bullet for each other without a second thought. Or at least take one for the team and dump a bedpan or two. It's a compatriotism that only those who have genuinely fought back death and won, ultimately altering the course of someone's destiny, can fully appreciate.

As much as I'd like to leave it on that intrepid high note, that's again not the whole story. Throughout my career, I have found that every positive experience is balanced against, not necessarily a negative one, just one that lets the air out of your balloon. A dampening of one's enthusiasm as it were.

Toxic nursing cultures definitely exist. Scathing jealousy, unchecked ambition, laziness, ignorance, every ugly human fault is present at all times in direct proportion to humanity's better attributes. Contrary to popular belief, we are not, in fact, an army of mini Florence Nightingales. We are ourselves. Fully human, and capable of some pretty despicable and unsavory failings, however, I like to believe that without romanticizing it too much, we are more so at our core, good to ourselves, each other, and our patients, far more often than we are not.

*

Year two began with slightly less uncertainty, and a gradual lengthening of space between panic attacks than when my first year started. Perhaps my greatest achievement, apart from my academic successes, was that I actually got my driver's license. And, by staying on campus for Thanksgiving, and working full time through the break, I had managed to get a solid jump on my savings for a new-to-me vehicle of my very own.

In what was perhaps one of my most fortuitous encounters in life, I had a customer who came in and left me a two hundred fifty dollar tip on a nine dollar and seventy five cent plate. It was the most I had ever gotten in one shot, by about two hundred forty dollars. He was an older gentleman who had asked if I was in college. When I told him I was a nursing student, he explained that he was a cancer survivor and that he was alive today because of the nurses who took care of him. I thought that was the end of our interaction, because once I brought him his dinner, he ate silently, paid his bill without any pomp or circumstance, and turned and left without saying goodbye. I went to bus his table and found the cash and a hand-written note on the back of his napkin that read: *Good luck in your studies. Be kind.* When I ran out to thank him he was already gone. I have come to believe that the only explanation for his generosity and humility was that he was an angel.

Once I pulled my empty Café Bustelo can out from behind my thick winter jacket in the back of my closet, and totaled up my earnings from the past year (less what I had spent on my insatiable appetite for Wegmans sushi) I had just over thirty five hundred dollars.

I had been searching the Swapsheet for cars for sale since I had amassed just over my first thousand. Finally, I found it. A1996 Subaru Outback. It had a hundred thirty thousand miles on it already, but the rust hadn't eaten her away too badly, and the owner assured me she was great in the snow. I bought her. Cash. Five hundred less than asking price. For the first time, I realized how limiting it was to shrink your world down to a walking radius, or as far as you can bum a ride off a friend until they resent and avoid you.

Once I got the plates for it, and it passed inspection, and all of the other surprise accoutrements required to get the thing street legal, I went to the mall. It was such a small thing, but putting the radio to the station *I* chose, singing at the top of my lungs in the sanctuary of my own space, knowing that no one was in the seat beside me grabbing the "oh shit" bar above the window, it was the single most freeing experience of my life. I felt alive, independent, and adult for the first time all at once. I was so fucking proud of myself.

CHAPTER SIX

Finding My Way

I could write an entire book just on that final year of nursing school. It was one of those transformative, singular experiences so nuanced, so distinct, that any mention of isolated events or experiences puts you right back in it, no matter how long you've been a nurse. Without diminishing the pivotal nature of what took place in my time there, I will say, I got through it because we had each other. Every set back and struggle was salvaged by some other member of our class. We supported each other through every test, every paper, and every single competency check off. We held each other through breakups, financial hardships, academic struggles, roommate problems. It was all absorbed communally, and the pressure of the moment was distributed over many shoulders, which made it all seem not quite so bad.

The culmination of our efforts was savored the night before graduation, when we all met for our pinning ceremony to commemorate our journey. Mami pinned the emblem of my nursing school to the breast of my o button down shirt. She cried. I beamed and whispered *gracias Mami* into her salt and pepper waves of hair, now more salt than I remembered. The ceremony was short and sweet, and it took place in one of the lesser conference rooms with the lights slightly dimmed. We were all given electric tea lights as a symbol of Florence Nightingale being the Lady with the Lamp, that we held in our hands, as opposed to a live flame. We could be trusted with a life but not a candle. I smirked at the irony, but there was no denying that something about our pinning ceremony felt sacred, holy, like a prayer circle, or a séance. Either way, it felt like something in the universe had shifted to make a way for me to be here. It felt like a beginning, like something bigger at work than what I had accomplished solely by the sweat of my brow and the work of my hands.

When we finally assembled behind the school in the amphitheater, preparing to walk the stage for graduation the next morning, we all sat scattered throughout the risers, straining to maintain visual contact with each other. I had assumed we'd walk out in formation, arms linked, in a public display of unity and glorious accomplishment. But we were winnowed out, and landed according to our place in the alphabet, without any distinction of what we had just survived, and nothing to distinguish ourselves as graduate nurses. It was over before I had a chance to realize what was happening.

Afterwards, I ran to meet William who was standing at the far end of the lawn with his parents and grandparents. I looked at his grandmother and wondered fleetingly if she was aware that I got laid on the couch in her screened porch. She gave me a look as if she did.

William and I hugged, and Mami and my sisters and I posed for a picture his mother took of us. And then it was over. I gathered my things from my dorm, turned in my key, and the place vanished in the rearview mirror of my Subaru.

Mami and I found the one Mexican restaurant in town and went there for a celebratory early dinner. Mami cursed the food in Spanish for its lack of seasoning as if every staff member there didn't understand Spanish.

I looked around the table at my family. Marisol and Valentina looked like pillars. Carved from gleaming marble but vibrant and full of life and benevolence. Our chatter was a dull din, but somehow it felt natural and free flowing.

I should probably stop rambling now. I know you get the point, but this feeling, this state of being, was one that I had never felt before. We were all here. We'd all made it, despite the forces that threatened to tatter and rend us apart.

Mami had cut to only working two jobs, one of which was only part time, and she made her own hours. She slept until six these days and looked and felt better than she had in years. I nearly spit out my *flautas* when Mami said she started taking a Zumba class. Every Thursday she meets with "her girls" and they Zumba. Who knew?

Valentina was clean. She didn't say it, and I didn't ask, but it was there. There was a clarity to her gaze, her hair was shinier, the apples of her cheeks were fuller and flushed with an apricot glow, the content of her speech was more ordered and subdued. She was the same, but more, I don't know, real? Maybe that's not the word, but that's all I could put my finger on. She seemed like the realest version of herself, not the one that threatened to spontaneously combust.

Marisol was her usual polished, washed, and pressed self. Imperceptibly removed but participating as if her whole heart was in the conversation, even though there was a thin veneer between herself and the rest of us. Like having sex with a condom. Or so I'm told.

They looked good. They looked whole and wholly like a reflection of my soul. We were all various permutations of the same ancient ancestor. The same heart beating within a different form. It was oddly comforting. It felt like the four of us were all different keys to the same lock.

I momentarily lauded myself for having the power to draw these three busy, distracted, important women out of their respective realms and into what I had made my own. I had hoped to hold this moment a little longer, but it dissipated like smoke nearly as quickly as it had accumulated. Marisol apologized, and demurely excused herself to return to the animal hospital, which, knowing that it was Saturday and that she would not have accepted call starting in the middle of the afternoon, I silently accepted that she had had her fill. I kissed her cheeks and thanked her for my card that she had tucked a crisply folded hundred dollar bill into, and off she went. Back to Ithaca. A place I again promised to visit one day, even though she had never formally extended an invitation.

Mami and Valentina were staying the night in the hotel by the lake. Having turned in my key to my dorm, I now had no place to go that was mine. I had about a month on my hands to figure my life out before I had to sit for my state nursing board exam. I was too nervous to apply for jobs yet, even though a handful of my classmates had had positions lined up for them around the city since at least March. It just seemed like bad luck to me.

What if I failed, and I had to be demoted? Everyone on my unit would know that I failed and lose confidence in me. I decided to not even look at job postings until I got my test results back.

I considered briefly, going back to Manhattan and taking a reprieve until I could test and get some solid ground under my feet, but somehow, in the churning activity no one had offered. And, something about it didn't seem right. I had changed. I wasn't the tough, brash, Latina from the two-one-two I had believed myself to be when I arrived here. I don't think I ever truly was her. In a lot of ways, I was still trying to decipher who I was.

I had defined myself through the eyes of my lovers, and through the constant glare from the eyes in the back of Mami's head. Now I didn't know how to define myself.

Robin and I had fizzled out the semester before I graduated. She went off to pursue her teaching degree in Binghamton, not far from where my sister lived. I had commuted back and forth between clinicals and work, but the absences grew longer, and there became less and less to say beyond, how's work? How's school? Our bodies started to forget how to settle into one another. It was the typical autumn of any dying thing. Awkwardness where silence once felt sacred, hands that failed to bend into each other's negative spaces, all the empty, hollow, longing things. For me, our parting was amicable and felt very mature somehow. None of the tears or histrionics that punctuated the dehiscence of my relationship with Jenni. It was just a night when I couldn't make the three-hour drive. Robin said to me over the phone, *this isn't working.* And I said, *I agree*. We thanked each other for the memories, and said maybe when life fell into place, we would find each other again, but we both silently decided within ourselves that we wouldn't.

And that was it. I got up, went to work, and planned my weekend. That's not to say our time together was trivial, or without deep feelings or emotion. We knew what we had. It was wonderful but it was out of place in the mad dash to the finish line of who we were trying to become. It felt liberating to not be completely controlled by my feelings, and to give myself permission not to feel everything and be crushed by it. I took a deep breath and jumped into the last push to pass my boards.

*

At two thirty in the morning, sharing a queen sized bed with Mami and Valentina, and me sweltering between their sprawling bodies, because they were too cheap or too poor to spring for a second room, underneath the faux down comforter, I texted William.

Me: *Can I crash with you after my mom leaves?* I was shocked to get a reply two minutes later.

William: *Yeah sure thing.*

Me: *Cool. Thanks.*

And that was that. I drove Mami and Valentina to the airport and headed back to meet William and move my box and backpack into his grandparent's guest room on the lake.

The only requirement of my stay was that I open the windows for an hour a day to air the place out, weather permitting. That was it. No discussion of rent, no admonishments of "no boys, no drinking, no loud parties." Perhaps they knew the boys would not be a problem. Perhaps they actually trusted me. Or perhaps this was what friendship actually was.

*

I was completely checked out at work. I found it difficult to care about the specials when I was trying to steel myself for the biggest test of my life. As soon as I'd get off shift I would rush back to the cottage, pull out my books and rifle through text books, and flash cards, and struggle to keep from going cross eyed from hours spent reading and rereading the furious scrawl of my notes. I had signed up for my licensure exam, the NCLEX, and I was a disaster, just a flaming dumpster fire of nerves and self-doubt. William came over one night for a lighthearted study sesh, and took one look at me and said, "you're done studying for tonight." I almost cried. He put his hands on my shoulders and looked me in the eyes and said, "Daniela, you're the smartest girl in our class. The money's in the bank. You're done. You know everything you need to know." I agreed to stow the books for one night and we went bowling. I know, bowling...

I had never bowled before. It was just as seedy and cliché as I had hoped it to be, but to my absolute dismay there was no Dude, and no Lebowski.

There were horrible shoes, stale beer, and a guy in a plaid shirt with the sleeves ripped off twirling a toothpick with his tongue. That was mesmerizing.

Between the ambiance, my ridiculous approach with the bowling ball clutched to my chest, and my wide shuffling gait, like I just shit my pants, it was enough to have us all dying of laughter. Just the ridiculousness of it all, the whole thing struck me as being absolutely hilarious. It was exactly what I needed. I hadn't realized that I had completely forgotten how to have fun. Just two years ago I was this kid, who didn't need to schedule fun into her life, it was all around me always.

My life had become so fixated, so singular. I was an adult, with pressures and expectations and deadlines. It was bizarre, and final, and surreal, but that was the precise instant that I knew I had left the old me behind completely. For some inexplicable reason, I marked the milestone with a click of my tongue. As if to say, "it is finished."

In the open window of that realization, I made a determination within myself to embrace the notion of it, willfully and consciously. And in my newfound infinite wisdom, I embraced this moment of fleeting pleasure, and surrendered to the mental reprieve, knowing that the days of friends and shenanigans would soon be another gauzy memory as we all scattered to the wind after graduation.

I had planned to take my NCLEX two weeks to the day after graduation, as my professors had assured us that we would be eligible to do so once we received our official Authorization to Test from the state nursing board.

Well, that didn't happen.

It took nearly a month before I was able to get a testing date.

I took my NCLEX on a Wednesday. I barely slept the night before. My coffee was now churning and curdling away in my stomach, threatening to eat through me like Draino. I was absolutely certain that I had a peptic ulcer.

I felt like I started out the test strong. The questions seemed basic at first. I nearly tricked myself looking for deeper meaning in the prosaic multiple-choice answers I was being lobbed. But then somewhere in the middle, just as I was considering that perhaps I had over prepared, the questions seemed to get abruptly harder. Hemochromatosis what? Tetralogy of fallot huh?? I felt like I was stabbing wildly in the dark. By the time my test shut down on me I was sure I failed.

We were informed that it could take up to forty-eight hours before our test results would be made available. I didn't even care at that point. It was over, I tried my best, and if I failed, I would have to wait three months to retest, so there was no point in worrying about what was happening today.

I checked the state licensure website before I went to bed that night, certain that my test would take the entire forty-eight hours to result. I typed in my name, and four Daniela Martinez' down, I found my birth date, alongside my very own license number. I looked, and reloaded the webpage, and looked again. And there it was. Daniela Martinez, Registered Nurse, and my very own license number!

I frantically called William, and I just screamed into my phone when he picked up. He screamed back. I finally did it! Where most students celebrated after walking the stage at graduation, I had to wait over a month to finally breathe the sigh of relief I hadn't realized I was holding in.

*

I called the nurse recruitment office the next day. I got an automated message stating essentially *fill out an application online and don't call us, we'll call you.*

William had passed his test the week before me and had already dropped some applications. We were both determined to get jobs on the same floor at the University trauma center, but he had warned me ahead of time that the pickings were slim. The state still hadn't passed the budget for the fiscal year, and they were several months late, leaving non-privatized, state funded hospitals in limbo as to how much money they would have to work with in the coming year, so things like hiring new nursing staff was on a critical need basis only, and training brand new baby nurses was expensive. I have heard it estimated that it costs approximately forty thousand dollars to put a new graduate nurse through their initial residency to get them up to speed as a fully functioning RN, so the first thing to go when money is tight are jobs for new grads.

During my first year, nurse recruiters from all over the tri-county area would turn up at the college, pizza and cake in hand, heralding the benefits and amenities waiting for us at their particular institution. It was there just waiting for me to pluck it from the vine, like low hanging fruit, once I was street legal at the end of my nursing program.

Throughout nursing school, I had been under the delusion that hospitals were throwing themselves at my feet, and that having a choice job fresh out of school was a foregone conclusion. By the time I had reached my last semester, and was finally in that glorious position of being able to savor the benefits these state-of-the-art facilities had been dangling before me, I quickly learned that the pizza train had stopped running entirely some months before my final semester, completely derailed due to New York State's inability to pass a budget that guaranteed funding to the very hospitals and healthcare centers that had been wooing me throughout my college career. The top spots in the ED and ICU had all but vanished. By the time I came to the table, the only unit offering slots to new grads was a single med/surg unit that had opened up the year before.

Med/surg. It was the phlegm in the back of the throat of every new grad nurse. Just the words, *Medical/Surgical floor* spirited a cold wind through your newly minted scrub top to find purchase deep within your soul.

Bedpans, nursing home kickbacks, bed baths galore... It was everything we had been led to believe was your consolation prize if you didn't get one of your top pick positions.

I was assured by the now withholding recruiter who, just months before, had materialized in our student lounge, stuffing us full of carbs until we were glassy-eyed and agreeable, and all but patted my head and asked if I wanted another slice of olive peperoni. She now held my future nursing career in her clutches, nearly Cheshire cat smiling as she explained to me that med/surg was all she was authorized to offer me.

I agreed to a four-hour shadow experience, followed by an interview and a chance at one of only twenty-three positions being offered hospital wide, despite boasting nearly a thousand bed capacity. The previous graduating semester, the hospital had taken in nearly two hundred fifty new grads alone. This year, amidst the budget woes, twenty-three positions were all that they had. Beggars would clearly not be choosers under the current economic circumstances, but I was definitely not too proud to take what I could get at this point.

I arrived to my shadow experience forty-five minutes early. I couldn't help myself. Like Mami, my internal alarm clock was now hardwired to bolt me upright in bed at two minutes to 0500. Jolting me awake as if I were about to miss the last train out of Jersey.

I tried to pace myself. I prayed for traffic, or that I wouldn't find the parking garage. But by 0615 I was standing outside of the darkened nurse recruitment office, in scrubs so heavily starched they could likely stand on their own. I had two copies of my pitiful resume tucked under my arm hopefully. I tried to smile politely to the nurses shuffling past me on their way to or from their units. They all looked hurried, determined, unseeing as they passed by me as if I was an apparition.

I tried to imagine myself counted amongst their ranks. I tried to see my face in their hustling gait, but I couldn't quite place myself in that vignette. As I contemplated a lifelong career in waitressing, a young-looking nurse passed by and gave me a little smile and nod, restoring my resolve for a little while longer.

As the top of the hour approached, and I drew nearer to the time I was actually supposed to be darkening the door of the Nurse Recruitment office, the flow of the oncoming shift had started to wane, and my awkwardness at being the only human standing still while everyone else churned around me, was beginning to subside. Just as I relaxed my back against the cool of the cinder block wall, the office secretary pushed by me and let herself in through the door without acknowledging me loitering there. I followed her inside sheepishly as she put up her jacket, put away her keys, took a swig of coffee, and reapplied a layer of mauve colored lipstick.

I stood there intently, unsure if she had seen me and chose to deny my presence, or if she was so enthralled with her routine that I was incapable of breaking her trance. I cleared my throat as unassumingly as I could. She capped her lipstick and only then looked up in my general direction.

"Name?" She asked.

Her abruptness caught me off guard and I had to take a moment to formulate a response.

"Daniela. Um, Daniela Martinez." It sounded like I was asking her instead of telling her.

Without looking up she told me to have a seat.

Shortly thereafter, four other nurses filed in and were giving the same frosty reception. At least it's not just me, I thought with a slight bit of relief.

I was looking down when the polished nurse recruiter Diana Leone, RN, BSN breezed in without so much as a glance in our direction. I'm sensing a theme here. She returned moments later with a toothy smile hung high on her face.

"Welcome!" She nearly demanded. "Alright everyone, remind me of your names again."

We round-robined our reintroductions to her, and she thumbed through a short stack of manila folders with our names scrawled across the tabs.

"Alright, let's roll out," she declared.

We followed along like ducklings, and she dropped us off at our respective units. Radiology for Evan, MICU for Janet, Ortho for Helena, CCU for Jeremy. I was the last stop, perhaps because I was likely the only new grad, or perhaps because Diana sensed my apprehension, but more likely because I was the farthest walk from the elevator.

Before we turned for the unit, she looked at me for the first time. Her lack of ability to emote genuine human emotion was more likely a therapeutic effect of her carefully aimed Botox and less to do with her coldness, but she looked directly in my eyes and handed me my folder and said,

"You're going to do great." For some reason, despite the flat note in her voice, I felt reassured.

Upon walking onto the unit, I again found myself with my hands pinned at my side waiting for yet another secretary to acknowledge that my painful awkwardness was due to my need for assistance, and not simply my desire to bother her.

"Can I help you?" *Janelle*, I read off her name tag. I looked at the smiling face of her picture printed on her badge and I thought it was a mistake. This girl did not look capable of such a smile.

"Yes, I'm Daniela Martinez, I'm here for the shadow," I said too softly causing me to have to repeat myself.

She looked me up one side and down the other and sucked on her teeth before responding.

"Lemme get the charge nurse," she said as she turned in her wheeled office chair and peered around the corner.

"Michelle!" She snapped loudly.

A wild red head rounded the Formica countertop of the nurses station in a rainbow and unicorn scrub top.

She came around the desk and introduced herself as Shelly and put her hand out to shake mine once I stated my business on her unit.

Shelly took the clipboard off the desk and glanced over her roster a couple of times, weighing her options.

"I guess we can put you with... hmm. Layla," Shelly finally decided.

Layla was a warm and welcoming Filipina who looked to be in her mid to late twenties, but her face was so cherubic and child-like she may have been thirty. I couldn't tell. From the second we made our introductions I determined that I liked her. She was getting report from Dom, the off going night nurse who chatted back and forth with her in bursts of chirpy Tagalog as they gave report.

Layla translated for me once Dom picked up his belongings and vacated the section of countertop we now occupied.

"We have five patient assignments on days, but at night you can flex up to as many as eight," Layla explained to me as she widened her eyes for me to emphasize that that was a heavy assignment. I likened my eyes in kind as if I understood the full weight of what that meant.

"So today we have rooms 23, 24, and 25. Most of our rooms are semi-private, but 25 is an iso room so we only have one in there. Mr. Martin. He's hospice but they're renovating the hospice unit, so we're taking all their overflow. Don't worry, I don't think he'll die on our shift," she chuckled.

"Hopefully not," I murmured, suddenly nervous.

"23A is a sickle celler, 23B is pancreatitis, 24A is a Crohn's flare, and 24B is a GI bleed going for a colonoscopy later today, so we'll be on poo duty until he cleans out," she explained.

"Well let's go update our boards and meet everyone." I followed her into 23A, and watched her butterfly script uncurl on the whiteboard as she wrote down our names. Layla washed her hands and did a brief assessment of our first patient.

"Daniela, look," she said. "This is kind of interesting actually. Ms. Winters do you mind if I show Daniela your port?"

"Help yourself," Ms. Winters said.

Layla pulled back the layers of blankets to reveal an implanted vascular access device on the inside of the patient's thigh.

"You don't see this very often. Ms. Winters how many ports have you had?" Layla asked loudly.

"Twenty-seven," she reported unenthusiastically.

"Wow," I said. "I've only seen one, but it was in someone's chest."

"That's where they usually go, but Ms. Winters has had sickle cell her whole life and she's running out of spots," Layla informed me.

"Since I was two years old," Ms. Winters, now forty-seven, nearly geriatric for her particular type of sickle cell disease, Layla later informed me.

"Wow," was all I could manage to say. That is a very long time to be in pain, was all I could think.

We moved onto our next patient, sitting up in the chair beside her bed, one thin curtain over, politely acting as if she hadn't heard our entire conversation.

We followed the same routine. Introduction, assessment, then pearl of wisdom I had failed to learn in nursing school.

Our B bed patient, Mrs. P, her preferred name since it was ungodly trying to listen to the nurses struggle through her full name of Kathy Panagopoulos. Mrs. P had idiopathic pancreatitis from a gallstone that had been retained after having her gallbladder removed. For weeks she returned to her surgeon complaining up worsening right upper quadrant pain after her surgery. Her doctor just thought she had a low pain threshold, but Kathy had birthed three sons without analgesia, and she knew this was not straightforward post-operative pain, as her surgeon had claimed. She finally returned and demanded another CT scan. When she had one, they found that not only had she retained a stone, but her pancreas was now inflamed and cystic. By the time they ran amylase and lipase levels on her, her numbers were through the roof and resulted at the upper level of measurement, meaning they were so high they didn't even give an exact result because they were off the scale. She was promptly admitted for acute pancreatitis, which can be fatal as the pancreatic digestive enzymes leak into the delicate pancreatic tissue. If left untreated, those enzymes can leak out of the pancreas and effectively eat you alive from the inside out.

Mrs. P., like her counterpart in bed A, was on a PCA pump for pain control, but in her case, she was on complete and utter bowel rest. Even ice chips were off limits. She hadn't taken anything at all by mouth in twenty days, receiving her fluid and nutrition parenterally through the PICC line in her bruised and tender looking arm.

I took in the suffering in this room alone and quickly realized what an immense gift being healthy is. Living in crippling pain your entire life was something I couldn't fathom. And I had never appreciated what a privilege it was to enjoy a cool glass of water or to simply satiate your hunger. It seems so mindless, so innate, and yet here was a woman who, by no fault of her own, had to lay in a hospital bed apart from her family while the foundation of her body's needs, lipids, amino acids, electrolytes, glucose, vitamins, were dripped into her arm, far away from her lips, far away from any sort of sensation that could be interpreted as enjoyment.

We met and assessed our other patients and returned to the nurses station to begin gathering medications for the first of several med passes of the shift.

Just as we were a quarter of the way through our first patient's laundry list of meds, some of which were encroaching on "overdue" territory, one of the gentlemen in room 24 hit the call light.

Layla looked me in the eyes and said,

"And so, it begins."

We went in to 24B and found our eighty-four year old Santa Clause-esque patient, finger painting his call light and headboard with maroon-black tarry stool. The fact that he had accidentally pushed the call light was no small miracle, since we had been in there not five minutes before, and he was nowhere near the sorry state we found him in now. The contrast spoke volumes for the quickness with which a patient can go from clean, fed, and content, to shit-covered, tangled in blankets, and half-way out of the bed.

Layla passed me a blue plastic gown and some size small gloves and cleaned out the cabinet of folded linens and wipes she had squirreled away from the last clean-up she did.

"Smell that?" She asked.

"Uh, yeah," I said sardonically. I was pretty sure the entire fourth floor could smell it.

"Well, now you'll never forget it. It's the smell of GI bleed. Digested blood. You can smell it a mile away, and if you ever smell it again you need to call the doctor right away."

As I was watching Layla wipe and talk, I had Mr. Stevens turned toward me, business end to Layla, and before I realized what was happening, he had vomited all down my blue gown.

"Oh," was all I could manage to say before Layla flipped him on his back and was checking for a carotid pulse.

"I NEED SOME HELP IN HERE!" Layla shouted in the most authoritative way I had ever heard someone speak.

Standing in Mr. Steven's black coffee-ground vomit as everyone rushed by and began grabbing and jostling, was the most useless I had ever felt in my entire life.

I backed away to make space for those that knew what they were doing.

Soon an overhead page had gone out, calmly calling for the Code Team to come to the unit. Seemingly within seconds the room was full of residents, nurses, a respiratory therapist, and I'm not even sure who else.

The only cognizance I managed to retain was to take off my soiled gown and gloves and take up as little space as possible. I watched the commotion from the doorway as Layla pulled the roommate's bed out of the room to make space. She caught my eye and said,

"Come on!"

I fell in line with the entourage and followed them to the ICU.

Mr. Stevens I would learn, had an episode of vasovagal syncope. The stooling and blood loss had caused him to be hypovolemic, and increased his vagal tone, causing his heart rate to plummet into the twenties when his constant violent defecation stimulated his vagus nerve. They gave him IV fluid, and atropine, and transcutaneously paced him on the way up to the ICU, where he could be started on the massive transfusion protocol and possibly a vasoactive medication infusion to help with his blood pressure I would learn.

I followed Layla out of the unit, and we made our way down the hall quietly, until we reached the elevator, when Layla turned to me and said,

"Well, that was fun," Layla said with a breezy smile.

I looked back at her and blinked.

"We may have different definitions of fun," I told her. That was when she filled me in on what had just happened clinically. All I could do was shake my head and say, "I still have so much to learn. I just thought he threw up. I just wasn't expecting all that at all."

"You'll figure it out. We were all there once. So, what do you think of the unit? Are you going to come work with us?" She looked back at me hopefully.

"I hope so," I said. And I meant it. I got the offer to shadow the unit and felt a little put out being that it was med/surg, knowing that far less "accomplished" graduate nurses than I were getting jobs in ICUs and EDs in other hospitals. Suddenly I realized just in the few hours I had been there how diverse a patient population we had within our own assignment, and how little I knew about any of it. Even in report, when we heard about our GI bleed patient that crumped on us, when Dom, the night nurse, was telling us our patient had a bleed, Layla cut him right off and said, "what's the H&H?" I realized later H&H was hemoglobin and hematocrit, and thought to myself, "what a great question!" I need to know these things, and I didn't even know what I didn't know at this point.

When we returned to the floor, Melissa, the manager of the unit was waiting in the nurses station for us.

"Fun day huh?" She asked and extended her hand to me to make her formal introduction. I thanked Layla for everything she taught me and for taking the time to show me around, and I followed Melissa back to her office.

She kept her office extremely dimly lit for someone who intended to accomplish anything, but it gave the room a cloistered, deceptively cozy feeling.

Melissa had my résumé out on her desk in front of her, and she strained her eyes to read it back to me. She nodded as if she was interested in any of the seemingly frivolous details of my work and education history. I became self-conscious, and acutely aware that nothing in the entirety of my life's experience had even remotely prepared me for what lay in wait for me here. Not even nursing school had scratched the surface of teaching me what I needed to know. I felt like I knew so much when I graduated. So fucking much. But in this arena, with real people actively dying in front of you, none of that amounted to shit.

How did Layla know to ask about H&H? How did she know that a man shitting and vomiting meant that he was actively trying to die on us? How did she remember where to press when palpating one's pancreas? I felt like I should know this stuff, and in the silent moments Melissa spent mulling over my inadequacy, I felt myself lose my nerve. I almost considered apologizing for wasting everyone's time and walked out.

Melissa sniffed deeply and looked up at me abruptly.

"Daniela, let me start by telling you a little bit about our unit. We're brand new, but the depth of experience of the nurses on the floor is incredible. Like I'm sure you'll find on other floors, we have a lot of new grads, but when I agreed to open the unit I intentionally restricted the number of new nurses allowed on the floor because I wanted to create a culture of mentorship. I wanted to make sure the new nurses coming in would have a soft place to land, where preceptors weren't spread so thin, they didn't have time to educate and invest in the nurses just starting out. I know no one comes out of nursing school wanting to work med/surg. They all want a shot at the top in ICU, or peds, or L&D, or something along those lines. Am I right?"

She looked at me but didn't pause for an answer.

"Daniela, I've been a nurse twenty-three years now, and I'm not going to lie to you, starting out as a new nurse is hard. When I was coming up, nurses ate their young. If you didn't know an answer you were laughed at. I've actually seen nurses set each other up for failure by stealing equipment, or hiding supplies, just awful stuff to make their life a living hell. I fought through that and when I agreed to take this job, my one request was that I have final say on every nurse hired. I had to work twice as hard to get information that should have just been given freely. I want you to have the best possible start, and even if med/surg wasn't your top choice, I want to give you a launch pad to have a solid foundation clinically in whatever you ultimately choose to do. Even though I know a great deal of our nurses will do their year and move on to seemingly bigger and better things, I want you to see that there's more here than meets the eye, and a that great work and learning environment is essential to who you become as a nurse. I hope you will consider joining us."

I paused for a moment, and considered my words carefully, as if I felt like speaking them aloud was incanting a life of my own creation.

"Where do I sign?" I said.

CHAPTER SEVEN

Med/Surg

So, I signed the paper.

Twenty dollars and sixty cents per hour, decent benefits, rotating shifts, and a one-year contract.

At the end of the day, they could have said to me, *bitch you're lucky we let you in this door, we ain't paying you, but we'll let you come back, sign here,* and I would have gladly signed it. I was in! I was a real nurse!

I made plans to move into an apartment closer to the city. If I had learned anything in my two winters Upstate, it was that you sure as hell don't want to get stuck in a snow storm on the interstate and have to make your way home any longer than you had to. A thirty-minute drive could easily turn into an hour and a half or more when the roads were bad, and that presupposed that they didn't close the highway all together, or that you didn't crash along the way. As a new driver, these driving conditions were a hazard to my life and limbs, and I wanted to give myself the best possible chance to make it to my first paycheck.

William had gotten into the orientation class exactly one month ahead of me, so by the time my good news made it to him, he had plenty of tips and pointers to lend me.

Bring this paperwork, get this stethoscope, brush up on this topic, but mostly he was just excited to be in the position to be lending advice. He got a job on the ortho unit one floor up from where I was going. Technically, it was med/surg too, but his official offer letter said *Orthopedics*, so in his mind he was a step above me, which I was fine letting him believe that if it made him feel better.

William had met a girl on a dating app in our final semester that was an LPN working on getting her RN, who was nine years his senior. His infatuation almost caused him to fail our pediatric clinical since he was too googly-eyed over this chick to look at his books. He was already talking about moving in with her by the time he took the job, so he was holding out that his next apartment would be one that he would be sharing with a certain lady friend of his. I had my doubts, but I was happy to bring him along while he window shopped.

We found a spot in the South Wedge. It was a cute, hipster, up and coming little neighborhood that reminded me of a very small version of Williamsburg before it exploded and gentrified to the point of being oversaturated, and almost a cartoon version of what it once was. I liked it. I didn't need much, just a pad to crash in after an exhausting shift, and quiet neighbors so I could sleep during the day when I was working the night shift. I found a place over a shared studio space that the owner promised me would be low traffic, and a reasonable decibel level during the day in case I was sleeping after a night shift.

After handing over first and last month's rent, along with my security deposit, I was handed my first set of really-mine keys.

That afternoon I packed my box, and now my other box that was stuffed to the gills with new scrubs and nursing books. I aired out the cottage one more time, and left a heartfelt note flooded with my deepest gratitude, and I pulled my Subaru out of the driveway one last time, watching the lake shrink in my rearview as I headed for a life I had more questions than answers to.

When I arrived back at my new apartment, I hadn't actually realized I had to call the electric company to have my power turned on, so I had to move in and make a quick assessment of my surroundings before the daylight faded, since they couldn't come out to turn it on until the next day.

I made a run to the store for some tea lights and a lighter and ate Chinese takeout by candlelight my first night there. It felt surreal. I had nothing. Two boxes did not account for the life I had created to this point. It would be depressing were it not for the fact that it all felt like crackling potential energy. Like the studio downstairs. With the proper tools and supplies you can create anything.

That night I slept so well on my little floor bed that I almost missed my alarm. By the time it registered what was screaming in my ear, nearly twenty minutes had gone by. I was too late to take a shower, so I gave my underarms an extra swipe of deodorant and piled my hair into a staticky knot on top of my head and pulled my scrubs on.

I lived less than two miles from the hospital, so it wasn't the drive that took long, it was finding the orientation room that made me late.

New nurses were still ambling to their seats when I skidded in breathlessly. I signed the attendance sheet and found a spot in the back.

Class started with a train of presenters. Safety officer, security, benefits. All the usual suspects. By the end we moved into some skills orientation, and actually got to put our hand on some of the equipment we would be using.

The next two weeks would be filled with more of the same, with a ratcheting up of the difficulty of information we would be presented. I loved it. It felt real, and practical, and like I was being given the tools I needed to do my job.

My first day as a nurse came to a close in a massive classroom, with more to come. It was good. We got out early enough for me to go home to change and head out for some essentials. I had absolutely nothing in the apartment. No paper towels, no bowls, no bed, let alone anything else that would make my tiny studio look like anyone besides a squatter lived there.

I gathered the basics, and even picked up some food other than takeout. It was pre-packaged, but hey, at least I was making an attempt.

I came home to lights that turned on with a flip of a switch, and it felt a little bit like magic. Evidently, they had turned my power on when I was at work, and it was the best housewarming gift that I could have asked for.

After eating dinner atop one of my overturned now-empty boxes, I called Mami. Our chats were getting farther and farther apart. Having been the lone straggler at home after my sisters moved out, and staying behind to watch her sit by the phone wishing, willing it to ring with news of her girls, and night after night seeing her reluctantly tuck herself into bed with not so much as a phone call to see how she's doing, when she had given us everything, had broken my heart on a nightly basis, and I swore I would never do that to her. But, as the days passed, and my curiosity regarding Mami's daily routine became less and less of a driving force to pick up the phone, before I knew it, I was losing stretches of days, even weeks without calling her. As the space between us widened, I found myself forgiving my sisters for their inconsideration. Life gets in the way, I get that now. But it doesn't absolve me of the guilt.

*

The following day in orientation, I finally got up the nerve to approach a girl in my class who was going to the ED once orientation was over. I was instantly jealous, but also in absolute awe of the *cajones* this girl possessed to go into such an angry hornet's nest of a unit directly out of nursing school, still wet behind the ears.

Her name was Sabine. She was a tall (at least six foot), lanky, French Canadian nurse, with an accent that was more French than Canadian, which was especially charming, and a dark dry wit that I just loved. She looked like a giraffe that had gotten turned around in the labyrinth of hallways in the hospital, and accidentally wandered into graduate nurse orientation. She was hilarious. She would make these really obscure observations, like, hey, doesn't this presenter look like the type of gentleman who would pay a prostitute to sit and eat dinner with him at Denny's, just so he could feel a genuine human emotion other than his raging self-loathing? And somehow, inexplicably, she would be one hundred percent correct. If there were ever a man who would pay a prostitute to have dinner with him, it would be this guy. Absolutely.

Lunch was even more entertaining. We sat together and spent our full thirty minutes people-watching and coming up with a backstory for everyone in the cafeteria.

"So, this is Janice. She's a selfish lover and cries after sex, and tithes double on Sunday's to compensate for the fact that she's a closet sex addict."

God, the backstories were amazing! Sabine was hilarious, and I was incredibly grateful to have someone so entertaining with me to make the next two weeks to make the time go by more enjoyable. It went a long way in easing my anxiety and grounding my nervous energy.

Sabine's backstory, from what I could gather over our entirely too short lunch, was that she was married, had one kid, Benji, six months old, he was born during nursing school and she almost got kicked out of her nursing program because she missed so many days while he was in the NICU after being born full term at only three pounds from IUGR. Her husband, Allen, was a helicopter mechanic for the Army Reserves, and he was currently on orders in Japan for the next four months. Sabine was certainly a woman with a lot on her plate. Clearly, her best coping mechanism was her sense of humor.

We made our way back to the classroom and settled into an underwhelming lecture on insulin and heparin protocols.

The rest of our week went by like that. Lectures, teambuilding exercises, carefully measured doses of HIPAA, OSHA, and other JHACO mandated talking points.

Making it to the weekend was no small feat. Despite sitting in classes, and being acutely aware that these two weeks would be the easiest of my nursing career, the mental strain of being acutely aware of the responsibility I was now weighted with, just doing the damn thing, was a mental exhaustion in and of itself.

When Saturday finally rolled around, I blew past the 0500 circadian rhythm wake-up call I'd been a slave to since starting nursing school. To my shock and bewilderment when I finally cleared the fairy dust from my eyes it was already 0830. I hadn't slept like that since, I didn't even know. Maybe never.

I had had so many plans for my first day off, and now I was three and a half hours behind. I leapt up from my pile of blankets on the floor in my living room in front of the television, and went to make coffee, planning a harried flurry of activity to catch up for time lost, but as the coffee maker sputtered and percolated, I realized I was in a rush to go nowhere. I had no deadline, no one waiting for me, no appointments or assignments, I was…free. It felt oddly disconcerting. I realized how institutionalized I had become, or I suppose I had always just been. Before nursing there was Robin. Before Robin there was work. Before work there was school. Before school there was Jeni. Before Jeni there was theater. Before theater there was Mami. Before Mami, there was nothing, I suppose. I had always been beholden to something, or someone. My time had never been my own.

It should have been a relief, but it felt disorienting. What did I want to do? Who the hell was I? What did I even like to do?

I poured a cup of coffee, black, like Valentina used to make. I inhaled the steam undulating from its surface, and I closed my eyes. Food. Water. Shelter. I had those, but not much else. I decided to spend my day off making myself a home.

I had a small amount of savings left from my waitressing job at Schooners. It wasn't much, but it would get me some essentials and a few comforts until my first paycheck came in. I had promised myself that I would hold back a little bit of money to plan a trip back to the City, but I knew I was still several weeks away from being able to afford the time away. In the meantime, I decided to focus today on being home.

I finished my coffee and peeked at the smattering of the few grounds at the bottom of my cup that had escaped the filter, and tried to discern a fortune, but alas, I did not possess that gift. Mami did, and so did Valentina. Coffee grounds, tea leaves, palms, cards, all whispered from beyond my purview in a voice so hushed I was sure there was nothing there, but perhaps I just had never learned to listen. Mami only consulted with this voice in times she was in grave need of guidance, when Mother Mary and the Saints were either too busy, or too slow to otherwise direct her steps. I don't know what had gotten me seeking answers from the great beyond, but I was suddenly aware of my own need for guidance, or maybe it was just a need for comfort that this was ok. That I was ok. Either way, I started my day feeling vulnerable somehow, but also full of possibility.

After a quick shower and some indecision over whether my jeans were making my hips look too wide, or if my hips were just too wide for my jeans, I set out in search of those essential elements to insert myself into this place, and possibly some new jeans.

After a few missteps, I returned with a bed that I could dress up like a couch by day, a dresser, a small round table with hairpin legs that I fell in love with, and two hopeful chairs, and an assortment of kitchen utensils I was unsure if I would ever need or use. Overall, it was an exceptionally fruitful excursion.

I spent the next day nesting. Arranging and rearranging until the seemingly unrelated elements decided to cooperate, and suddenly it all gelled into a space I wanted to occupy.

I was exceedingly proud of myself. I had created a life. Not just a life of survival and barely making it. I felt like I was thriving. Like I was on the precipice of something great. I wasn't entirely clear on what that was, but I knew that it would be better than what I had left behind me in Manhattan.

*

The next few days of classroom orientation went by uneventfully. By the end of it, I was feeling that itch I felt at the end of nursing school. Like if one more lecturer came through and asked us to recite our name, the unit we were going to, and a "fun fact" about ourselves, I was going to spontaneously combust. I would rather light myself on fire than come up with a "fun fact" to share with the group.

When I finally got to my unit at the end of the introductions, and pleasantries, and policies and procedures, I was worn a little thin. Although I was ecstatic to finally make it to my floor, I was not met with the same warm fuzzy vibe that had danced within my heart when I was here before. I tried to take note of the stress level of the nurses, whether the smiles looked forced, and if the nurses helped each other and appeared to genuinely like each other. I had determined that all of the above were true when I was there shadowing a few short weeks ago, but now I couldn't see it.

Furled bows and sharp answers abounded. Call lights were sounding in a tumult of ringing that seemed to be drowned out only by the screaming of IV pumps, heart monitors, and unanswered telephones. It was jarringly over stimulating.

I wasn't with Layla as I somehow assumed that I would be. I was with another nurse, Justine. She had been a nurse for fourteen years, the last three of them were spent on this floor. She had that air about her that she was here, but not by choice, and orienting someone who didn't know their ass from their elbow probably landed solidly next to "shag a hand grenade" on her list of priorities.

When I approached her and held my hand out for a handshake before the Purell on my hands had a chance to dry, she looked at it like it was something I had pulled out of a garbage disposal and offered to her. She looked me up and down, and then up and down again to be sure she got the complete picture of what I was offering, and she was left wanting.

"Rule number 1. Don't touch another person's body part without gloves if you didn't birth it or marry it. Rule number 2. If it's wet and not yours, don't touch it at all."

"Duly noted," I said under my breath.

I sat down beside her in a nervous pose so electrified from the caffeine and anxiety that I came to a near hover above my chair. We got report from Roberto, a total gym gay. He was the über buff, impeccably groomed type of homosexual man that would have every *abuelita* not in-the-know thinking he was the pinnacle of manliness and masculinity, ready to pussy slay entire zip codes of ladies, when in reality he was just looking for some girthy *salchicha* to choke on.

Roberto gave us our assignment and told us he would be back that night. We had five patients, all of whom were seemingly stable, and two were completely independent. One was a thirty-six year old with a PE on a heparin drip, the other was there for IV antibiotics and a debridement after he had failed three other courses of treatment for his diabetic foot ulcer. The rest were an assortment of nursing home maladies that were there for observation or as social admits.

We went through and met and assessed everybody and checked foleys and linens to see who was peeing and how much. Once we circled back around to the nurses station, we started with the first set of medications. Justine grilled me on every medication I was pulling. I knew maybe twenty percent of what I was getting out, and that was being optimistic. Anything I didn't know off the top of my head, she made me look up. When I couldn't find it, she made me call pharmacy and speak to the pharmacist. I felt like a fucking idiot. I knew she was judging me. I was convinced she would report me to the manager for being incompetent. Every time I said I didn't know she waited, and waited, until I gave her something. I was nearly in tears before our first set of meds made it into to the patient's mouth.

While I stood there spooning Mr. Lewiston his chunky, pill-laced vanilla pudding, Justine spared me the indignity of standing in the med room staring blankly at the drug guide, and she went ahead and grabbed meds for two of our other patients. By the time I finished shoving pudding in Mr. Lewiston's gaping O of an edentulous mouth, Justine came and got me so I could get a move on our other two patients.

Those weren't quite as bad. I had actually heard of most of the meds, and it wasn't quite the laundry list I had for Mr. Lewiston.

We went in to give our last patient, Mr. Donaldson his meds, he was reclining leisurely in his Posey tent, looking absolutely relaxed and carefree. He was the most pleasantly confused man I had ever met.

"Well hello there, ladies!" He said chipperly.

"Good morning Mr. Donaldson. Do you remember us? We were just in here a moment ago. We went to get your medicine," I said proudly.

"Now my dear, I must have dozed off a bit. I do apologize, but I seem to have forgotten where I am. Are we camping together? We must be camping. This is just lovely," he said dreamily.

Before I could correct him to help him reorient, Justine interrupted me.

"That's right Mr. Donaldson. We're all here camping by this stream. We just came to bring you your breakfast."

I looked back at her surprised. They had taught us in nursing school to never reinforce a patient's delusions, it only made their confusion worse.

"Well I do thank you kindly. That is awfully nice of you," He replied.

Justine unzipped his tent to hand him his breakfast tray. I hadn't noticed but she had mixed his pills in with his juice and encouraged him to drink up.

When we came out, I tried not to ask Justine why she had lied to him like that, but my curiosity began to boil over and before I could restrain it, I started to say,

"In nursing school, we…" but Justine cut me off abruptly.

"You're going to see a lot of stuff they don't teach you in nursing school. It's best to just watch and learn. If you're talking about Mr. Donaldson, the best policy is to just tell him what he wants to hear. Are we going to cure his dementia?" She asked me pointedly.

"Well no, but I…"

"No. No we are not. So, we can't fix him. If you try and reorient him too much, he starts asking for his wife. His wife is in Cabo with her pool boy and hasn't visited him in a year. She's the only thing he cares about, so we just try to avoid it, and tell him she's with his children, who also haven't visited. When he gets a lucid moment, and realizes his whole family abandoned him here, he just wails in anguish for hours. It's fucking awful. Work smarter, not harder, dear. Trust me." I jotted myself an asterisk punctuated mental note to do just that.

Patient care wise, the morning was relatively uneventful. No GI bleeds being raced up to the ICU. I thought we were in the clear to ride out the last four hours of our twelve-hour shift, until our girl on the heparin drip got rowdy when Justine wouldn't let her take a shower.

"What the fuck you mean you won't "let me" take a shower? I'm a grown ass woman, bitch! I don't need you to "let" me do nothing!" She shouted at Justine.

"Miss Evans, it's not a matter of permission, it's a matter of the dialysis catheter in your chest, and it's a process to get it secured so you don't get water in it and get an infection. They are on their way up right now to take you to dialysis. When you get back from dialysis, we can talk about it, but you can't just jump in the shower, unfortunately," Justine stated, calmly, evenly, completely in control. But whatever control Justine thought she had was a quickly shattered illusion.

The patient paced in front of us like a caged tiger, debating if she should rip our arms off and beat us with them, or run for the shower.

"Fucking bitch, watch me!" she said abruptly.

Pause.

This was not an idle threat. This woman was on a heparin drip. Heparin is commonly known as a "blood thinner" but it's a bit of a misnomer. Heparin interrupts the clotting cascade and makes you less likely to continue forming clot, which prevents an existing clot from getting bigger, and allows the body more opportunity to break down whatever clots are already there. Great for clots, not so great if you start bleeding though, since you are artificially less able to produce clots to help stop the bleed. Even the smallest nick from shaving can leave your sink looking like a crime scene.

The other thing about this situation that is capital "B" BAD, is that this dialysis catheter in Miss Evan's chest is a Hickman. It's a large, tunneled catheter that is inserted into one of the largest blood vessels in the body, the superior vena cava. It is typically only removed by a physician and removing it in an uncontrolled manor can cause you to suck air into the opening, creating an air embolus. If that happens, you die. Quickly.

End pause.

She pulled it out.

She fucking pulled it out!

And the blood. Oh God, so much blood.

Justine screamed. I blinked. I looked for gloves. I looked for help. I looked for a reset button. Fucking A, this bitch pulled out her tunneled catheter while on a heparin drip, just because Justine asked her to wait for a shower until she finished her dialysis and she didn't wanna. I had never seen such unbridled, deliberate, retaliatory self-harm in my entire life. Just the level of pettiness this woman was willing to go to all for a shower she could take later this afternoon I think shocked me the most.

Shelly called overhead for the Code Team not knowing what else to do. Stephanie got her to lie down and put her in reverse Trendelenburg and slapped some Vaseline gauze on her chest so she wouldn't pull air through the gaping hole and directly into her SVC. She wouldn't let Justine near her so Justine had me hold pressure while she ran to page the doc and run over to Ortho for some Combat Gauze.

I would love to ruminate on this case and tell you after this happened it was the worst thing that happened that day. I would love to tell you the nursing gods took pity on me following this travesty and the rest of my day was a complete breeze once this cluster fuck had been squelched. However, that simply was not so.

After an emergency call to the physician, and a puppy-kicked call to the nephrologist to notify him that the patient's HD cath was acrimoniously discontinued, we took the disgruntled patient to see the livid nephrologist in Interventional Radiology for placement of another one.

All of this and not a single task waited for us. Med passes, linen changes, call lights, none of slowed down to accommodate the unanticipated disaster we had going on.

Just when I thought I was firing on all cylinders, and had managed to handle the lion's share of the hand we had been dealt, I looked up and saw Mr. Donaldson in his room directly across from the nurses station, and I suddenly understood the reason why we kept our merry camper Mr. Donaldson in the Posey tent.

Mr. Donaldson was beating the walls of his Posey tent, foley catheter taught and swinging from his penis, stark ass naked, covered in excrement, screaming "lemme outa this fucking cage!" at the top of his lungs.

I looked at Justine, eyes wide as saucers. She, on the other hand, was completely nonplussed, and looked across at him with an apathetic flat affect that can only be explained as an absolute lack of surprise.

"Its 1800. He's sundowning," and with a deep and heavy sigh, she got up to make a B52 cocktail.

A B52 was 50 mg Benadryl, 5 mg Haldol, and 2 mg Lorazepam all mixed together in a syringe and shot in the ass of a wild patient. Enough sedative to stop a horse, or in this case, what was once the most pleasant man I had ever met in my life two hours ago.

Once we quelled the beast, we had to all but climb in the tent with him and wipe the shit from the netting walls while we tried not to wake him. Just as we were elbows deep in it, Roberto walked in.

"Fun day huh?" He said. If looks could kill, I would be 007.

*

What a fucking clusterfuck of a day.

I don't even remember what happened the rest of the shift. I don't even remember the drive home, or what I ate, or even if I ate. I just remember that shower. That purifying, cathartic shower.

I stood there with the scalding water flowing over me until I felt absolved of everything that went wrong today. From Justine's judgy, pinched face, to not knowing my meds, to being so far behind I couldn't even medicate my one patient in the time she medicated two, to the fucking catheter and the blood. God, so much blood…I could still see it when I closed my eyes. I squeezed them shut tight enough for it to fade to black for a moment.

I pushed my forehead onto the cool of the tile, and finally forced myself to reach for the shower handle to turn it off.

I threw myself onto the bed and pulled the blankets over my head. Maybe this was a mistake. Maybe nursing was a bad choice. Maybe I wasn't cut out for this. Maybe barfing out a career path to my guidance counselor in high school isn't actually how you chose a career.

I thought about calling out the next day. I thought about emailing my manager and telling her she made a mistake. I thought about joining a commune. I wanted a hug. I wanted sex. I wanted to be drunk or knocked out. I wanted to feel anything but this. I did the only non-self-destructive thing I could think of. I picked up the phone and called Mami.

*

"Hey Mami."

"¡Heyyyyy *niña*!" She said, as if she had been waiting by the phone. "How was your first day?"

My "fine" caught in my throat and I nearly choked. I coughed, and the coughing turned to sputtering, and the sputtering turned to sobs.

After placating me and allowing a few seconds to cry it out, Mami stopped me.

"Daniela stop it!" She demanded sternly. The finality of her tone arrested the flow of my tears, which collapsed into gulping, gasping breaths. "What, did you think, this would be easy? Did you think they would just let you in and say, 'save this man's life,' and you just wouldn't be scared? *Dios mio* girl, this isn't some kind of joke! This isn't dressing up and playing nurse like you're still at theater practice! You need to toughen up! You have real people in front of you. Get it together!"

I stopped and took a jagged breath.

"Ok, that's better. Daniela, *escuchame.* This is real life *mi amor.* Nothing worth doing is ever, ever going to be easy. Do you think I had it easy even one day in my life? *No*. Every day is a struggle. This *blanquita,* this Justin *o* whateva, this girl is nothing. She's no one to you. You earned the right to be there. You were top of your class. You passed your boards on your first try. You got this! So, a patient did something stupid and reckless. How is that your fault? This girl, she was acting a fool and she knows exactly what she done. You gotta let that go, girl. That's not on you. Now, tell me you're going to do me this one favor, as your mother, promise me. Tell me you're going to eat something, and you're going to get a good night's sleep, and wake up in the morning looking all fresh and fly, and you're going to show this *puta* you're there to work! You handle it Daniela. I didn't raise no quitter! Get it done tomorrow. *¿Me escuchas? Te amo.*"

And that was it. We said goodnight and I padded out to the kitchen and ate some Ben and Jerry's in front of the open freezer. After that, I went to bed and slept like a dead woman.

The next day, I did exactly as Mami said. I fixed my hair. I put on my lucky hoops. I even put on a flush of lip gloss which I only saved for special occasions. When I came into work the next day, I stomped down that hallway like I had the *Rocky* theme playing behind me.

*

In my struggle to find my way here, outside of the city, I had somehow lost my essence. I had lost the very thing about me that made me feel great. It was my voice, my presence, the swing of my hips, the expanse of my hair, the vibrancy of my being. I had quieted myself and toned all those things down until I looked like everyone else around me. I spoke more softly. I didn't point out when someone else fucked up. I looked the other way when someone did me wrong. I tried to vanish into this blonde haired, blue eyed tide that had come in all around me, and I did everything in my power not to stand out. And I lost myself.

I suddenly realized that this wasn't high school. This wasn't college. This wasn't proving myself to anyone. This was my reset, and the person I project myself to be in the coming weeks and months is the person I will be for the rest of my career. I needed to get my head right to create a life that could sustain me. As I looked around our unit, I noticed a pained cellophane veneer across the eyes of every one of the nurses there. They all looked spread too thin. They all looked like they were trying too hard, or like they were one glass of spilled milk away from crying. Except one.

Vanessa Miller. She was a Rubenesque middle aged black woman. She was one of the senior nurses on the floor, who often filled in as charge. She seemed sage. Wise. Like she had seen everything and remained unmoved. She had braids down to her full hips and she rearranged them about her shoulders like a mantle. I had noticed her the very first day I shadowed on the unit. She stood out to me because my very first time on the floor, she was there when our GI bleed patient went down. When everyone else was freaking out, she came in, and without being told, without even knowing the story, she calmly set up suction, started another IV, and strung up fluids on a pressure bag. She didn't ask for details, she didn't look frantic, if anything, she looked like she was floating while everyone around her was moving in fast forward. Yet, she was the only one actually *doing* something. I remember locking eyes with her as I stood frozen. It was like she looked inside of me, as if to say, "you ready for all this?" I wanted to answer "yes" but in my panicked, disoriented state, all I could do was answer back with my eyes, "I don't know."

Vanessa wasn't working my first day, so she didn't see my disastrous initiation, but I was determined to be ready for the pitch today. My heart fluttered briefly when I entered the break room and she was sitting at the table making a hushed phone call. It sounded like she had a son, and something happened, but I tried not to eavesdrop.

I crumpled my jacket and stuffed it into my bottom locker and remade the mental note to get a lock.

I shuffled out the door and felt her eyes on my back. I was early, and chances were likely that Justine wouldn't be in yet.

I walked out onto the floor and looked at the assignment sheet. I glanced at our rooms and searched for the nurse we were relieving. It was Layla.

I sat down and began checking my email while I waited on Justine. While I sat there hyper focused on the meaningless spam that I had been sent, Vanessa walked out in front of me.

"Cat got your tongue?"

I blinked and looked back at her.

"I'm sorry?" I said.

"That's right. You can't walk onto a unit and just not introduce yourself. It's not," she curled her lip while she searched for the word, "neighborly."

"I'm sorry I-"

"You've already said that. I'm not looking for an apology, just wanted to say hi, and welcome. I'm Vanessa," she pushed her hand towards me to shake it, and I reached back awkwardly.

"I'm-"

"Daniela. I already know. Welcome again," and she zipped off to find her night nurse.

Before I could figure out what I had just encountered, I realized I was still extending my hand, as if shaking hands with a ghost, which may have just happened.

Just as I was drawing it back in to myself Justine blew in. Hasty, frazzled, and two minutes late.

She sat down and set her coffee cup down on the counter.

"Freakin' 490. Traffic is a nightmare," she smoothed her hair and pulled a compact out of her pocket and checked her makeup quickly.

Just then, Layla appeared.

"Daniela! You made it! I'm so happy you're here!" She exclaimed warmly and sidled up for a shoulder hug.

"Thank you!" I said, matching her welcoming tone. "I'm happy to be here."

"That makes one of us," muttered Justine.

"Oh, hush up you!" Layla teased. "Don't corrupt a new nurse! She's going to be one of the good ones," she gave me a wink.

Bolstered by Layla's vote of confidence, I took a deep breath and determined that today was going to be a great day.

We got report, went through the same routine, met the patients, did the assessments, passed the meds, and answered the call lights. I was still struggling with the computer charting system. It seemed like there was layer upon layer you had to look at to find the information on your patients. Doctor's notes were in one place, labs were in another, radiology reports on another. It seemed like I could never keep track of where to go. There were systems within systems. You had to print a handoff sheet anytime someone went off the unit, you had to access the ED board when a patient came up from there as an admission. It seemed a little crazy, and it was hard to sort out.

We had a discharge today, which evidently was a big deal because according to Justine, our patient had been on the floor with us for four months.

When the discharge order came in, and her ride was there, Justine and I went in to remove Miss Sally's IV and Vanessa followed us in.

We reviewed her paperwork, and Justine let me take the IV out. Her skin was so thin and fragile, I had to pull the tape back a millimeter at a time while applying counter-traction, so it didn't tear. I had never seen skin like that, translucent and fragile as wet tissue paper. Justine later explained to me that months of high dose steroids can do that.

While I was holding pressure on the discontinued IV site, Vanessa had sat down on the bed beside her. She looked in Miss Sally's eyes and smiled broadly.

"You did it honey. You made it out of here alive," she laughed a rich and boiling laugh, smooth as coffee. "But, honey did you ever give us a run for our money!" With this they both laughed, and Miss Sally had tears rolling down her hollow cheeks. "You take care of yourself, you hear? No falling, and don't you dare get up without someone nearby, you understand?"

"Yes ma'am," Sally promised. Vanessa reached out to her and she gave her a bountiful embrace.

"All right now, that's enough of that. You go on home and enjoy those grandbabies," Vanessa helped her to her feet and got her situated in the wheelchair.

Everyone on the unit came out to wish Miss Sally luck in her recovery. She had survived breast cancer, but she was nearly killed by a cold. She spent a month in the ICU with septic pneumonia and came to us after she was extubated. She had thrown a clot on our unit and it lodged in her mesenteric artery. Vanessa had her the night she went down. She had been vomiting and stooling uncontrollably. She needed an emergent bowel resection, because a portion of her bowel had become ischemic from the clot. If Vanessa hadn't been there to bypass the resident when he blew her off, and called the attending at home, she probably wouldn't have made it. Miss Sally was leaving with an ileostomy, but she was going home. Thanks to our unit. Thanks to Vanessa.

I felt undeserving of the task, but I took her out to the discharge area in the wheelchair, and helped her into her daughter's minivan, helped get her seatbelt fastened, and gave her a final wave goodbye. I saw her face light up and look twenty years younger the moment she took her first breath of fresh air and felt the sun on her face for the first time in months.

I walked back slowly to the unit. On the way up I ran into Sabine, the new grad I met in orientation who went to the ED.

"Hi!" We both said in unison.

"How is it? How's your unit? How was your first day?" We both rapid fired questions at each other neither one of us had time to answer. We exchanged contact information and agreed to meet up for coffee soon.

"You should come to the ED when you're done playing in poop!" She teased.

"You better be careful what you wish for!" I joked as we parted ways.

It was hard to imagine moving on when I still had so much to learn. Every patient contact felt like a unique set of problems. No two of the same diagnoses were ever exactly alike. It was overwhelming, but after Mami's pep talk, and actually leaving the unit that evening feeling like I nearly knew what I was doing, I went home with my chin held a little higher than the day before

*

Four weeks in, I had my first evaluation, and I met with our manager Melissa to talk about how things were going. She went over Justine's notes and she asked me my thoughts on the unit, and if I was happy here.

"I am. I feel like this was the right decision for me. I feel nervous, but I think if I wasn't a little nervous, I'd probably be missing something," I said.

"You're absolutely right. And I think you're right where you're supposed to be. According to Justine, you have a good bedside manner, and you're starting to put the whole thing together, which is important. From your evaluation scores, it looks like right now, your biggest hurdle is going to be time management and getting more proficient with the charting system, which is right on target for you. I'm going to recommend that we start rotating your shifts. As part of your contract you agreed to rotating shifts, and the sooner you get going on them the better. Nights are a completely different animal. It comes with some unique challenges, but I think you're in a good place to take them on. The next schedule I'll start you working nights, and you'll come back to days in three weeks. We do three weeks days, three weeks nights, so moving forward you can plan on that," she explained.

"Ok, sounds good," was all I could gather to say.

I felt excited that I hadn't bombed my first eval, a little put out that they felt like I was still struggling with my time management and computer charting, and I was definitely nervous about moving onto nights.

Nights were certainly their own animal, as Melissa had said. There were no visitors, no scheduled tests, or PT, or OT, or speech evals, no management walking around, but also less staff, fewer doctors in house, and fewer resources if shit ever got real. In that regard, nurses had to be resourceful. They had to patch things up until morning and maintain until reinforcements arrived. It was a huge change of pace and objective.

My first night shift I slept for twenty minutes and that was it. Most of the challenge wasn't the patient care, it was the pure physiologic struggle of forcing your body to keep moving when literally every cell in it is starving for sleep. It is total anguish. You start to appreciate weird shit you took for granted like, cozy socks, taking your bra off, being horizontal. It is a battle just to hold your ever-closing eyelids in a semi-open position from about 0430 until you leave at 0730-ish the next morning. Whatever shift differential they're offering isn't worth it. No one can quantify how good it feels to draw your blackout shades, turn your nightstand light off, or to wrap yourself in a fluffy comforter.

Despite the disorienting day/night changeover, the night shift does afford you some comforts. Loose lips abound once you're a little loopy from sleep deprivation. You get to know your coworkers in a completely different way at night than you ever would during the day. You learn who's in a good marriage and who's cheating on their husband. You learn what secret plans or ambitions someone may have. You learn who's struggling financially. It's oddly intimate once the overhead lights go down at eight p.m. and the only light in the place is the low glow of the nurses station and the med room. Music comes on softly. Everything becomes hilarious once you get a little punchy. It really feels completely different than being on days. But that relaxed atmosphere can lull you into thinking your patients are sleeping when they could be dying.

After I had been on nights for two weeks and was finally adjusting to the tachycardia and faint essential tremor I had developed, I was sitting in the nurses station doing my nightly chart audit when Stephanie, the nurse next to me suddenly looked up when her patient across the way put his call light on.

"Thant's weird," Stephanie looked at me and said.

"What's weird?" I asked, not sure what was unusual about one call light being on in the never-ending call light show we seemed to be watching.

"I've been with Mr. Dotson the last three nights and he's never put his call light on."

Stephanie pulled herself to standing with a groan and walked slowly over to room 19, favoring her right hip ever so slightly. She flung the seafoam curtain and disappeared behind it.

Mr. Dotson was a seventy-six year old male patient who came in to the ED after his daughter found him face down in his bathroom, unresponsive and barely breathing, with blood flung in every room of his home. She thought he had been shot. Once they got him intubated and stabilized, they got his lab work back and it showed a hematocrit of 9. No, not a hemoglobin. A hematocrit. Of 9. It seemed impossible. They re-ran it, they thought it was contaminated, or exceedingly dilutional, but no, his crit was 9. Normal hematocrit for a male is between around 38-48, depending on the facility. His was 9. I had never heard of a number that low.

His CT scans were all normal. He didn't appear to have any type of injury. They couldn't find a tumor or any indication of cancer. They finally did a tagged red blood cell study where they take a sample of blood, separate out the red cells, and "tag" them with a radioactive tracer they mix in with the sample, then reinject it all back into a vein and scan you to see where the tagged cells go. If they go outside of where they're supposed to be, it means there's blood where there shouldn't be. It came back normal. His colonoscopy came back normal. His daily stool tests for occult blood came back normal. After the mass transfusion protocol and about a dozen more transfusions, his blood counts normalized, and he was able to be extubated. When they asked him what happened, he said he didn't remember. They chalked it up to a bizarre fluke in his hematology and downgraded him from the ICU to our unit.

He had been in bed for the past four weeks and was still working with PT while he waited for bed placement at a rehab facility to get his strength back to make it home.

One thing about Mr. Dotson, he didn't ask for much. He used his urinal, he waited until the nurse was at his bedside to make any requests, he fed himself independently, though not strong enough yet to ambulate, he was able to reposition himself and scoot up in bed. For our population, he was a dream patient.

For Stephanie to call it strange piqued my curiosity, so I followed her into his room to see what he needed too.

"Good evening Mr. Dotson, what can I do for you?"

He was sitting bolt upright in bed, pale, diaphoretic, his hair mussed and matted with sweat to his temples, eyes wild. He was staring straight ahead at the wall in front of him. After a second, he slowly turned his head toward us, and then snapped it back forward, violently projectile vomiting coffee ground emesis so aggressively it sprayed the wall on the opposite side of the room. His eyes rolled back in his head and he flopped back into bed like a dead fish.

"Jesus!" Stephanie yelled, and hit the code blue button on the wall.

She quickly checked for a pulse and started CPR.

With a brief assessment of the room, Roberto figured out what was going on and took over compressions while Justine wheeled in the crash cart and sent me for a suction setup and told me to pull out intubation meds.

"What are intubation meds?!" I yelled back.

"Succs and Etomidate! They're in the med dispenser!"

I ran to the med room, pleading with my badge to let me in. Succinylcholine and Etomidate were the only meds that came up under that prefix. I overrode them and ran back to the room with a suction set up.

The Code Team was already in there and yelling for RSI drugs. I passed them off quickly to Justine.

After suctioning out two hundred fifty cc's of black from his mouth and oropharynx they got him intubated, but we didn't get him back. We coded him for thirty minutes, but it felt like hours.

The night swing doc looked through the chart in the nurses station as he prepared to call Mr. Dotson's daughter.

"He must have been a closet drinker. He had to have popped some esophageal varices and bled out. There was nothing we could do. You can't hold pressure on it, and there's no way GI could get here in time to band it," he said.

"Wow," was all I could manage to say.

I helped Stephanie with the post-mortem care. We cleaned and wrapped Mr. Dotson in a shroud. His eyes were now forever frozen in that horrified stare, no matter how many times we tried to close them, they popped right back open as if alerting us to an unseen specter.

Once packaged, transportation came and wheeled him to the morgue. The room was such a gruesome scene, we had to wheel Mr. Dotson's roommate out into the hall while we cleaned it up. We scrubbed clotted blood out of the light switch and doorframe. The splattered ceiling tiles were a lost cause. We called facility services to come and replace them, but they wouldn't be there until morning. Mr. Dotson's roommate had the memory span of a goldfish and was too confused to remember watching Mr. Dotson die in front of him just an hour before, so when we finished deconning the room, we wheeled him right back where he came from before Mr. Dotson's bed was even cold.

Stephanie was distraught. She questioned herself on everything, thinking she had missed something. Roberto rubbed her shoulders and reminded her, "you can only do what you had orders for. If you're only ordered to be checking vital signs every four hours, it's hard to catch an acute change. And Mr. Dotson was so soft spoken he never complained about anything, so he hadn't mentioned that he wasn't feeling well until it was too late." Roberto had such a sweet undulating Puerto Rican accent when he spoke. He always knew what to say.

Our crazy night had given way to a wicked adrenaline hangover. It was like we all had our coffees laced with Benadryl. We were zombies by the time day shift rolled in. When we told the oncoming shift what had gone on the night before there was a collective gasp that went up around the nurses station.

Night shift codes are always the worst because it's just you, a new resident covering upwards of one hundred fifty patients hospital wide, and the remnants of whatever skeleton crew you have left lurking in the hospital. I've heard tell of codes so under-staffed that nurses have to be pulled from other units just to help do compressions. It's crazy. But with my first code notched into my belt, I felt like I had faced my worst fear and lived to tell the tale.

As we all huddled into the break room to grab our purses and jackets, a handful of us decided to meet at the one dive bar open in the city that served alcohol this early.

I had quietly celebrated my twenty-first birthday alone in my apartment the month before. Mami and Valentina had called me to sing their hyper-enthusiastic version of *feliz cumpleaños* while I blew the candle out on my cupcake. Mami sent me a sweater that I opened while I talked to her, and Valentina said my present was still in the mail and should be there any day now. It still hasn't arrived. Marisol sent me her usual sparkly Hallmark card that left glitter all over your fingertips and inexplicably made its way onto every surface in the apartment. She let the card speak her sentiments for her, and her upright narrow scrawl of a signature emblazoned across the bottom served as her endorsement of the notion, reinforced with a crisp hundred-dollar bill inside.

I had to work the next day, so the opportunity to let loose and make regrettable decisions was essentially off the table.

After a particularly heinous nightshift filled with one insatiably mastrubating homeless man in DT's, and a bilateral amputee who tried to scratch whatever flesh she could get her witchy talons in, our collectively sleep deprived huddle decided to finish out our "day" with some greasy food and libations.

When we got to the wonderfully dimly lit dive, we were surrounded by tables full of sleepy nurses that had the same idea. 4 South, 7 North, Obs, OR. We all gave each other a knowing nod as we made our way to our seats.

We sat down and ordered drinks before food. This was the first time I had ever legally purchased alcohol for myself now that I was finally of age to do so. I didn't even know what I liked. I ordered a beer because I didn't really know what else there was without seeing a drink menu, which was currently being poured over by Steph and Justine.

There was something bonding and decompressing about the camaraderie that comes from seeing your coworkers outside of the sterile walls and stale air of the hospital. Everyone's face softened, their shifting eyes stilled and focused, they were warmer and more genuine.

When we got our drinks, we toasted to 7:30.

"To 7:30!" We clinked.

In case you were wondering, alcohol hits you like a freight train when you're sleep deprived, dehydrated, and underfed. It hits you especially hard when you haven't had an alcoholic beverage since last fall's bonfire rager.

Luckily, my poached eggs and hash sopped up most of the alcohol, and I was able to make my way out of the cramped dining room vertically. I made it home and crashed hard, belly full and head swimming ever so gently, and fell into a dark and dreamless sleep.

When I awoke, it was five p.m. I had completely slept the day away. I had worked my three shifts for the week and had back loaded my next week, so I had a stretch of five days off before I had to flip my schedule back to days.

I made plans with William to get lunch the next day. It was my first time seeing him since we both started working our real jobs.

William met me at *Roux*, a cozy Creole comfort food joint in one of the meticulously preserved historic homes on East Ave. I ordered a luscious étouffée and William got some spicy crawfish croquettes. It was the nicest meal I had ever had, and I felt vastly underdressed for the occasion in my jeans and fleece jacket.

William and I reminisced about college and contrasted our lives back then, to the hustle and flow we were being jostled through now. We talked about his girlfriend, Lisa extensively. She was working on her RN and was hoping to graduate this spring. William was planning on asking her to marry him after graduation. They had moved in together two months ago. Lisa was his first serious girlfriend, and, though he didn't say so, I suspected she was the first girl he had slept with, and he was actually talking about marrying her.

"William, I'm really happy for you and all, but, I mean, we're twenty-one. Our lives are just starting, don't you think-"

"She's the one Daniela. Trust me. And we're not rushing. I'm going to wait until next year. It will be great," he assured me. Lisa was thirty going on fifty-two. I was afraid William, sweet and innocent and very much possessing the emotional intelligence of his given age, would not hold Lisa's attention for the lifetime he was promising. Time will tell, and I wasn't willing to make this relationship a battleground between William and I when we had been through so much. Besides, I was here for William, and if Lisa was only boarding the train for a season, I was willing to see William through the rest of the ride.

"William, I just don't want to see you get hurt," I conceded. He reached across his entre and squeezed my hand reassuringly, and we left it at that.

We finished our lunch and thanked each other for taking the time out of our respective busy schedules to meet up. It was great to see him, but there was an obvious rift. We were in very different places in our lives. William was talking marriage, and I hadn't even looked at a woman since Robin. It's like I had dried up. I wasn't even interested in sex. I've heard it said that women think about sex approximately eighteen times per day, on average. I don't think I had thought about it that many times in the last four months, if I was truly being honest.

In my own defense, I was busy. Really fucking busy. The rotating shifts sucked, and it was hit or miss if I slept at all. I was so hyper-focused on keeping my head above water at work, that I hadn't even looked around and smelled the proverbial roses in God knows how long.

*

I was nearing the end of my orientation. I felt like I was still relying on my preceptor for a lot of things, and the thought of going it alone seemed overwhelming to me still. But, on the bright side, I felt like a different person since I started working as a nurse. I would often look back on my day, and just hold a moment of awe to reflect on how much more I knew, and how far I had come in a few short months. I couldn't wait to see what I knew after my first year.

A week before orientation ended, I had a final meeting with my manager and my preceptor. We all sat down in Melissa's dim office and she gave Justine and I each a copy of my evaluation. I scored well in my bedside manner and my critical thinking, but despite the work I had done to be more efficient and manage my time well, I still had *approaching proficiency* in the comment section. I had a moment of genuine concern that they weren't going to release me off orientation if I didn't hit the official *proficient* mark prior to my established release date.

In the end, Melissa and Justine agreed that I was ready. I had been taking the entire assignment myself for five weeks now. I struggled to stay afloat sometimes, but it was always within reason, and I knew how to recognize when I was drowning and ask for help. Ultimately, at the end of my shift, I always managed to get my work completed. My time management problem was actually a problem of spending time building a rapport with my patients, and not a lack of time management. I had questions, I wanted to hear stories, I wanted to understand illnesses, I wanted to find common ground, and that took time, which is the one thing you are not given in this profession.

The person on our unit that always managed to find that sweet spot of talking and tasking better than anyone was Vanessa. Vanessa created a partnership with her patients. She had a way of saying, *we're in this together*, and patients who appear to be "medically unsalvageable," are able to find some degree healing with her help, even if it was just while they were under her care. She walked them, and dressed them, and gave them their dignity back. She was the nurse that would ask the doctor for a pass to take her patients outside when the weather was nice, or let an old man have his beloved cat lay in the bed with him while he was dying, when every other charge nurse insisted it was against hospital policy.

Although if asked in a court of law I will deny it until my dying day, the kindest thing I ever saw one human do for another was what Vanessa did for her twenty-six year old patient who had pancreatic cancer. He came in a week ago and was placed in a room toward the back of the unit. He had come into the ED with a concern that he had suddenly turned yellow. Not just a little golden, like highlighter yellow. So yellow that when I went to clean his skin with an alcohol swab to start a new IV after his last one blew, it came up yellow. The bilirubin was literally leaking out of his skin. When they did a CT scan, they found a pancreatic tumor so large it had invaded his liver and metastasized there. The disease was so advanced, surgery and chemo weren't even discussed as an option for him, so he came to us for palliative care. Apart from the jaundice, he looked like your average blue collar twenty-six year old construction worker, with a fiancé he was clearly very much in love with. So much so, that the nurses would frequently find her in bed with him and shoo her away citing hospital policy when they told her she was not allowed to lie in the bed with him. Making up stories that it exceeded the weight limit of the bed frame, or some other rule that they believed her to be breaking. Vanessa heard about their wagging fingers and made a plan the next night when she picked him up on her assignment. She brought in some little battery-operated tea lights and an old CD player with a couple of Sade CDs she brought in from home. She plugged it in and placed it on the bedside table and introduced herself.

"My name is Vanessa, how you feeling hun?" She asked.

"Good, considering," he replied as he straightened himself and motioned for his fiancé to get off the bed while the nurse was in the room.

"Oh, honey don't trouble yourself at all. You're welcome to stay the night. I looked through your chart, and there is not a damn thing I need from you tonight. If you all want to relax, I'm going to close your door and your curtain, and let you all have some privacy and hopefully a good night's sleep. I promise not to bother you unless you ask me to. Just put your call light on if you need something, otherwise no one needs to be in here until seven o'clock tomorrow morning. Is that alright with you?"

"Yes ma'am, that sounds wonderful."

Vanessa did just as she said she would. She pulled the curtain and left them to do as people in love about to lose each other forever should.

Vanessa smiled to herself as she charted over the ever so quiet squeaking of the hospital bed that went on late into the evening.

Where others saw a rule to be followed or a policy broken, Vanessa knew when fuckery was about and people were using policy as justification for exercising their control over another human being. That night, Vanessa did what no one else would have even dreamed to do. She gave them privacy, and space to be human, and it was the most humane thing that anyone did for that man his entire stay there.

He died three days later.

She was one of the good ones. I couldn't imagine anyone commenting on Vanessa's time management and forcing her to sacrifice that bond in the interest of metrics and timetables. Unfortunately, however, healthcare is a business, and ultimately no nurse was immune to the crush of the time clock. Even Vanessa's healing touch was measured and quantified. She knew where to trim fat though, and somehow, she managed to fly under the radar. Or perhaps above it.

I started following her around the unit, as discretely as possible. If her patient put the call light on, I jumped up to answer it. She would usually materialize behind me right when I was fumbling or saying something completely asinine. She never mocked me or belittled me. Even when her patients would say, "it's alright, I'll wait for my nurse," Vanessa would appear and say, "easy now, don't be so quick to turn away help. This one is just as capable as me at doing that," and with gentle ease, offer me encouragement and cut herself a break if she was tied up with something else. She always had the perfect answer. I just wanted to absorb that energy any way that I could, even if it just meant putting her patient on a bedpan.

As I put in work for Vanessa, I didn't expect to find myself in need of a favor so soon. I was trying to play my hand slowly before I had to cash in my chips.

I had this patient who was a quadriplegic and covered in bed sores and was contracted into an immovable pretzel, making his dressing changes nearly impossible by yourself.

Mr. Legree had been on our floor several times for recurrent klebsiella UTIs, due to his chronic indwelling foley catheter. He had had multiple strokes, which according to his family, had left him completely aphasic.

I got done what I could up until the point that I needed a separate pair of hands to pry his frozen legs apart to get to the other bed sores. I came out to the nurses station to see who might be available to help me, but it was a ghost town. Only Vanessa was sitting out there charting quietly. I squirmed. I didn't want to ask, but I was desperate.

"Um, Vanessa?" I asked timidly.

Her typing abruptly stopped, and her fingers hung suspended above the keys.

"I have this patient in 19, I wondered if you could help me hold while I-"

"Yeah, no problem," she said as she clicked off her chart and was four paces ahead of me before I got to the room.

We gowned up together, and I gave her a superfluous account of Mr. Legree's past medical history. She knew him well. She had cared for him many times in his frequent visits, so I kept it short and just explained I only needed her to help me hold his legs apart so I could put a foam dressing between his knees where his cachectic knobs were rubbing.

When she got down there, she saw the condition of his penis after the traction and pressure from his foley had nearly fileted his entire shaft.

"Oh wow, I knew it was like that, but that looks much worse since I had him. It must be getting pulled upward and extending that tear. He really, really needs a suprapubic catheter, but his family keeps refusing. I'd love to bring them in here and see if they'd appreciate having their penises split open. It's like a highway for infection down there." Vanessa shook her head and her braids fell over her shoulders gracefully.

As we were examining the sorry state of Mr. Legree's phallus, we heard a croak come from the head of the bead.

Mr. Legree was staring directly at us intensely, and almost looked like he had something to say.

After a long and very pregnant pause, he was able to forcibly and very distinctly say:

"Suck my dick."

Vanessa and I looked at each other and then back at him in shock. We had to have heard him wrong. We were told he was without a doubt, completely and utterly aphasic. Absolutely mute, both by the physician notes and by his insistent family.

We were both about to dismiss it as a misunderstanding until he locked eyes with me and said clear as a bell,

"Suck. My. Dick."

I stood there, mouth agape, completely stunned.

After a few bewildered blinks, Vanessa said firmly, "No sir. No thank you."

She peeled off her gloves and gown and threw them on the bed and walked out. I followed behind her for the simple fact that I was absolutely shocked and had no idea how to respond. I followed her to the supply room where we both stood there silently for a moment. I opened my mouth to speak again but finding myself still stunned speechless, I quickly shut it. Just as I did Vanessa busted out in peels of completely unhinged laughter, and I suddenly couldn't contain my own.

Through heaves and wheezes Vanessa stopped laughing long enough to say,

"And baby's first words were: *suck my dick*!"

I almost peed my pants I was laughing so uncontrollably. God, if it had been anyone but Vanessa, I don't know what I would do. This job is completely ridiculous, I thought to myself as I tried to dab the tears streaming from my eyes with the shoulder of my scrub top.

*

That winter we got hit hard with the flu. Between influenza A, B, and H1N1, the local nursing homes were emptying out directly into our unit, and these patients were *sick.* Sepsis, pneumonia, UTIs, C-diff, pretty much every complication known to plague humankind was coming along with it. Even our nurses weren't immune.

The flu hit even before the annual vaccine was even being offered, back in September and even as early as August, which was seemingly unheard of. When it was finally was released to the general population, there was a national shortage.

No one saw H1N1 coming until it was at our doorstep barging its way inside. Our unit was packed to the gills with elderly, infirmed, completely dependent, extremely medically fragile patients. There were no ICU beds, they were holding sixty plus patients in the ED, and the house supervisor was practically beating down our door to get patients in. We were putting patients in the hallway the moment we got a discharge or transfer order, whether we had a place to move them to or not. It was chaos, and to make matters worse, Melissa's presence on our unit was increasingly absent.

Schedules were coming out late, emails were going unreturned, staffing shortages were getting scary. On one particular night, Roberto and I were the only ones to show up for our night shift after Stephanie no call no showed due to a scheduling change she insisted she was unaware of. Shelly was in charge and stayed with us until eleven, but she had to be back for work the next morning. She left multiple messages on Melissa's home phone, but her cellular voice mailbox was full. She called the house supervisor who was "working on it," but had absolutely no flex nurses available to cover. Shelly had already called everyone on our roster and even called in some favors from friends on other units, but everyone was either sick, already working the next day, unavailable, or just plain burned the fuck out.

When Shelly left, Roberto and I divided up the twenty-three beds on the unit, Roberto took the odds, and I was on evens. We all but made a blood pact to knock this shit out and whatever happened, happened. Night meds, linen changes, down and dirty bed baths consisting of a quick wipe of pits and groin and a diaper change, three rounds of vitals, and eleven sets of a.m. labs were done by six. We survived. Barely.

That morning, Roberto bought me a beer.

"*Salud.* To *us*," Roberto toasted. We clinked glasses and dove into our greasy breakfasts.

"Girl, you were a rockstar last night. I couldn't have done it with anyone but you. No, literally no one on our unit has hustle like that. I like your style. I'm almost glad Stephanie didn't show up," he said smiling devilishly.

"Thank you. That means a lot. If someone had told me when I had to interview that I'd be taking eleven patients, I would have run."

Roberto laughed.

"You're doing really, really well. What are your plans after your contract is up? You sticking around, or are you moving on up?"

"I don't really know yet. I'd like to see what else is out there, but I feel like I still have so much to learn. "

"You do. You do. But this isn't a parking lot. You're too early in your career to set up shop in med/surg. If you see something you like, go for it. I'm working on my Bachelors right now. Once I get that done, I'm looking at some of these manager positions. I want out of this bedside game. I wish I was Melissa right now. Must be nice to just turn off your phone."

"Yeah, what's up with that? I haven't seen her in weeks."

"Girl, I do not know, and I love some good gossip, but something is up. Word on the streets is she has some trouble at home, but she's been in the game too long for that. But, you're absolutely right. Something is up."

I pulled back the last of the foam in my glass and I started to say my goodbye when Roberto leaned over the table and got a serious look on his face.

"Danicla, can I ask you a personal question? You don't have to answer if you're not comfortable,"

Oh God, I thought. I had worked hard in my ten months there to stay in my lane and just keep my head down and get my work done. I didn't want my personal life to mix with my professional one. Despite Roberto's proclivity for gossip, I trusted him. He was friendly with everyone but very much separate. He was also a proud Latino man and I found comfort in his flowing vowels as opposed to those harsh, grating Upstate *a*'s.

"Yeah, what's up?" I said, feeling the danger of exposure crackling though our now interlaced fingers.

Roberto flashed his whitened and straightened to perfection grin and squeezed my hand.

"Alright, I'm just gonna say it. *Mami*, are you *gay*?" he asked, eyes dancing. I looked back coyly.

"Girl, are you?" I asked, arching an eyebrow in his direction.

"Oh honey, I'm as gay as a maypole," he laughed wildly. His laugh was infectious, and I smoothed down the baby hairs haloing my forehead, and said,

"Girl yes," and let out a big sigh and started laughing. We both kind of squealed at the sudden kinship we had finally put words to what we had always assumed.

Every time I came "out" to someone felt like the first time, but each situation felt like removing an ugly, itchy sweater I didn't realize I was wearing. This was a leap for me. I had gone back and forth about how I would handle this moment that I broke the seal and confessed my true identity at work. A large part of me felt that it was no one's business but my own, and I didn't want that to factor into what anyone thought of me as a person, but I ultimately realized this was just code for fear. I had been justifying my hiding based on what I assumed someone would feel towards me, but the vast majority of the time, my assumption was wrong, and I was in fact still in the closet, much as I wanted to deny it. I had my moment a few months ago where I set my mind to scrubbing off the whitewashed veneer I had been wearing since I had moved out of the City, but I realized that part of that was denying who I truly was.

*

That Monday, when I was finally off, after putting in sixty grueling hours of being shit on, coughed on, and vomited on, I woke up determined. I was going to take care of myself and focus on finding my way back to the fiery girl I was before I came here.

First thing's first, I needed a creative outlet.

I was a creative being. I needed a vessel to pour that energy into. I loved theater, and my long-term goal was to get back to that, but I needed something that was a little more flexible since my schedule was dictated by my unpredictable hours. I decided to ask my landlord about the studio space that lay right below my feet on the first floor of my apartment building.

My landlord was Evan. He was the classic artist-type. Wiry, tortured, hungry-looking eyes, and a style I like to call *homeless chic*. I ran into him when I was walking home from the coffee shop that morning. He was just opening up the studio. He waved to me and I think it was the flash of his chunky, sterling silver rings glinting in the morning sun that most caught my eye, but for whatever reason, I back stepped a few paces and went back around the corner to meet him.

"Morning!" I sang, thanks to the coffee still optimistically coursing through my veins.

"Morning, my little nurse in residence! How's the new job going?"

"Good, good. Not so new anymore. I like it. I think I'll keep it," I joked. "Hey, so Evan, I have been meaning to ask you, do you have anyone here that teaches art lessons or anything like that? I was kind of thinking about getting into painting, or something. I just need to do something creative to balance out this crazy work schedule of mine."

"Yes, absolutely! That would be fantastic! A few of my artists come to mind. Do you have a particular media you were looking to work with, or a style of work you'd like to focus on?"

"Oh, gosh, I really hadn't thought that far ahead. I guess I'm just looking for someone who is supportive and fun and can give me some pointers on what I need to get started."

"Excellent. Well, actually, I have just the artist for you! Let me check on her availability and pricing and I'll get back with you. Will you be home today, or are you sleeping or what's a good time to get in touch? You seem to keep drug dealer hours," he laughed, which was actually hilarious, because it was completely true.

"I'm free all day! I don't go back in to work until Wednesday, so call me anytime! Thanks!"

I felt refreshed, rejuvenated, awakened! This was the best thing I had done for myself in years, maybe the best thing I had done for myself ever, besides going to nursing school.

Evan called me back that afternoon. He had an artist, Jade, who could teach me on a flexible schedule who he thought I might "grow well" with.

He sent me her contact information and I texted her and met her downstairs as she was finishing up.

Jade was gorgeous. Not otherworldly gorgeous like Jenni, like earthy, motherly, tangibly gorgeous. She had skin like creamy hot cocoa, and locs sprawled out all around her with delicate gold cuffs and colored thread woven into them. She had a small gap in her front teeth that was the most perfect and fitting imperfection I had ever seen. It made me smile. I could already tell we would grow very well together.

"Daniela! Hey honey, welcome to my space! Come in, come in, let me show you what I've got cooking!" I liked how my name sounded in her mouth.

"Hi! Yes, thank you for having me!" I said, trying to match her warmth but falling just slightly tepid, not quite knowing what energy to bring into her space.

"So, this is just some of my work. I have a style I like to call "ethclectic," kind of ethnic, kind of eclectic," she laughed richly at her quip. "My work is an effort to pull from what is inside of me and give birth to it on the outside. I draw from my emotions, my heritage, whatever moves me, I really try to capture that in in its purest and sometimes rawest form and bring that into this realm. Art for me is an inheritance and a destiny. I feel very cosmically connected to what I put on canvas. Its deeply personal. If that doesn't scare you off too much, I'd love to help you do the same."

I was captivated. Jade had given words to everything I had been longing for, crying out for. She was an absolute revelation to me how she was able to manifest everything I felt my soul had been crying out for. I felt detached, disconnected from who I was and who I wanted to be. I could see her, she was out there floating in the stars, I just need a way to get to her, and I felt like maybe Jade could be the Sherpa that gets me there. No pressure.

I made a motion with my hands to demonstrate that she just blew my mind, and kind of laughed at my ignorance and inability to add to anything she just said. She told me everything I wanted to hear.

"Wow, Jade, that's…everything. I don't even know what to say, I'm at a loss for words, but wow, just, thank you, I guess. Yeah, thank you."

"The universe provides," she said in a way that sounded like the universe answering back.

"When can we start?"

"Right now, if it feels right."

Oh, it felt right. Everything felt right. We had the studio to ourselves, so the lights were turned down in the other spaces, and Jade's spotlights were beaming just on our little corner. Marvin Gay was laying down some *Inner City Blues,* which sounded conspiratorial, revolutionary, and velvet all at the same time. This paint and this canvas felt like a revolution. My revolution. And I was ready for it.

"So, Miss Daniela, tell me the story of you."

"Well, I was born in Manhattan," I began.

"No baby, not with your words, we'll get to that. Tell me with your colors. What color is your soul?"

"My soul? I guess if I had to pick," My eyes bounced around the studio in search of something that looked like it suited me, but I didn't see what I was looking for, until I did. I picked up a tube of oil paint sitting precariously at the edge of Jade's palate. I picked it up and turned it over in my hand. I held it out towards her. Alizarin Crimson. "I think it's this color."

Jade smiled and nodded as if I had just spoken words in her language.

"Beautiful," she said grinning as she turned the wrinkled tube over in her delicate fingers.

She rifled through a pile of blank canvases she had stacked against the wall.

"I think this is you," she offered, and set a medium sized rectangular canvas, almost double in length than width. About the size of a wall mirror. She set it up on her paint caked easel.

She took the tube of paint from my hand and squeezed out a dollop of paint onto the square of grey glass she used for her palate. She turned to me and asked,

"Is your story more darkness, or more light?"

I considered this a moment, and finally said,

"It started in darkness, but now it's more light."

"I'm glad to hear that. Now pick your shape. What shape speaks to you? Angles and edges, or is it more flow and twist?"

"I think in the beginning, when things in my life were pretty bad, and I was trying to fit into everyone's expectations, everything was sharp, now it's getting to be round and soft."

"Do you kind of feel this inside you? Is this sounding real for you? Do you want to start manifesting some of this together, or do you want more time to kind of sit with it and speak it into being?"

I closed my eyes a moment. I licked my lips and felt something stir within me.

"No, I think I can feel it. I think I'm ready."

"Alright. Decisive. I like it!" She smiled glowingly.

Jade started adding some additional colors to the palate. Pthalo blue, cadmium yellow, Mars black, flake white. She showed me how to combine colors to make shadows and highlights and encouraged me to play with some combinations to get a feel for the strength of the colors. When I was ready, she had me lay in some colors roughly with the palette knife I was blending my colors with. As the color emerged and became smooth, she had me pull some of it onto the edge of the knife and lay in my strokes in a way that connected to what we had discussed.

Jade lit some candles as Van Morrison was softly crooning *Into the Mystic*. I felt mystic in that moment. I remembered Valentina's wild, haunted way of creating, back in her darkened disheveled apartment in Hell's Kitchen, and it felt so unbridled, so out of control and possessed. This felt measured, composed, gentle, and safe. It felt more like giving birth and less like committing murder.

I started in the bottom left corner with my darkness. I felt scared, and angry, and small. I painted a series of peaks, like shark's teeth in pthalo blue, and a brooding violet I created with just a crumb of the alizarin crimson. As I wound my way over and up, I let the crimson build up its strength, and my brush strokes grew longer, and I allowed the flow of the paint as it dragged across the canvas to help me find the end of my lines. Jade showed me how to build up depth by developing an impasto in my brush strokes.

By the time I had pushed paint into all four corners, Jade walked me back ten paces and positioned the lamp in such a way that it caught the crests of the impasto, creating shapes and juxtapositions I wasn't aware that I had made. It took my breath away.

"I see you," said Jade from over my shoulder. I felt her warm breath pass by my left ear and move my hair slightly.

I covered my mouth with my hand and drew a breath to clear the lump from balling up in my throat. I turned to Jade, who didn't retreat when I entered her space.

"Thank you," I said, and I hugged her, or rather, she hugged me. It was so encompassing and absorptive. I didn't feel it coming, it was like a mist that gathered to make a light rain, but I was crying before I had a chance to reel it back in. Jade held me solid as an oak and didn't relinquish one bit of her solidity until I was completely finished.

"God, I'm so sorry, I am so embarrassed, I'm not usually like that," I laughed, shocked at my lack of propriety.

"Nah. Don't do that. Don't ever apologize for being real. What we created here tonight was an exchange of something bigger than ourselves. Don't apologize for you, unless you're prepared to apologize for the whole universe."

"Ok, then I will just say…thank you."

"No, thank you. Thank you for letting me share this with you."

Jade and I made plans to meet again next week and try some different mediums. We embraced again and I left her in her studio to finish the Chris Isaak song that was smoothly unwinding in her space, while I returned to my apartment with my painting.

When I saw the green glare of the clock above my stove, I realized it was past midnight and I was still too wound up to sleep. I paced the length of the apartment a few times and finally forced myself to lay back into bed. My hands found their way over the rise and fall of my belly and down between my thighs, to find that I was wetter than I had been in months, if not years. I navigated my familiar topography until I found my rhythm and rose to a crescendo and found that magnificent release that I desperately needed. Breathlessly, I drifted off into the most luscious sleep.

CHAPTER EIGHT

15th Street

"Daniela, are you home?" Valentina's voice came unsteadily and urgently through my phone while I was at work. I never took calls on the unit, but something told me this was important.

"Valentina, hi! No, no, I'm working, I'm at work. What's up? Wait. What's wrong? What happened?" I asked pointedly, feeling the panic rise in my chest.

"No, Daniela, I need you to go home, it's an emergency, I need to talk to you."

"Valentina, you need to tell me now. What happened? Are you ok? Is Mami ok? Is it Marisol? What? What's happening?"

Valentina imploded and let out a guttural wail.

"Mami's dead Daniela!" She screamed.

I dropped my phone. Everything started to go dark. I dropped to my knees in the back hallway and caught myself on the crash cart and let out a yelp.

Layla and Dom heard my clamor and came running around the corner to me. Layla helped me into a chair, and Dom retrieved my phone for me and held it back up to my ear. Valentina was still crying on the open line.

"Valentina how? What happened?"

Valentina took a stridorous inhale and said, "I don't know! I don't know what happened Daniella! She didn't show up to work and they called me at the bar, and I went to the apartment, and she was just there on the floor in the living room! She was laying in vomit and snoring and wouldn't wake up! She wouldn't do anything! It's like, her eyes were open, but she couldn't see. I ran out and yelled for help. Mrs. Lopez came out and called 911. They put in a breathing tube, and she got a scan of her head when we got to the hospital, and when they moved her back to the room, she just…*died*! They were pumping on her chest and yelling, and they kicked me out of the room, and came back twenty minutes later, and just said that she was dead! She like, had an aneurysm or some shit!

Like, what?! What does that even mean? You're a nurse, like what the fuck Daniela?!" She fell back into gasping sobs.

"Valentina I'm coming! Ok? I'm on the next flight out! Call Marisol and I'll be there as soon as I can!"

Layla looked at me and just said,

"Go, go, go. We're fine, we got this, you go home, and I'll tell Melissa you're not coming in tomorrow. Drive safe!"

I tried to give a hurried report, but Layla wouldn't let me.

"Girl, I can read, I'll figure it out, go to your family and call me if you need anything!" I grabbed my purse and left my jacket still hanging in my locker and sprinted for the parking lot.

My head was spinning. I wanted to cry, but it felt like a yawn that evaporated before it reached my throat.

I bought a one-way ticket to Manhattan from my phone on the way to my car. The flight left in an hour. I had just enough time to make it to the airport from the hospital and hopefully I could squeak through security before they closed the door to the plane.

I just barely made it.

The forty-five minute flight felt impossible. I felt like I was sliding down in my seat. I felt like I was being strangled by my lap belt. I felt like my hands were numb. My lips and eye lids were tingling. I realized I was hyperventilating and tried to consciously slow my breathing.

I pictured Jade's soothing voice, trying to imagine the universe and that Mami was still in it, and that she would meet me on the platform on 14th Street.

Our decent from altitude seemed to compress the air in my lungs, and I felt like I couldn't get a full breath. When we finally deplaned at JFK, I half ran, half walked to the sky tram. The A train was running local to14th because MTA was working on the C line for some reason, and the ride from JFK to downtown alone took longer than my whole flight from Rochester.

The shuffle of passengers seemed to flood in and out around me like I was a rock in the middle of a stream. It felt surreal. I began to question if Mami was dead or if I was. None of this seemed like my life. None of it felt real.

When the train stopped at 14th, I ran out of the15th Street side of the station to the end of the block where our soot stained building stood, same as always. I caught the security door just as a faceless man was walking out, and bee lined to our apartment at the end of the hall. I fumbled with the keys and then realized the door was open and I pushed my way in.

Mami's vomit was still on the floor, but Mami was gone. I don't know why I expected her to still be in the apartment knowing the timeline of events, but somehow, I thought she was there waiting for me.

Valentina was crumpled and despondent on the couch. I climbed into her lap and threw my arms around her while she fell apart. I tried to hold her like Jade had held me the other night until I emptied. I waited and waited for my presence to be enough to pull her back, but it didn't seem to be working.

When there was a break in her heaves, I finally asked her, "Where is she?"

That set her off again and it was fifteen minutes before she wailed, "In the *morgue!*" And sobbed so primally I thought she would puke.

Just then, Marisol came through the door. When she saw the pathetic state of the apartment, and the remnants of our family, she broke down too. I don't think I had a single memory of Marisol crying, and the sight of it is what finally triggered me to break down. We sat there collapsed upon each other until we had physically run out of tears.

I untangled myself, and being the only one with the gustatory fortitude to clean up the emesis that was now crusting to the floor boards around the edges, I went and got the towel off the bathroom floor that Mami used to catch the drips from her wet body after she would step out of the shower, and I gently placed it over the mess. I gathered it all up and threw it in the trash and went to the kitchen for some disinfectant. I asked Valentina if there was a number the hospital had given her for the chaplain or a social worker. She fished around in her pocket and produced a business card that had been haphazardly creased from being carelessly carried home. I realized the small miracle of it making its way back from the hospital with Valentina in the state she was in.

I took the card with me into the bedroom and called the hospital chaplain. I made arrangements for Mami's body to be sent to the nearest funeral home. Mami had a brother and her mother still living back in D.R. I called them, having not heard my *abuela's* voice since I was a teenager, and tried to explain as best I could in Spanish what had happened. I would have to wait to see if they could pool resources to come to the states to say their goodbyes.

To my knowledge, Mami didn't have any friends. She was married to her work. So, I called her job to say she wouldn't be coming back. There was a collective gasp that went up like an offering every time I notified someone of her passing. After making the few immediate notifications I needed to make, I quickly realized the business of dying was slightly outside of my scope, and made a mental note to contact a lawyer and figure out how to close a bank account and contact Social Security, and see what we needed to do with the apartment on 15th that we had all been raised in.

I was compartmentalizing. Taking on one task at a time like rungs on a ladder to try and gain enough perspective over the horror of the situation to figure out where we had all landed.

When I emerged from the bedroom, Valentina was sleeping hard on the couch, and Marisol was sprawled over her protectively like a cloak. She straightened and gently peeled herself off of Valentina's legs, trying not to wake her. We retreated to the kitchen to talk in hushed tones, while Valentina fitfully slept through the worst of the shock.

Marisol opened her mouth to speak, but no words came out.

"I called *abuelita* and *tio* Fernando."

Marisol nodded.

"Thank you," she said finally. "I didn't think Valentina and I would be relying on our baby sister to handle this stuff. You're so grown up now. I keep forgetting. How's the new job? Do you like nursing?"

"I do," I admitted. "It's challenging and overwhelming, but I'm off orientation now and I'm finding my way. I like Rochester. There's a lot of art and food and stuff so I feel like I'm staying busy."

"That's good. I'm proud of you. I could never do it. Animals are so simple. It's expected, even when it's not. I think I just get along better with them."

"How's Ithaca? You still have to take me hiking."

"Yes definitely. It's beautiful. You should come and stay for a weekend. You can bring your boyfriend, or whatever."

I think the mental dump of everything that just happened had completely removed my filter, and without thinking, I bluntly said to this sister of mine that I barely knew,

"How about my girlfriend?"

She turned to face me, "she's more than welcome to come too," she said genuinely. Then smiled and said, "you can finally meet my husband." Now it was my turn to be shocked. We both started laughing.

"I'd love to," I said.

The inappropriateness of our laughter woke Valentina, who shuffled over, sleep drunk and holding her head.

"You guys. Holy fuck," she said in a gravely voice.

"Has anyone eaten yet today?" We all looked at each other realizing how unaware we were of our basic human needs under the crippling circumstances.

"I'll order us some Chinese," I said as I pulled out my phone.

"I need a drink," said Valentina. Marisol nodded.

The only alcohol Mami had in the apartment was a dusty bottle of *Mamajuana,* Mami no doubt had only touched medicinally, and a fifth of Crown Royal, still in its purple pouch.

I reached for the Crown and pulled three of our faded plastic drinking cups we had sitting in the cabinet since we arrived in the United States. I poured out a few fingers of liquor into each cup and passed them around. Yellow for Marisol, green for Valentina, red for me. Our cups made a dull clink, and Marisol raised hers and said, "to Mami."

"To Mami," Valentina and I lamented.

That night we sat on the floor and pulled out our old photo albums and poured over grainy faded Polaroids and snapshots. Mami and baby Marisol on the beach in D.R. Me in my frothy Christening gown. The three of us on the stairs of our stoop arranged by height. There was a notable five, or six year hole in time following Ignacio's death. No birthdays, no Christmases, then suddenly, an older, triumphant Marisol holding a single rose after her chorus concert, followed by *quinceañeras,* a small flurry of me in full theater makeup, and finally, the three of us at my graduation Upstate.

We somehow made it to bed around three a.m. after a few more rounds of the Crown Royal. Marisol and Valentina slept in Mami's bed and I took the couch. We slept with the lights on.

When the harsh glare of morning streamed through a crack in the blinds and directly into the corner of my left eye, I awoke disoriented, still in my scrubs from the day before. The day brought with it both a physical and emotional hangover. Phone calls, funeral arrangements, and the chore of dying was almost worse than the vacuum of Mami's absence.

We buried Mami on a Tuesday. Only a handful of coworkers, restaurant regulars, and Mrs. Lopez were there. *Abuela* and *tio* couldn't get a flight in time, but they called, and we all promised to go to D.R. soon to visit.

We met with the lawyer and made an accounting of Mami's modest assets, and Valentina assumed possession of the apartment on 15th. Her lease in Hell's Kitchen was about to be up the following month, and the drain of working in the bar while she fought a daily battle for her sobriety had finally worn too thin to continue with the façade of being a party girl that didn't partake in the party.

It was Mami's final gift to her. Valentina had been focusing more on her art and was looking for a way to make a creative life her reality, and more than just a hobby. This was the start she needed to shift the direction of her path. The apartment was rent stabilized, and the monthly cost was about a third what she had been paying in Hell's Kitchen and offered her more light and space to create her work.

Marisol and I helped her haul her few possessions to 15th Street, and I got to see the full spectrum of what she was capable of creating. It was stunning, and represented Mami's success in life, raising three daughters, all on separate but meaningful paths, living lives that were independent and fulfilling. We were a testament to the *fait accompli* of her 0500 wakeup calls, overtime, *chancla* whippings, and regimented and austere upbringing. Shc loved us right. I couldn't have asked for a better mother.

CHAPTER NINE

Following the Clinical Course

I checked in with work the day after Mami's funeral. It sounded busy. I had to wait for Shelly to come to the phone because she was in with a patient, which probably meant that she had to take an assignment, which probably meant that we were still short staffed and over capacity. I told her I'd have to miss one more shift and I'd be back the following day I was scheduled. I'd already used up my three days of bereavement, and whatever meager vacation time I had saved since I got off orientation. It didn't matter that I wasn't emotionally ready to return to my sick and dying patients, I was expected to be there, and they desperately needed the help.

Leaving Manhattan felt like Mami dying all over again. The three of us being winnowed and tossed to the wind, apart from each other once again felt like being drawn and quartered.

Marisol and Valentina walked me down to the entrance of the train station. They hugged my neck as a tall passerby rudely bumped my shoulder, causing us to momentarily separate and gather, holding on tighter. Valentina was crying. Marisol looked like she was crying on the inside. I was trying not to, because a distraught girl on the train was a target. I wanted to stay invisible as long as I could stand it, until I had a chance to fall apart in the sanctuary of my own bed.

"How are we supposed to do this?" Cried Valentina. "How are we supposed to just go on like nothing happened? Mami didn't teach us how to survive this!"

"What are you talking about Val?" Marisol retorted. "Don't be stupid. Mami taught us nothing, if not how to survive. Pull yourself together. Throw out the last of that Crown Royal and get your shit together. Paint. Draw. That's how Mami taught us to survive. Find a way to clear out a little corner for yourself, and you fucking post up there. Now, let Dani catch her train so she doesn't miss her flight." The forcefulness with which Marisol scolded Valentina echoed her authority as the big sister, and it was a tone that I had never heard her take. She hugged me tight, without the vail. Real and genuine. I hugged her back with all my might and hugged Valentina the same. I took a big gulp of air like I was about to go under water right before I headed into the train station. The ride home passed by my window, but I didn't see any of it.

When I made it back to my apartment there was a small, wilted flower arrangement and a card outside my door that read, "*Sending light and love to you and your family in this difficult time. Love, 4 North.*"

I pushed open my apartment door and found everything as I had left it the morning I went into work and didn't return home for a week. My milk was curdled, and my garbage reeked, but otherwise, I felt a huge weight lift off my shoulders the moment I collapsed into my bed.

My chest ached. I felt empty and alone. The first thing I wanted to do was call Mami, and it struck me like a bolt lightning through my heart that she would never pick up the other line again. I began to cry, first as a whimper, and then quickly gathering into gulping, convulsive waves. I cried myself to sleep with my boots and clothes still on.

I awoke at three a.m., parched, like I was dying of thirst. I went to the sink and greedily chugged glass after glass of tap water until I finally felt satiated. I took off the boots and jeans that I was still wearing, that I had borrowed from Mami's closet since I arrived to the City without anything to wear but my scrubs.

Mami's clothes felt tight on me. She was at least an inch shorter, and at least a size, maybe two smaller. I held them to my face and tried to inhale her smell, but by now it was fading and absorbing my invisible scent. I wanted to cry all over again, but I had nothing left.

I lay in bed until I couldn't stand it anymore. I got up at 0430 and took a long shower, and finally shaved my legs. By the time I emerged, I felt slippery and new, and like I had just now managed to skim the last of the grit and smoke of the City from my surface.

I turned on the news and it was nothing but shooting, stabbing, shooting, shooting, car wreck, and I quickly turned it off. I bet the ED was slammed last night. I made myself some coffee and rummaged through the fridge for something to eat that wasn't fuzzy or funky smelling. I found a yogurt that was only two days past its expiration, so I had that. I made a mental note to go grocery shopping after I got out of work at 1900. I looked back at my stove clock and it was only 0545. I felt like the walls were closing in on me, so I decided to head into work early.

When I got there, nightshift was just starting their frantic tucking and boosting and straightening of patients, to create the illusion that they were ready to start their day for the next shift. I glanced over the assignment sheet and didn't see my name. I looked for Vanessa who had been charging all night.

When I found her in room twenty-three, she was coaxing blood from a dry vein, and it kept collapsing on her. She rotated the fragile hand over and hung it down over the side of the bed to allow the blood to refill the feeble vessel, and finally struck red gold, filling the three tubes that had been ordered. I waited for her to finish, not wanting to scare off whatever luck was shining upon her. Without ever glancing my way she said,

"Daniela, how you doing love? Welcome back." She looked up from her work and held my gaze solidly. "I am so deeply sorry about your mother. That is one of the hardest losses in life, and it just broke my heart to hear about it."

"Thank you," I cleared my throat and tried to formulate a more substantial response, but it was all too fresh and raw to know how to reply, so I left it at that.

"What's the matter with the schedule baby? Don't see your name?"

"Um, no, that's what I was coming to ask you."

"Look at the top baby. You're in charge today."

I looked over the schedule I was sure I had scoured already, but there it was. Top of the page, just like the lady said.

I looked up, mouth agape.

"You been here long enough to do it. You were actually scheduled all last week, but you were gone, so we moved you on to this week," She retracted her needle and activated the safety and finally looked back at me carefully. "Close your mouth child, there's germs in here. You got this. You're ready."

I followed her out in stunned silence.

Vanessa patted the chair next to her and motioned for me to sit down.

"The biggest thing is making the assignment, so I'll do the first one with you, but you'll have to fill it out for nightshift before they get here tonight. You're actually really lucky, we've got good staffing today so you can just focus on charging and you shouldn't have to take an assignment unless someone doesn't show."

Vanessa walked me through plugging names with room numbers, returning nurses to the patients they had the day before for continuity of care. Then she briefly ran me through a laundry list of line items I had to accomplish. Check the crash cart, fax the house supervisor our census, go to the bed board meeting at 0800, and probably five other items I promptly forgot.

As dayshift filed in, they all looked curiously at the unfamiliar handwriting on the assignment sheet and settled in to get report. I took a deep breath and waited for everyone to settle into their usual routine.

I tried to help keep everything flowing until the admissions started rolling in. One was an obvious misplacement. It was a patient on a heparin drip with a massive LV thrombus that had q1 hour vitals ordered. We punted him straight up to the ICU where he belonged. There was another one that came in that was a bariatric patient who weighed three hundred and fifty-five kilograms. Not pounds. Kilograms.

He was admitted with increased output from his ileostomy secondary to c-diff. He was just awful, not because of his size, or because of the c-diff, but because of his propensity to throw his ostomy bag at nurses who didn't immediately give him what he wanted.

I went in and gave him my best "mom" voice. I informed him that intentionally flinging infected fecal material at nurses amounted to assault and was considered a federal offence in the state of New York. I asked him who changed his ostomy bag at home for him, and he defiantly answered that he did it himself. At that point I placed a box of ostomy supplies and wipes on his bedside table and told him that we would not be changing it for him any longer. He called me a bitch and several other choice names. Channeling my inner Vanessa, I explained to him that we were here as his partners in healing, and not as his punching bag. We wanted to help him get the care that he needed so he didn't get dehydrated, or any sicker than he already was. I explained I knew the doctor ordered labs for him that they weren't able to obtain in the ED, and that if he stopped cussing and flinging his stool at us, I was willing to help him with that, but he had to show some understanding that we were fighting the same battle together, and that I was willing to fight with him if he was willing to fight for himself, and that meant not fighting the ones trying to help him. He reluctantly agreed, and within three minutes I had his labs. He thanked me and turned his whole attitude around, at least for the moment. Behavior like that was never really corrected, just redirected for the time being, but if it got me through my shift, that was a win in my book.

There were a few more fires that cropped up that I quickly squelched before they got out of hand. I almost got into it with Stephanie when she came in and started complaining about her assignment, but she zipped her lip when I told her I can call Melissa and ask her to straighten it out for her if she likes.

When Vanessa returned that night, she gave me a big hug and told me I did good. I handed off the unit to her, and walked out to my car exhausted, numb, and with a surprising sense of normalcy about my life. The fact that a patient threw an ostomy bag full of c-diff at my face didn't even phase me. The fact that I was in charge for the first time didn't even give me pause. All of my anxieties and obsessions and self-doubt seemed to have vanished. I just didn't have the mental energy to devote to such petty worries after Mami died. Life was obviously too short. I think I was still in shock. But with rent to pay, and work to do, I just didn't have the space to unpack all of it right now.

*

I had been doing charge now for a couple of months, and I had finally settled into a tenuous comfort zone with it. Melissa had gotten more unreliable to the point where our entire unit was essentially just fending for themselves. I had gone from rotating shifts to pretty much working straight nights since I needed the differential and the overtime to cover my student loans, and since no one else seemed to ever want to work them.

I met with Layla for lunch one afternoon when I managed to be vertical before 1300.

"So, what do you think is going on? Are they going to fire her, or do you think she'll resign?" I asked, genuinely curious.

"I don't know. Something's got to happen soon because we're running out of supplies. No one is ordering anything. Shelly's been trying to take over payroll and scheduling, but she's not authorized to do much else. After Dom and Amanda left, we're really hurting for staff. I'm already looking for something else. Don't say anything," She shot me a sharp glare.

"Who am I going to tell? Seriously. Honestly, I think I might too, once my year is up in June. I need to get started on my Bachelors since I have to matriculate into a program within two years to keep working here. I don't want to be in school and wondering if our whole unit is going to fall apart, and I also don't want to do it working sixty hours of nights per week. Something's gotta give."

"You're absolutely right girl. Where are you thinking of transferring?"

"ED," I said as I sopped up the last of my cioppino with a corner of my crusty bread.

'ED? Girl, you must be crazy! Do you even know what it's like down there? You've seen what they send up here! It's a disaster! If you're looking to settle down so you can get through school, that is not how you do it!" She admonished.

"Oh, ye of little faith," I said as I smiled into my glass of Riesling.

*

I had been back to see Jade a handful of times. Each time we created something together it felt like we were making love. She would draw out the most intimate details of my life and show me how to carry them over to my canvas and lay them down gently.

One sultry summer night the AC had quit, and the studio was absolutely sweltering. Jade had taken off her cardigan, and then her flowing scarf, and stood before me in just her threadbare white tank top. She wasn't wearing a bra over her tiny breasts. I could see her nipples hard and angulated in my general direction. I saw a blossom of hair under her arms, and instead of looking unkempt, it looked like a secret garden that only I was meant to see. It was evocative of pubic hair, and just the peek of it I had gotten me savagely aroused. She was fanning herself with a paper she had folded into an accordion and pinched into a fan at the end. I watched a drop of sweat roll slowly down her long neck, pooling in the well of her graceful collarbone. In my lust, the only thing I wanted in life was to lick it off of her before it had the chance to settle there. I stopped myself, but it was the last straw. I couldn't focus, I couldn't paint. I couldn't take her breathing and sweating so close to me.

"Do you want to come upstairs? I have working air conditioning and cold beer in the fridge, and it's hot as hell down here. We can finish another day."

Jade tossed the willow switches of her delicate locs behind her shoulder and laughed.

"Girl, I thought you'd never ask."

We washed the brushes in the sink, hands lathered and bumping into each other clumsy yet calculated as we rinsed them free to paint again. Jade grabbed her Kente cloth satchel and scarf and followed me up the separate entrance to my cramped but cozy apartment.

When I fumbled with the keys, Jade came up behind me and put her thinly veiled chest on my back. I held my breath.

"Is this alright?" She asked into the nape of my neck.

"Yes," I breathed jaggedly, and turned to face her.

She caught my lips with hers and kissed me passionately when I turned around, sliding her bubblegum tongue forward to meet mine.

Now I was desperate to get the door open, and when I flung it ajar, the knob punched a perfectly round hole in my wall.

I only paused to push it closed with my pointed toe just an instant before Jade grabbed me and pulled me over to the bed.

She kissed and sucked and licked me ravenously, and I did the same to her, searching thirstily for that drop of sweat I had followed down her chest earlier.

We made love to each other ardently on my bed, both of us climaxing hard in each other's hand.

We laid there breathless and trembling before Jade turned on her side and drank in the shape of my face with her eyes. I gazed back in awe, as if I were looking across at galaxies.

"It would be unethical for me to continue as your teacher at this particular juncture," she said. We both laughed and I pulled her into my chest, and we drifted off to sleep in the afterglow.

*

Shelly was put in the position of interim manager after Melissa officially stepped down. She finally acknowledged that some personal issues at home had spiraled out of control, and she could no longer fulfill her obligation to our unit.

It's a hard way to watch someone you looked up to and respected bow out. It's incredibly telling of how you can have all the tools in place to be successful, but years of packing away baggage and never finding a suitable place to put it, can cause all the fractures to finally give way and shatter out from under you. Melissa was a strong and accomplished nurse. It really was unsettling to know that if it could happen to her, no one is immune.

Shelly was slowly putting the pieces of our unit back together, but I couldn't wait around and risk going down with the ship. I felt hungry to learn and to grow, and as Roberto had once said, med/surg wasn't the place for me to set up shop.

I had learned everything I knew about nursing there. Assessment, pharmacology, wound care, time management, prioritization, leadership, even something as simple as learning how to talk to people, I had learned by buzzing from room to room on this unit. It was invaluable, and ultimately, I loved the people I worked with. But the itch to grow and see if the grass was actually greener, became too much of an insatiable curiosity not to explore.

CHAPTER TEN

Welcome to the Dark Side

Working in the ED is a little like teaching Kindergarten. You have no control, there are no adults around to ask for help, and when it's time to go, no one can find their shoes.

When I started down there, I was told I would have four weeks of orientation. Then four turned into three, three turned into two, and three days before my two-week mark, we were short staffed, and I was unceremoniously informed that I was coming off orientation.

The first words anyone spoke to me down there were, "*Welcome to the Dark Side,*" and I can think of nothing more apropos than that.

Unlike on the floor, you have no forewarning of what you're getting into your rooms. You may have six patients, you may have twelve, or more, depending on how the night goes. You are completely at the mercy of the needs of the department and the needs of whatever hellfire was coming down in the city at the time. And nothing is ever as advertised. There is always more to the story than the chief complaint, or what you get in report. Always.

Assessment and communication are two of the most valuable skills you can possibly possess in an environment where at any given moment, a patient that arrives with a completely innocuous complaint can die on you without any overt warning, unless you are constantly assessing and communicating.

Assessment is every single miniscule observation you make. Are their hands cold? Are their nail beds pink? Are they convex or concave? Do they have hair on their lower legs? Do their ears sit low on either side of their head? Have they bathed recently? Is their lipstick on straight?

Seasoned ED nurses have their own set of assessment findings that you won't find in any book or taught in any class.

"Holy fucking shit dude, your patient in room 8 just crossed his feet, you better get in there!"

"He crossed his feet? Like, he crossed them and left them there, or he had an itch and moved them back?"

"Nah bro, they're just sitting there crossed and he ain't crossin' 'em back."

"Aw fuck, roll me the crash cart."

Or, *"Yo, your man just said he saw a train."*

"A train? Like, he said he saw a train, or he was about to get on a train?"

"Yo, he's got a ticket, you better get in there."

"Goddammit."

These were the subtle sixth sense things that only experience teaches you, and every interaction is a lesson.

Moving to an environment of completely unhinged, uncontrolled, chaos from one of managed, categorical, controlled chaos, is not an easy transition. It's a stripping away of hard won, meticulously rehearsed, best practices, to those practices that fit into the category of, *you do whatever you have to do, by whatever means necessary*. That's not to say that the rules don't apply, it's just that the rulebook changes when life and limb are on the line.

I started my orientation with Kathy, a seasoned, burly, Brünhilde of a woman, built like a brick wall. I was completely intimidated of her because she looked like she absolutely could and would crumple me up like a wad of paper if I did anything at all out of line.

I had heard Kathy was a sweetheart once you got to know her, and every year for thanksgiving she made the best homemade cinnamon applesauce in the department, maybe in the whole hospital, so it paid to be on her good side. I could hardly picture a woman like Kathy doing anything remotely domestic, in fact, it was hard to picture a woman like that outside of the ED at all. She was swift, efficient, and she could place an IV so fast you'd have to watch three or four of them before you could even register how it got there. She was a wealth of knowledge too. Murphy drip, Morgan lens, magic mouthwash, this woman knew things I had never once heard of. She would be setting up for a procedure before the doc ever even saw the patient. She just had really, really good instincts, and she worked so effortlessly she was five steps ahead while I was still sorting out step one. Although my time with her was abruptly cut short, she had been the one to give the ok that I was ready to come off orientation. Unlike my climactic signoff from orientation on the floor, Kathy simply said, "You'll figure it out kid," and walked off to get report.

I very apprehensively made my way over to my zone to take my assignment. I kept adjusting my stethoscope around my neck, I checked my pockets for my trauma shears, and for my pen and collection of alcohol swabs. Stood at the desk in zone seven. Randy, the nurse I was relieving was typing away furiously. He looked back at me and said, "hey new girl," then went back to typing. I sucked in a breath and cleared my throat as subtly as I could. Randy paused, and looked back at me.

"Where's Kathy?" He asked seriously.

I smiled nervously. "Just me today," I shrugged.

"Wait, who's precepting you?"

I cleared my throat again, as it had suddenly gone dry. "No one. I'm on my own today."

"Oh wow, well that was quick. You must be a real badass," he said generously, but the apprehension on his face was pretty apparent.

"I think we were just short today," I said dismissively.

"Nah, if Kathy didn't think you could hack it, she'd have walked your ass out to the curb and said, 'better luck in dialysis,'" he joked. "Anyways, you ready to do the damn thing?"

"Ready."

"Alright, 21A is an MHA, he's medically cleared, just waiting for a spot in psych. B bed is in DKA, we're just waiting for him to finish his two liters and if his sugar comes down they'll decide if he needs an insulin drip. Keep A bed on his side because he keeps walking over there and getting into it with B bed. Just throw him some juice and cereal and he should stay out of your way. 22A, nursing home CHF exacerbation. She's puffed up like a little blimp after they served ham in the mess hall at the SNF last night. Anyways she's on BiPAP until she gets the fluid out of her lungs. She's a DNI, so if she goes down, she's SOL. B bed is a drug seeker. Some chronic pain bullshit. Her 'boyfriend stole her pain pills,'" he air-quoted. "Hopefully discharged soon. She's been up my ass all night for meds. 23A was found down at home by his old lady. She didn't know how long he had been down, but it must have been a while. He's in rhabdo, and his CK is like 43,000. He's getting fluid now. They want another liter when that one's done. B bed is empty. I'll be back tonight. Good luck!" He grabbed his coffee cup and jacket and walked out without even looking back to see if I had any questions.

I stood there a moment trying to straighten out everything in my head. On my first day I pulled out a sheet of paper and started writing down names, room numbers, diagnoses, and outstanding tasks in neat little rows, as I had done every day I got report since the day I became a nurse to help organize my day. Kathy pulled it out of my hand and said, "lemme see this." She looked it over briefly and ripped it down the middle in front of me. "You gotta learn to do this in your head. When a doc comes screaming, you're gonna have to know what to say without reading it off your pretty little paper. Keep up buttercup!" I stood there, mouth agape, no longer knowing how to proceed.

I had that same feeling now. I didn't know where to start. I logged into my EMR and assigned myself to my patients. I looked up what was late and what needed to get done first. I checked on my BiPAP lady and found her soaked in urine. She had gotten 120 mg of Lasix and had no foley to catch the pee now spilling off her bed. I wanted to cry. Her lungs still sounded wet and her pCO2 on her ABG was 80, so she wasn't turning around any time soon. I knew that would be a project, so as long as her breathing was ok, I had to check on my DKA patient. I know they were optimistic about him turning the corner with some fluid and his subQ insulin, but his anion gap was 26, and his room smelled like fermented Fruit Roll-Up hooch as soon as you walked in. He was breathing about sixty times a minute and was super lethargic.

As I walked in with the glucometer to check B bed's sugar, I was immediately accosted by his neighbor.

"Hey there little lady, where you going with all that? Where's my stuff at girl? Your boyfriend Randall said you'd give it to me. He said when that juicy Latina gets here, she'd give it to me. He also said I could give it to you. You down with that?"

I walked right back out to where I came, too afraid to go back into that room.

Just then, Kathy swooped in like an angel and put her arm around my shoulder.

"Hey kid, how's it going?"

My chin poked out and quivered imperceptibly.

"Ok, ok, whatchu got going on here?" She scrolled through my assignment. "DKA, rhabdo, CHF, bullshit, bullshit, and an empty. Ok, I'll tell you what, let's get in there and knock this out. What's your priority?"

"My lady in 22A is wet, she peed all over-"

"Don't give me that horseshit girl! These people are sick! Get your head out your ass and try again! No one's dying from having pissy sheets! ABCs, what's your priority?"

"21B is real sick. I went in to check his sugar, but A bed came at me all threatening and I-"

"Ok, ok, I got him, you go do what you gotta do."

I went back into 21B and checked his sugar. Critical high. *Shit.* He barely moved when I poked him with the lancet and he was breathing like a freight train chugging.

I heard Kathy on the other side of the curtain.

"All right my man, I don't know what Randy told you, but we've got some ground rules here. Your nurse Daniela is going to work on getting you upstairs. For that to happen you need to be on your very best behavior. She's got people dying over here and she's got stuff to do. I need you to stay on your side of the room, stay out of her way, and wait patiently while she gets things in order so you can get where you need to go. You got one minute to tell me what you need, and I'll get it for you."

He thought for a minute, and said, "Just juice."

"Just juice it is then," she said as she turned towards the kitchenette.

"Oh, and crackers, crackers, crackers."

"Anything else? You get one shot at this my man."

"Yeah, juice and crackers and we're straight."

She returned and handed him all the juice and crackers she could carry back from the kitchenette, and he took them excitedly.

"It says 'high,'" I told her.

"Ok, did you tell the doc?"

"Not yet," I said waiting for my tongue lashing.

Kathy sighed and rolled her eyes.

"Anything else you want to tell him while we're up there?" She asked.

"22B needs a foley."

"Yes. Yes, she does, that's my girl!" said Kathy as she walked up on deck with me where the docs sat. She nudged me forward.

"Doctor Reynolds?" I asked cautiously. A brash and boyish looking sandy-haired second year resident looked up at me.

"I just wanted to let you know, Mr. Davis in 21B is still critically high on his sugar and he finished his two liters."

He ran his fingers through his wavy hair, irritated.

"Ok 10 of Regular insulin IV push, and I'll put in for the drip. I'll have to call MICU, fuck."

He turned back to his computer. Kathy nudged me again. I cleared my throat. He looked back more irritated than before.

"Um, also 22B needs a foley. She got 120 mg of Lasix and she's just dumping fluid. We need to keep track of her I's and O's." I said, giving my best pitch.

"Yes, to the insulin, no to the foley." And turned around definitively. I began to turn to walk back to my desk, but Kathy grabbed me by my forearm.

She tapped him on the shoulder with her heavy sausage finger. He turned around more irritated than ever.

"So, that's not gonna work. This lady is full of fluid, she's like the Michelin Man in there, just peeing everywhere and we can't lay her flat to change her. She'll suffocate. Do you want to suffocate her, or do you want us to put a foley in her and let her diurese in peace?"

"Dammit Kathy, you drive a hard bargain. Fine. Foley. Anything else? I got a sepsis workup to put in."

"That'll do for now doctor!" Kathy said cheerfully and spun on her heel and headed back to my zone. She turned to me, "you good for a little bit kid?"

"Yeah, I think so. Thank you so much Kathy," I said emphatically.

"Sure thing. Grab me when you get that insulin ready to go," she said, halfway down the hall already.

I went and drew everything up, and Kathy co-signed it with me.

"Grab another liter and hang it slow. He's going to need some maintenance fluid. His cells are all shriveled up and it's gonna take more than two liters to plump 'em up. He's probably been like this for days rationing his insulin," she said, looking on him with genuine pity. Insulin is expensive. Like, six hundred plus bucks a pop, if you're lucky. When you have to choose between feeding your kids or paying your rent, the stuff you see takes precedent, but what goes on unseen in your own body is that you are slowly dying. As a nurse it really is one of the most infuriating things about our healthcare system. No one should have to choose between a life-saving medication or having a roof over their head.

I checked the clock and planned on rechecking Mr. Davis' sugar in a half an hour.

I went back to 22B with dry linens and a foley kit. I briefly thought of just doing the damn thing myself to avoid pulling Kathy away from her patients any longer than I already had, but if this patient's ankles were any indication of what her labia looked like, I'd have a better shot of threading a needle with a hotdog. I walked to the next zone over. It was Brittany. She was standing at her desk talking to another nurse Yvonne. They both stopped abruptly and looked me over.

"Hey, sorry to interrupt. Are either of you free to help me with a bed change and a foley?"

Yvonne stared back at me blankly and said, "I think I hear my patients calling," and walked away.

I smiled back at Brittany pleadingly.

"Ok fine, but you better have everything ready to go when I get in there."

"Yes." I said, dying on the inside, hating to feel dependent on another nurse to accomplish my work.

22B, Mrs. Lawrence was a rotund older woman, but in her fluid overloaded state, she was downright pillowy. I untucked the linens on my side of the bed, pulled down the front of the diaper, and opened and readied my foley kit. As if on cue, Brittany came in with gloves already donned.

"Alright," she said, "let's do this."

She hoisted an inflated thigh upward, forcing a bend in the knee, and her hip cracked sharply as it elevated. I tried to tuck the leg on my side similarly, but I was limited in what I could do with my elbows without contaminating my sterile gloves.

Once we got Mrs. Lawrence fully exposed, the view of her urethra was nonexistent. It was just swollen, bloated skin down there and I didn't want to go searching and risk giving her an infection.

Brittany hoisted, lifted. She overturned a bedpan and tucked it under her bottom to elevate her pelvis. She pulled out a headlamp (I'm not even joking) from her cargo leg pocket and tried illuminating the area for better visualization.

"Fuck it," she said. Luckily, my patient remained blessedly confused. "Just shoot your damn shot and see what happens."

Boom. Liquid gold. First try.

"Yessss," I cheered.

"Congratulations. Let's get these wet sheets out."

We tucked and pulled and boosted Mrs. Lawrence up as best we could. When we finished, I was huffing and puffing almost as bad as my DKA patient. Before I could thank Brittany for her help, she was already doffing her gloves and pulling the curtain.

"Thank you!" I called after her, but she was gone.

I felt better already. I had never had such a difficult procedure before. On the floor, if you can't get it, you can't get it. You call the physician and write a note, but the stakes are much higher down here, and this wasn't even necessarily a life-saving procedure, but it certainly was a back saving one.

When I emerged, my orders were piling up and I still hadn't seen two of my patients, and there was one slated to come to my empty bed.

I quickly circled around and checked another glucose on my DKA patient. 467. Progress, I'll take it. My insulin drip was still being made in the pharmacy, but the next step was getting that up and running so I didn't lose the small bit of headway I had made on this sugar.

When I looked over at my psych patient, he was still drinking his juice. Or so it appeared.

I quickly saw my rhabdo guy and took my back pain her discharge papers. She refused to sign and said we had done nothing to help her and threw them in my face and said she wanted to talk to the doctor. I went to let him know she wanted to talk to him, but he was nowhere to be found. I asked her to wait, and I would have him see her as soon as he was available. Unhappy with that answer, she grabbed her IV and ripped it from her arm and tossed it at me, blood gushing down her forearm.

I grabbed gloves and tried to chase her to the exit, but Kathy caught me by the elbow.

"Let that one roll, girl," she said.

"But she's bleeding everywhere."

Kathy shook her head, and said, "not everyone wants help. All she has to do is hold pressure on it for about twenty seconds and it will stop. Either way, it will stop on its own. When someone refuses help, you gotta let 'em go. You can't save everybody." With that she pulled out a Cavi wipe and dropped it on the blood and started wiping the floor with the toe of her worn clog.

I was still standing there watching her. She looked back at me and said, "I got this, you go see that rhabdo patient, he doesn't look so hot."

I went back to the room and found him looking toxic in the bed, his wife sitting at his bedside looking concerned.

I introduced myself and listened to him with my stethoscope. His lungs sounded wet, with fine crackles throughout his lung fields. I looked up at the dry bag of IV fluid. It was his third liter and it seemed to be overwhelming him. I looked up his labs, and we hadn't gotten any kidney function studies since 2200 last night.

I told Mr. and Mrs. John's I was concerned about him and would talk to the doctor about getting some more labs. I did just that and returned to get some blood.

On my way up to the tube station to send Mr. John's labs, out of the corner of my eye, I saw 21A refilling his juice cup with alcohol hand sanitizer from the dispenser on the wall next to his bed.

"Excuse me!" I yelled and marched over to see if I did in fact just see what I thought I saw. I did, and he quickly tried to swallow the last glob of sanitizer in his cup.

"What are you doing?!" I shouted, louder than I intended.

21A hiccupped, and said, "Jusss drinkin' some juissss…" he slurred.

"Oh my God." I said. "Oh. My. GOD!" I shouted, unintentionally loud.

My raised voice caught the attention of Brittany and Kelvin who was the other zone over from me, as well as Dr. Emma Stevens, one of the first-year residents.

"What happened?" Everyone asked collectively.

I let out a couple exasperated sighs and pointed at him with my outstretched arm.

"He drank the hand sanitizer," I said not fully believing it myself.

"Oh God," gasped Brittany.

Kelvin doubled over laughing, and even Dr. Stevens was attempting to smother a smirk.

"How much did he drink?" She asked.

"I don't know. I don't know how much was in there to begin with." I pressed the tab on the dispenser and only got a sputter from the bottom of the bag.

"Well, get an ETOH level. He's not going to psych anytime soon," she said as she walked back to her computer desk.

I wanted to cry. I wanted to wring his scrawny neck. I hated this assignment.

The day rolled on like a maelstrom. MVC, sepsis, sepsis, my rhabdo patient was in fulminant renal failure. He wound up going to ICU. My DKA patient also went to ICU, but not for over six hours which left me there checking his blood sugar every thirty minutes. We ultimately ended up moving my psych patient out to the trauma bay to be intubated for airway protection after he projectile vomited all over himself.

I was done. I was so fried by the time Randy came back in. I shot daggers at him with my eyes as he walked by my zone to pick up from zone eight. He just laughed and said, *fun day, huh?* As he kept walking past me.

Kathy walked by on her way out and slapped my shoulder and said,

"You survived! One down, thousands more to come!" And walked out to her car.

I gave report and headed over to Jade's house. She lived in a rough area of the city. Her run down rental house was just a few blocks from the so-called "fatal crescent." It is a chronically impoverished area rife with drugs, gangs, and all manner of crime you could think of. It is an area where seventy five percent of the city's murders take place. It is rumored that cops, fire, and EMS won't even go in there. Supposedly, if a drug deal goes wrong, or rival gangs start squaring up, they won't hesitate to turn a gun on whomever is responding, in an attempt to "finish the job." Allegedly, if a victim is sick, or in need of assistance, they have to be taken to a safer area outside of the crescent to be picked up. If there is a structure fire, supposedly they just let it burn. Anyone covering that area wears Kevlar, fire and EMS included.

I hated going out there, especially after a long day of work, but Jade didn't completely understand what I did, or how I could be completely exhausted by seven thirty in the evening. I tried to explain it to her, but I don't think I could have understood before I started working here either. Also, Jade was a creative being. She was fueled by inspiration, and she didn't find human suffering particularly inspiring. When I would start to tell her about a case that I had, or a particular disease or diagnosis, it wasn't far into my story before she would lift her hand and say, "*darling, content.*" It was one of her favorite little sayings. 'Content' meant, "don't talk to me about anything that contaminates my aura." To her credit, she worked hard to build a protective positive atmosphere around herself. She was able to maintain that even during dry spells between art and teaching jobs, which is no easy task, but defining my work and my experiences as being "contaminating," is incredibly isolating. I've never been one to have a lot of friends, and I don't need anyone's approval, but at the end of the day, you want to share your stories with someone. The problem with being a nurse is that, for the most part, only other healthcare workers, or first responders, or maybe military members, could really even begin to comprehend your stories. Even when someone has a strong constitution, they don't really understand it. Not really. That's why so many in healthcare wind up having marital problems and seek solitude in the arms of someone who grasps the moment by moment struggle of lifesaving. Between that and the sleep deprivation, ungodly hours, and constant overstimulation, maintaining a healthy relationship is hard anyway, but being with someone that minimizes what you do, or blatantly disregards it as "just a job," is a death sentence.

I swung into Jade's driveway and found her not at home. Or so I thought. I texted. I called. She didn't answer. I was freezing standing on her stoop, and it was dark already, and I felt exposed in the faintly green-tinged porch light.

I turned to leave, thinking her gone, but just as I had stepped down onto the driveway, she suddenly answered the door in her red and turquoise kimono, hair wild and flung about.

"Daniela, what are you doing here?"

"What do you mean? I just got out. I came by to see if you wanted to get something to eat."

"No, sweetie, I already ate. It's late, I was just about to shower and go to bed. We can go out tomorrow."

I was already suspicious, but this was ridiculous. Accusations were popping off furiously in my head. Seven thirty wasn't late to Jade. Hell, twelve thirty wasn't even late to Jade. I took a step closer to the door, craning my neck to see if someone was creeping around in the house.

"I came all the way out here, are you just going to leave me on your front step?" I said.

"I think we should talk in the morning when you have a chance to rest after your shift. Your energy is off, and I think It's best for us to have this conversation another time."

"What conversation Jade? I came here to see my girl and get a bite to eat. I didn't think we needed to have a conversation about that. But you're not being very conversational tonight. I texted you. I called you. Where have you been Jade? What's going on?"

She started to close the door, but I caught it with my hand, and pushed back hard. Against all rational thought, I shoved my way in and jostled past her. As I did, my landlord Evan must have heard the commotion from the bedroom and come into the kitchen with his hands up, like I was going to come in shooting. It's a good thing I didn't own a gun, because in that moment, I would have.

I immediately knew what I was seeing in front of me. The seemingly unrelated puzzle pieces, Jade, Evan, unanswered texts, the kimono, they all made sense now. But suddenly, I didn't. I felt completely out of place, and needed to get out immediately before I suffocated, or vomited, or wet my pants.

Jade was still holding the door ajar.

"Daniela I-"

I put my finger up to cut her off.

"Don't." I demanded, and walked out, slamming my car door.

I peeled out, spraying her porch with gravel from the driveway, and nearly got sideswiped by a car I didn't see coming when I pulled out. He had to hit his breaks to avoid slamming into my driver's side door.

I drove home maniacally, crowding my steering wheel to see through my furious tears. I ran up the stairs to my apartment and slammed my door, and sat down on my floor, pulling my knees to my chest, and I began to rock back and forth slowly as the anger and humiliation and sadness began flooding into me, until the full weight of everything came crashing down on me and I couldn't take it anymore.

This had been years of stress that had just piled onto me. Ignacio, the fucked up nervous life we lived in his wake, watching Mami live this plebian life of unrelenting struggle and insecurity, my fragmented, partially unraveled relationship with my sisters, failed relationship after failed relationship, Mami's death that I had never had time to grieve. Now Jade. What else? What else could go wrong? I am twenty-two years old, and I feel like this life had aged me another twenty-two years. I didn't know if I could take it. It hit me like darkness, like the lights being snuffed out. I had an utter breakdown and just cried, and screamed, and pounded the floor. I let the rage, and sorrow, and grief spill through me like a sieve.

When I finally felt emptied and wrung out, when all of that hurt and pain found its way out of the prison I had been holding in, I lay there sucking in gasping, spasmodic breaths. My head was pounding. My eyes were nearly swollen shut. I reached up onto my bed and pulled down a pillow and fell asleep on the floor.

I awoke at 0545 to my alarm screaming in my ear. *Fuck.* I don't know at what point the responsible part of my brain kicked in, but I must have set my alarm at some time in the middle of the night to remind myself that I still have responsibilities that don't give a shit about my mental health.

I peeled myself off the floor and went to the restroom to wash my swollen face. I looked like garbage. I felt worse than I looked. Every fiber of my being wanted to call out. I had never done it before, and I really didn't even know what the procedure was. The reality of my situation was that I was going to be on probation for my first six months in the Emergency Department. I had just transferred down there. I had no usable vacation time. They owned me until I could hit that six-month mark.

To my surprise, I actually felt better. I felt like I had emptied myself. I knew sitting at home would be worse and only allow that anguish to re-accumulate. Especially if I crossed paths with Evan or Jade outside of the studio. I had a flashback to Jade's open robe, and to Evan's hands in the air. I squeezed my eyes shut until it passed.

I was certain of only one thing. I needed to find a new apartment. First thing on my list when I get back from work. New apartment. Absolutely.

I got to the ED that day generally irritated, and not in the best headspace for dealing with a constant influx of the sickest patients I had ever dealt with.

I sipped my coffee acrimoniously while I waited for the charge nurse to post the assignment sheet.

Zone two. Perfect.

I walked down to get report. I was still a little foggy and distracted, waiting for the caffeine to be taken up in my blood stream. Once I had taken over the zone, the night nurse sleepily shuffled off.

I went through and met and assessed everybody, got meds together, and started moving through my task list. No one appeared especially sick. One kid had come back to the ED with a headache after a lumbar puncture he had two days ago to rule out meningitis. I gave him our usual migraine cocktail. Benadryl, Phenergan, Fioricet, and the doc had ordered a caffeine drip, which sounded absolutely amazing. 1,000 mg of caffeine in a liter of fluid, mainlined directly into your vein. If that didn't work, we'd have to call anesthesia to do a blood patch. All of this was new to me. We never saw stuff like this on the floor, and I was momentarily bolstered by the excitement of learning something new.

I also had a patient who was seventeen weeks pregnant. G:1, P:0. First time mom. She started spotting the night before with no apparent warning. She said she stood up from the table and felt a warm gush of fluid between her legs. When she went to investigate, all she saw was blood. She nearly passed out. They called her OB/GYN and the on-call doc told them that she would have to go to the ED, and to have the ED doc page him if she required follow up.

The patient and her husband looked absolutely terrified. Their tension was palpable from the doorway. Suddenly, my breakup seemed completely trivial. These parents were fighting for the life of their unborn child, and my patient's life as well, and I was just a stupid twenty-something with a heartache. I felt my focus sharpen. I took a few deep slow breaths to help me relax, and to consciously made an effort to soften my voice and body language before I went in to meet them, knowing that they were stressed out and we were all in for a very long day. I wanted to let them know that I was there to fight with them. With a few gentle words, and an explanation of what our plan was, I drew her blood and started her IV. She finally relaxed once I got it.

"I didn't even feel that. You did really good. They usually have a hard time," she told me. I breathed a huge sigh of relief. I would have felt awful if I missed. Getting the IV is a pivotal point in a patient's stay. If you get it right off the bat, you've earned their trust and they are immediately more amenable to the idea of working with you. Miss it, and they automatically think you're incompetent and that you are actively trying to cause them needless suffering. Once that bridge is crossed, it's generally smooth sailing from there.

"I'm glad. Anything at all I can do for you, or if you notice any changes, please let me know. I'm going to send this to the lab so we can get some blood counts and a few other tests to see how you're doing. Also, if you can, we need a urine sample. They should be coming by in a little while to do your ultrasound."

"Honey, a pregnant lady can always get you pee," she smiled, and I set her up to give us a sample while I walked to the tube station to send her blood.

I had two empty beds, so I wanted to get a handle on the work I knew I had, before I got hammered with a barrage of orders on a new patient.

Things got busy as the city began to wake up. I got two new patients at the same time, and my headache kid wound up needing that blood patch, so I had to get everything set up for the anesthesiologist when he got there. The patient needed to lie completely flat afterward, and of course, five minutes after the procedure he decided he also had to pee. I had to stand there and hold the urinal for him, so he didn't spill it everywhere. Besides the fact that peeing supine is no small anatomical feat, he was nineteen, so the similarity in age gave him performance anxiety, so it took a little longer than usual.

I got sidetracked and never did get a chance to log in and see my pregnant lady's lab results. I was in with another patient when they came to the bedside to do her ultrasound. All I heard from the room next door was a swelling wail from behind her curtain. I pulled my gloves off and went to investigate. The ultrasound tech was just cleaning her probe off when I came in. She shot me a warning look, and subtly shook her head.

I looked over at them huddled in the darkened room.

After several moments pause, I was finally able to say, "can I get you anything? Blanket? Water? Are you in any pain?" Her husband shook his head silently. I went up on deck to find the doctor. It was Dr. Herbert today. He was a somewhat gruff middle- aged gentleman who was a former flight surgeon in the Air Force. His crew cut and regimented demeanor had stuck with him from his military days and made him an intimidating presence to work with. He seemed like the worst choice for such a delicate situation.

I went up to him and quietly notified him that the ultrasound tech was unable to find a fetal heartbeat. He nodded in acknowledgement but made no immediate effort to go down and console the family.

I returned to the room with tissues, a glass of water, and a warm blanket. It wasn't what they wanted, but it was the only thing I could think to do. I felt helpless.

I returned back to tending my other patients, until the husband came out to get me.

"Um, I'm sorry Daniela, I don't mean to bother you, but my wife is feeling some pressure, maybe. I'm not really sure."

I jumped up to see what was going on.

She was sitting up with her legs butterflied out beside her.

“Are you having any cramping? Are you feeling like you need to push?”

She was sweating and breathing heavily. *Shit.*

“I don’t know actually. I feel like I need to poop.” *Literally shit.* That was always the sign, not that a bowel movement was on the way, that a baby was.

“Whatever you do, don’t push!” I said too abruptly. “Doctor Herbert, *I need some help in here!”* I yelled up to the deck.

Dr. Herbert rushed down quickly and snapped the curtain shut.

“All right my dear, let’s have you lie back so I can take a look at what’s going on,” he said uncharacteristically gently.

She did as she was told as he pulled on a pair of gloves.

He looked directly at her and said, “Mrs. Finch, I am incredibly sorry to inform you that you are delivering this baby, and it will not survive. Now, I’m going to help you. I need you to look at me and focus on controlling how hard you push. Just bear down nice and steady for me.”

She let out a yelp and her breathing started getting out of control again.

“Ok, ma’am, the baby’s head is out now. You’re going to feel my hand touching you as I slip the cord from around its neck. I need you to not push for a moment,”

Her breathing intensified.

“Ok, good, good, the cord is free, now one more steady push just like last time for the shoulders to come out.”

With a gush, and more force than I anticipated, the slippery fetus was freed from her body. Dr. Herbert clamped the cord and cut it in one fluid motion and passed the stillborn infant to me.

I grabbed a towel and tried to wrap it as best I could and placed the pear-sized baby in her mother's arms.

She was purple, her feet black. There were no signs of life whatsoever. The baby must have died in utero several days ago, they just didn't know it.

The new parents took in the horror of their shattered hopes and dreams being placed squarely in front of them, they stared transfixed, in stunned, emotionless shock, while we waited for the gelatinous placenta to fully pass.

Dr. Herbert inspected the placenta and placed it in an emesis basin and set it by the sink as he washed his hands. He turned to the Finches and said, "I am so, incredibly sorry for your loss. I'm going to call the OB team down to assist you, and we'll have the physician check you out. If there is anything at all that you need in the meantime, please let your nurse or I know."

I followed Dr. Herbert out of the room and went and found the charge nurse Sharon in the trauma bay and explained what just happened. She called up to L&D to get a nurse from the floor to come down and assist with post-mortem neonatal care, and assess fundal height, and monitor the things we weren't trained to monitor.

We moved the roommate in the next bed out and into the next zone over and placed a purple butterfly sign on the curtain to allow them space to grieve. The thin curtain dividing the room was about as effective as my old roommate Bethany's blue masking tape at providing separation.

As the other patient was wheeled out, she said,

"I'll pray for you dear,"

"Thank you," Mr. Finch replied softly.

I was completely stunned by what had just transpired. It all happened so fast. It was shocking and heartbreaking all at the same time.

The rest of the shift was a blur. Nothing more that happened that day could compare to what had happened in that room. I gave sign out to Sabine, who had just come back after a brief leave of absence she took while her husband was deployed. I hadn't seen her since I started down there. I stuck to the script and let her know about the patients, and I walked the mile and a half home. I was completely drained. Emptied.

*

The next morning, I regrouped. I was a woman possessed. The previous day's events were now a launch pad for me to redirect my life yet again.

I called every apartment complex in the general vicinity of the hospital. I wanted the option to walk to work more consistently in the spring and summer, and I wanted a balcony I could have tea on when the weather allowed for it. I had been living this hungry, restricted life Mami had brought me up into, and I was finished with it. I had gotten a raise of another dollar and forty cents an hour when New York State finally got their shit together and passed the budget, and I had already gotten another forty cents an hour raise when I finished my contract on 4 North, and would be eligible for another raise once I came off probation after my six months were up in the ED, which was approaching faster than I thought. Between that, and the differentials from working weekends and overnights when I could, I was in a good place financially. Incredibly good, considering I was now twenty-two years old and I barely knew a single person in my peer group that was able to fully support themselves independently. It really was an incredible accomplishment, and I allowed myself a moment to savor it.

I found the perfect place. I texted Evan, and essentially said I was formally relinquishing my lease based on him breaking the terms of our contract by fucking my girlfriend. I knew he wouldn't be able to afford a lawyer to come after me for moving out a couple of months early, and if he had any conscience whatsoever, he'd know what he had taken from me already. Even if he didn't, I would pay every penny gladly, just to get out of the space that so much grief had consumed me in.

The place I found overlooked Highland Park, with a second-floor unit that had a tiny balcony that cantilevered out over the lilacs and let their perfume waft through the living room. Unlike my other place, this one also had a separate bedroom with a door and everything. It was perfect, and moving in felt like being reborn, which was exactly what I needed.

By the time I and got things situated, I was feeling more confident at work. I was actually enjoying the fast pace and all of the perpetually moving parts. Unlike on the floor, where you have patients for months, or even years in some cases, down here you only had your patients for your assigned shift, which had its benefits.

One difficult consequence of a prolonged admission to the floor, is that patients come through our door humbly, thanking everyone profusely, and never trying to be a bother. However, after a week or two without their freedom, losing control of everything from their meal schedule, to their ability to use the restroom independently, they quickly devolve into impatient, needy, and increasingly petulant residents. The honeymoon phase after their arrival goes out the window pretty rapidly as their health conditions and say in their daily routine spirals out of control. That sweet little old man or woman you used to look forward to caring for each day becomes a shadow of the person that walked into the unit. They're bitter, and resentful, and you're the only punching bag within reach. That still happened in the ED, but much faster, much less predictably, and in a much more incendiary way.

But, there are wins too. Even with the miscarriage, the outcome was horrendous, but the husband still came to me after and thanked me for caring for his wife. For the most part, I still choose to believe people want to do good at their core. Sometimes the spite and vitriol are a symptom of a much greater problem and have nothing to do with who they are as a person. It's grief over losing their health and freedom, and fear of losing more of it. No one wants to be sick. I get it, and I don't often blame them, but being on the receiving end of all that anxiety and frustration wears on you after a while.

*

When I returned to work the next day after I moved, I felt clear headed and ready to tackle whatever the shift brought through my rooms. Or so I thought. I received an admission from an outlying hospital that was supposed to be a direct admit to the vascular floor, but all the units were full, and the guy had to come through the ED to board until they could clear a room for him.

He seemed easy enough. Good looking, well groomed, normal guy, mid-forties, no past medical history, doesn't smoke. He takes a trip to Canada and when he returns, he has a nagging pain in the back of his knee. DVT, easy enough right? Well, turns out the clot is in the popliteal artery and not the vein like they originally thought. That's bad. But overall, the guy looks fine. He has a faint, dopplerable pedal pulse, and apart from some mild lower leg discomfort and a Heparin drip, he's really not asking for much.

At some point during the shift, the guy puts his call light on. I go to see what he wants and find him restless and thrashing his blankets around saying he can't get comfortable. As I'm taking this in and trying to straighten his blankets out for him, he kicks his leg and suddenly stops moving, sits bolt upright, and says, "*I'm gonna die,"* and his eyes get all big and roll back into his head. He falls backward into his pillow and turns purple from his chest up. I scream into the hall for the crash cart, and when I can't find a pulse, I start doing CPR. When I push on the guy's chest a couple times, he grabs my hands and opens his eyes, so I stop, and as soon as I do, he goes unresponsive again. So, I start pushing, and he again sits up and pulls my hands off. At this point I'm completely lost on what's going on. To everyone who just arrived to my room, it looks like we're fighting and that I'm assaulting him.

"I don't know what is happening!" I shout between compressions and grabs. "He was trying to fix his blanket and then he kicked his leg and goes, *I'm gonna die,* and goes unresponsive." I stop and he falls back into the bed again. I check a pulse and feel nothing, the monitor is showing PEA as soon as I stop compressing. I push and he shoots up like a jack-in-the-box and starts resisting me.

"Jimmy take over CPR, Ayanna get me some epi and dopamine drips, Keri call pharmacy and have them get tPA ready. Jimmy whatever you do, keep doing CPR, no matter how hard he fights you!" Emma, our first-year resident orders.

Ayanna, a salt-box Jamaican nurse who usually worked in the Trauma Bay happened to be walking by when this all started and got sucked into it. She passes me in the epi drip. I yelled back for an IV pump.

"We don't have one!" She yelled back in her undulating Jamaican lilt.

"Wha-what do I titrate the epi to?" I ask completely confused.

"A heart beat!" She yells to me daftly.

I attach the line and start running the drip to gravity. She hands me in the sulfur-smelling dopamine bag.

"Wha-what do I titrate the dopamine to?" I ask, afraid I already know the answer.

"A fucking blood pressure!" she yells back. *Aw balls*. I free flow that too. "Titrate to effect Daniela, titrate to effect! You run that shit 'til you get an effect, you hear?"

Just then, the pharmacist arrives with the tPA. She takes in the scene that looks like a roomful of nurses accosting a very distraught looking man and sees the wide-open vasoactive drips and just whispers, *fuck*, like a little church mouse. She hands me the bolus of tPA. I push it into his IV and we start rolling him to the trauma bay with Jimmy still on top wrestling him to try and maintain compressions. He needs to be intubated and at least have his drips run at a controlled rate.

After dropping my steaming pile of holy shit off in the Bay, I meander back to my room completely thrumming on what could I have missed, what could I have done differently, and wondering why the hell this guy would reanimate with CPR, and then die when we stopped.

Ayanna threw her arm around my shoulders and walked with me back to my zone.

"What in the cowboy fucking shit was that?" I asked with a gasp.

Ayanna threw her head back and cackled.

"What you've never hung that shit in a code before? Girl, just wait, you're just getting started!"

"Not without a pump! Never without a pump! I didn't even know how much I was giving!" I yell-whispered back.

"Daniela, does it matter? The whole point is to get the guy back right? Well you do what you gotta do. You gon' wait for a pump to come from hospital supply while that man dies? If you do you betta find you another job!" She said.

At that point I realized it. This wasn't a job for straight A students and book smart individuals. Did you need to know what the fuck you were doing? Absolutely. But did you need to intervene on the fly when the situation called for it? Abso-fucking-lutely.

He lived you know. The guy lived I found out later. They went in and did a thrombectomy. If it hadn't happened here, right in the ED with these badass docs and nurses standing by, he definitely wouldn't have made it.

I learned how to be an ED nurse that day. Not by being reckless, by acting when the moment called for it. After that I wasn't afraid. Or at least, I wasn't waiting for permission while a patient declined in front of me. That moment was the real start of my ED career.

*

I was settling in well to my life and role in the ED once I got through my probationary period. The slight bump in pay that came with it was nice too. I was learning a lot, happily single, and had even taken a vacation day to go down to Ithaca to see Marisol and meet the elusive husband.

Tommy was a botanist and worked at Cornell where Marisol had gone to vet school. They were two peas in a pod together, both quiet and reserved, and nerdy together in the most endearing of ways. She seemed softer somehow, less shifty. It looked good on her, and it warmed my heart that she had found her person, and a life she was justifiably very proud of. We talked about nursing, the City, and Mami. We went for a hike that afternoon to see some waterfalls. When I returned to work, I was a better person, and had noticed a considerable difference in my state of mind and general outlook on life.

I had started working on my Bachelors that fall, and I was muddling through my first semester. I was appalled at my limited attention span. I used to sit for hours poring over textbooks and journal articles. Now everything was such a struggle. I got through every assignment kicking and screaming, but I was glad I was doing it now and not a decade or two down the road.

As I was nearing my one-year ED anniversary, talk of orienting to the Trauma Bay began to circulate. Our department was setup in such a way that we had our main ED which handled all the usual suspects. Just your average, run of the mill ED patients, if there was such a thing. There was also a separate pediatric ED, a fast track area for all the subacute visits, a psych ED for our psychiatric patients to go after being medically cleared by us, and lastly, we had our Trauma Bay. No one saw the inside of the Trauma Bay until they had been road tested and proven competent in the other areas. If the patient met trauma alert criteria, or if a patient went deep south in the main ED and required either intubation or some sort of hemodynamic support, they went to the Trauma Bay. Other than that, you were on your own to figure it out with the rest of your patients.

I felt nowhere near ready to run that gauntlet. I felt like I was still learning something new every day, and like I was only now just barely managing to stay above water most days. As far as taking on what went on in the Trauma Bay was concerned, I was in absolutely no hurry to change lanes.

One day, late in the afternoon in the dead of winter, we got a multi-car crash in which several of the occupants in the vehicles involved were ejected and either dead on scene, or trying to die on the way to the hospital.

Death of an occupant in the same vehicle was a rock-solid reason to call a trauma alert, but for some reason, the patient that came to me didn't ring the bells. The medic gave me a quick report and said the patient had been the only restrained passenger in the collision. Her husband was the driver and was struck head on by another vehicle full of teenagers that crossed the centerline into their lane. The husband was DOA. They showed me a picture of the vehicle from the scene and it was just a tangled mass of metal that you couldn't tell where it began and the car it hit ended. They couldn't see any obvious injuries on her, apart from a few abrasions, and other than some wrist pain, she couldn't tell me anything specific that hurt, she'd just been non-stop screaming, *"I hurt! I hurt!"* When you would ask her where she hurt, she would yell back hysterically, *"I don't know!"* I chalked the yelling up to her being so shocked by what had transpired, and maybe she was a little concussed.

I gave her some oxygen so she would feel like we were doing something to help her, but I agreed with the medic. I couldn't see anything specific wrong, but something definitely didn't match up. Her pain was so disproportional to her injury pattern, I had a nagging suspicion that something more had to be going on. Ayanna was feeling froggy and saw the hot mess they were rolling my way, so she came over to snoop and help me get her settled.

She began cutting her clothes off, and the woman began swatting at her and saying, "*I can't breathe! I can't breathe!"* We looked up at her oxygen saturation and it was 100%, so Ayanna, in her thick Jamaican accent informed her,

"Ma'am, you are being very dramatic. You have to calm down. Your oxygen is 100% and you're yelling just fine, so I think you're breathing." I smothered a smirk at her typical petulance.

They came and shot a chest x-ray, and the physician, Dr. Harrison spotted the scout from across the way and bounded over fervently.

"Holy shit! Pull that up again for me!" The x-ray tech obliged and the doc again said "Holy shit! We need to get her to the Trauma Bay! *Now!*"

Slightly confused, I pulled her stretcher out and made tracks for the Trauma Bay.

"What? What is it? What did you see?" I looked back and asked as we were rolling.

"Diaphragmatic hernia!" He shouted back at me, eyes flashing.

I rolled faster. A diaphragmatic hernia is an acute traumatic emergency. The discrete space in the lungs maintains negative pressure that allows the lungs to remain inflated. The diaphragm is a tough sheet of muscle that separates that lung space from the rest of your organs. If that perforates, or straight up tears, every breath you take acts like a bellows and sucks your guts up through the hole and into your chest. Every breath you take strangles you with your own innards.

The trauma team descended on her faster than you can say 'hernia,' and whisked her off to the OR. Ayanna came over with her mouth covered looking every bit as mortified as she should have been.

"Oh my God, Daniela, I had no idea! Oh my God, I'm such a bitch!"

"You absolutely are," I laughed.

That day I learned that when someone's pain is completely disproportionate to their presenting injury, worry. Something's wrong until proven psych.

*

After Mami died, I took it upon myself to be the rope that bound me to my sisters. I went to Manhattan when I could, and I visited Marisol whenever possible. She was pregnant, scared shitless, but buoyant, ethereal, and everything she should be. Tommy was going to be a great dad. When we would settle in for the evening to digest the lovely meal he had cooked us, he would lay his head in Marisol's lap and sing softly, or read his plant books to her belly while she ran her fingers through the waves of his hair. It felt reverent, and I felt like an interloper in my very private sister's most intimate moments, but she grinned back at me, welcoming me into her space. It felt so healing to share this moment with them, and to bask in the glow of their love.

Valentina was a stronger version of her once flighty self. She had been in the apartment on 15th Street for over a year now and had really put her touch on it. It wasn't the temporary, gypsy abode we had crowded into growing up. She cleared out the plastic chairs and the trundle bed. She made it look vintage chic, as she called it, with a tufted emerald velvet chaise, plants everywhere, and some macramé tapestries she had knotted adorning the walls. Her art was selling well enough for her to only have to barista on Sunday's.

She had a gallery opening earlier in the year where she sold her entire collection. She called me after the showing, champagne-drunk and effervescent, and thanking Mami for looking down on her. I had so wished to be there, but I couldn't afford to miss class, and my work schedule was a nightmare. She ultimately confessed that she was glad that I didn't make it. She was so nervous for three days before that she hadn't eaten and barely slept, and she said if I had been there and noticed, she wouldn't be able to maintain her confident charade that she had cobbled together for the duration of the show.

She texted me pictures of her pieces with the proud byers, and it reminded me of a litter of puppies going to their forever homes. I told her how proud I was of her, and she agreed. She was actually proud of herself.

Things had tapered off a bit since then, but she took some of what she had saved back from the show and quietly went to Paris alone, to heal from some of the grief of losing Mami and to recover from everything else. She didn't say it, but I think she went just to be someplace that was three thousand miles from any sort of sadness. She went to the Louvre and fell in love with the morning light there. She's been studying French and hoping to take a sabbatical there for a month or two to reinvigorate her art. She estimated that she would need at least two or three more openings before she could safely check out like that, without leaving a shitshow of bills to come home to. I said a silent prayer that she would do it. I loved the thought of my wild sister sitting beside the Eifel Tower nibbling macrons, being wooed by a Parisian lover.

*

I decided to host Thanksgiving that year. I invited my sisters and Sabine and her kids, since her husband was slated to be deployed through Christmas. I flew Valentina out and spent a month watching Food TV episodes and pouring over Martha Stuart recipes for everything from sage chestnut stuffing, to honey bourbon brined turkey. We decided on a Dominican/American mashup with *mofongo* and *tostones* to complement our cranberry sauce and pumpkin pie.

Despite making a turkey that I insisted was dry, everyone swallowed it down graciously. Watching all of the most important people in my life, sitting together around my absolutely stretched-beyond-capacity dining room set, I realized we had never had this. We had never had such a cohesive moment of tradition, and family, and just gratitude, together at the same time. We agreed it wouldn't be the last. I just wished Mami was here to see it.

*

Not everyone was feeling the love that holiday season. Since I was off Thanksgiving, that meant I worked Christmas. Ironically, the holidays are synonymous with suicide season in the ED. We had wave after wave of drug overdoses, MHA's, and suicide attempts. One of them still haunts me.

I got pulled into the Trauma Bay because they were only running with one nurse and a tech, and they were getting hammered. The patient I got was a forty-five year old male status post self-inflicted GSW. It was his fourth attempt at committing suicide. The first was by cutting. He sliced his open wrists and hoped to slowly wash his life down his bathtub drain but lost his nerve before he managed to cut deep enough to cause the blood loss necessary to end his life by that means. We patched him up and sent him to the psych ED where he agreed not to hurt himself again. Following that, he tried swallowing a handful of pills, some of which were about a half a month's supply of his wife's Verapamil. At some point, he got frightened, perhaps because he was vomiting uncontrollably, so he called 911 and asked to be taken to the hospital. I guess they chased their asses when he got to us, and they ended up bolusing him with about four liters of fluid, 100 units of insulin, and were running non-stop dextrose, calcium, Dopamine, and Norepi drips. When they transferred him to the ICU, they were considering ECMO if his hemodynamics didn't stabilize, since they couldn't get a systolic above fifty. I had actually had him once in the main ED after a neighbor pulled him out of his car when he noticed smoke billowing from beneath his closed garage door, only to find him passed out behind the wheel. When I read through his history, I discovered that he was pathologically suicidal after his wife and four year old twin daughters were killed by a drunk driver three years prior. Every year, around the time of their death, he makes a gravely serious attempt on his life.

This time he shot himself in the head. Well, he tried anyway. People are rarely able to position a rifle adequately to cause a clean and lethal head shot. Most of the time, they flinch, or their arms aren't long enough to pull a riffle trigger while the business end is in their mouth. This gentleman was no exception, and as he pulled the trigger, the trajectory changed, and he only managed to blow off the lower portion of his face, nose, and sinuses, leaving his eyes to witness what he had done. After he awoke and realized he had again been unsuccessful, he called 911 and gurgled into the receiver until they sent help.

He rolled into the Trauma Bay sitting straight up with a yankauer stuck into what should have been his mouth hole, pulling a steady stream of blood into the portable suction canister. The docs kind of scratched their heads as I stood in stunned horror as he was pushed by, and they debated the best approach to manage his airway. They finally decided to give the induction, lay him down and see if he had chords left, or if they would need to cric him. In the most controlled way possible, we put him to sleep, and they took a look, but could only visualize bloody bubbles, so they aimed the tube for that and prayed.

I monitored him deeply conflicted. He was sick, obviously. But from a purely human standpoint, the man only wanted to be with his family. We could adjust his meds, maybe try some ECT, use whatever cognitive behavioral therapy we had available, but nothing that we do for him could fix his soul. This wasn't a serotonin imbalance. This was a man ripping himself in two to get off this ride, and we just kept strapping him back in. This time, he would continue on his self-destructive path without the face that I'm sure his girls used to kiss softly, and giggle at when they touched his scratchy beard. His lips that he whispered loving musings to his wife with were no longer there.

You try to compartmentalize. You try to tell yourself maybe the guy was an asshole, and he just needs to get over it.

You try not to think of such things as families, and lives, because if you humanize it too much, is begins to settle on you. If you don't stop yourself, you begin to place your family in those scenes. What if Tommy was left behind after Marisol and the baby died? Would he too hate this world so much without them in it, that he would do anything at all to get out of it? It's a razor's edge we walk to maintain empathy, without allowing the person's situation to affect us. In certain areas of nursing, you can almost justify what happens to people. This one got lung cancer because they smoked four packs a day. Note to self, don't smoke. This one had a heart attack because they ate McDonald's for every meal, and they have never seen the inside of a gym. Easy, eat healthy and exercise, done. But not everything that happens to a person is mitigated by controlling one's risk factors. Sometimes shit things happen, and in the case of trauma, sometimes moms driving their daughters back from ballet lessons get hit by drunk drivers. It wasn't fair, and I could barely imagine a fraction of this man's suffering. I don't know why, but this one got to me. For all the tragedy that I had seen while working here, this was the worst. For now, anyway.

*

My calm in the midst of the chaos of the self-inflicted gunshot wound earned me a spot in the Trauma Bay that I reluctantly accepted. Not that I was really given a choice. I was tasked with going through about a hundred hours of modules and getting my trauma certification, which I did as quickly as I was able, since they had me down to orient as soon as the next schedule came out. I worked my ass off, and completely forgot about my birthday until Marisol called, otherwise I would have forgotten it all together. Trauma orientation was a real cluster fuck. It basically consisted of, *here's how you set up an art line,* and *oh, you're getting a patient. Run up to the helipad and meet the flight crew with a stretcher.*

I was terrified all day, every day. The tones would drop, and I would instantly have to pee. It was Pavlovian.

I felt useless. My rock solid, Kathy-approved IV skills were suddenly shaky. I always felt like I couldn't remember where supplies were. I felt completely overwhelmed. I'd lay awake in bed at night staring at the ceiling, praying to Mami and every Saint I could think of to offer intercession on my behalf to help me drift off into a dreamless sleep. It was a dizzying, frenzied, fearful, transition. But I loved every second of it.

The cases were just so incredible. Necrotizing fasciitis, burns, toxic shock syndrome, papillary muscle rupture, amputations, ocular injuries, sucking chest wounds, a freakin' alligator bite in Upstate New York! And wave after merciless wave of every pathology you could think of. It was a trial by fire to be sure.

I can say without hesitation, in that first year there, I was absolutely a trauma junky. No doubt about it. The bloodier the better.

Every time we got a Level 1, I was all over it. MTP? Already called blood bank. Evisceration? I got your saline-soaked sterile gauze right here. Traumatic cardiac arrest? I had the contents of the drawers in the chest opening cart memorized.

I felt like I was immune to the horror of it all. Nothing got to me. An open tib-fib was child's play. I could hold stabilization and then go straight to lunch. We could code a nineteen year old for an hour, and once we were done wrapping her, I could be talking with the tech about my next haircut, not even thinking about the phone call her mother was about to receive. I didn't feel it happening to me, but all this death and lives torn apart in front of me was stealing some of my humanity in twelve hour increments.

There is a hidden cost to working trauma. You keep a loose hold on those that you love once you begin to see that no one is immune. No one is protected.

You start to imagine your reaction if some tragedy were to befall your own loved one. What if EMS rolled in here right now, and started giving you report on a late twenties female struck by a drunk driver, GCS of 3, and you realized it was your sister? What would you do? How would you react? Eventually you come to understand that you probably wouldn't react at all.

Upon that realization, you stop chasing the trauma. You start letting the orientee, or the charge nurse take the bloodier cases, not because you're going soft, because you've seen worse. Nothing surprises you anymore. Let it be someone else's turn. That's not to say that I don't love what I do, it's just that I didn't feel the need to charge in like a bull in a china shop every time I heard the main rotors chunking away on the helipad.

Around that time, I started hanging out with Dr. Emma Stevens. She was now a third year, doing her trauma rotation. We had kind of come up in our ED careers together. Plus, Emma was from Philly originally, and half Latina. Her mother was Puerto Rican. Anytime I would catch myself saying *you don't understand,* she had this way of just looking at me and waiting for me to realize that she did.

Trauma is messy. Both physically and emotionally. It's a completely catalytic environment in which the tiniest spark sets off an eruption of fireworks. Even people you don't think you could ever be attracted to suddenly look sexier, smarter, stronger, when endorphins and emotions are bubbling over. You need to vector that raw sexual tension and direct it somewhere, or else it manifests itself as anger or accusation when something doesn't go right. It's a fine balance to filter your tensions out to be positive, otherwise it's an environment where egos, shortcomings, and emotions can affect the outcome of a trauma. Everything happens so fast, you have to keep your head clear, and keep negativity out of the room, otherwise it ignites, and it destroys everything it touches.

Emma was one of those people with naturally good energy. Her excitement and nervousness came out as a really great dark sense of humor, or as playful flirtation. That's all I thought it was, until she asked me out for drinks after a particularly bad shift.

We had a guy come in one time who stabbed himself in the eye. The kicker wasn't necessarily the injury, it was the fact that he *drove* himself in. When he showed up in triage there were peals of collective horror that rippled through the packed waiting room.

When the triage nurse stood up to see what was coming in, he saw the scissors sticking out of the gentleman's eye socket and moving everywhere his good eye looked. In his shocked state, the triage nurse manhandled him into a wheelchair and ran him back to the Trauma Bay. Before he even got into the stretcher, Emma and I started working to stabilize the scissors and patch the good eye, so he'd quit fucking looking all over the damn place. Once we helped him onto the stretcher, and we asked him what happened, he told us the devil told him to cut his eyes out for watching porn, but he couldn't pull the scissors free to get to work on the other eye, so he asked if we could pull it out for him so he could finish the job. *Hard no sir.*

After Emma called that case out to optho, we got a shooting. A domestic. The mom was dead on scene, the daughter was brought in and we tried everything we could to code her for a while, but upon arrival she was already asystolic and ghostly white, with a hole through and through from her belly and out her back. She was gone before she ever got to us. Emma suspected an aortic injury. No matter how much blood we squeezed into her, we couldn't get her out of asystole. Initially the police arrested the girl's father, believing that he had come in and blasted everyone who happened to be home, but the mom's brother was found shot on scene as well, and just before the he passed away, he used his last breath to explain that it was his sister, the girl's mother, that did this. We spent the morning in lockdown until the police confirmed for certain that the killer was in fact dead on scene.

It sucks to not be able to make a save. There's a quiet truce one makes with the losses. Every nurse and physician has to face the futility of fighting death. Despite doing everything by best practice, and following sound diagnostic reasoning, there are just some cases that defy your every effort. At the end of the day, there are oppositional forces that don't follow the rulebook. Despite our most valiant efforts, despite the miracles of modern medicine, sometimes they just *fail.*

We were both ready for a drink after that domestic, and I think Emma sensed my ETOH deficiency, so she asked me out casually, almost like an afterthought. We stayed at the bar talking until it was nearly last call. At that point, I didn't even care if these drinks came with a happy ending, I just loved talking to someone who understood the deeper truths of what this job entailed. Plus, she was funny, and made me forget about those "deeper truths" for a minute.

For the record, the drinks came with a happy ending.

*

Emma and I dated through her last year of residency. It was a comfortable and easy life intertwined with each other. It helped me understand the politics and the push and shove of medicine. It's not just about being altruistic and doing right by the patient. It's insurance claims and a minefield of unspoken rules and protocols and interdepartmental politics.

Despite the ease of our arrangement, there was an elephant. We were existing together on borrowed time. Emma had put in for several attending slots across the country as she approached her graduation date from residency. She had been exploring openings everywhere from Maryland to Tennessee, to Texas and California. She could have her pick of anywhere she wanted to go. She had been a good medical student, and she made an even better resident, in one of the top residency programs in the country. I tried very hard not to sway her decision in any way.

In the end, she decided to go to Cali. She said she was sick of the sunrise and wanted to be where the sun sets for a while. She asked me to come with her. In the end she begged me to come with her. I wanted to, I really did. Nothing sounded better that riding off into the sunset with this feisty girl. But when I traced the lines of our life together, I could only see that she wanted to make me a kept woman. She wanted me to anchor her to something, because at present, all she had ever known was school and then work. Constantly being evaluated and judged. She just wanted a soft place to land, and she wanted someone to be there when she opened the door at night after a long shift. Who doesn't? But I had my own career to look after, and more often than not, our conflicts in schedule left her annoyed. She constantly talked about the future even very early on in our relationship. Settling down, cutting my hours, taking more vacations, kids and white picket fences. I had tried to tell her that I wasn't there yet. I tried to tell her the kid thing wasn't a foregone conclusion for me, and that I wasn't sure if I was done with my education. I had considered going on to advanced practice, but it was maybe five years down the road and where did that leave a family in the timeline? She would always change the subject from there, hoping that if she invited me along to enough baby showers and housewarming parties, I would see the timeline shorten considerably.

Ultimately, it was an afternoon spent looking at shared homes in San Diego that was our undoing.

We had flown out to California on a Wednesday red eye and had planned on staying through the weekend, driving out to Napa for some wine tours and to explore what all the West Coast fuss was about.

By Thursday, we were touring our fifteenth listing with our realtor who's heels clacked on the hardwoods so loudly everywhere we went that I thought I would have a seizure. I was exhausted. I didn't know what to do with a breezeway. I didn't care if we had a mudroom. I thought a butler's pantry was racist, or at the very least classist. I just felt completely overwhelmed. I sat down on the richly grained bench seat in the entryway to the Danish modern we had been touring. The realtor stepped outside for us to hash out whatever it was that we were quietly squabbling over.

"Emma, I don't know! I don't know how I feel about this stuff! I don't have an opinion about north versus south light. I don't give a fuck if we have a sink in the garage! I grew up sleeping five people in a one-bedroom apartment in Manhattan. My dad wasn't an orthodontist like yours. He was a fucking drug addicted, unemployed, rapist waste of oxygen! I'm just happy to have a bed to sleep in, so stop waiting for me to get all googly eyed over a reading nook, ok? I only want a home with you in it. That's it. That's literally my only requirement. They are all really nice! Ok?! Please baby, just tell me what makes you happy, because you obviously have thought a lot about this, and all I want is for you to be someplace that makes you happy, because when you're happy, I'm happy."

Emma broke down. Tears began to slide down her now splotchy pink cheeks. I got up and wrapped my arms around her.

"Daniela, I'm so sorry," she heaved. "I just wanted to find something that made you as excited as it made me. I just love you. I didn't think this would be so hard. I've been waiting to find something, because when we did, I wanted to ask you to marry me!"

I stopped, frozen, wondering if I had heard her incorrectly.

She was really bawling now. She began to lower herself down on one knee, but I met her there and began kissing her face, snot and all, and then I started to cry.

There it was. She was ready and I certainly was not.

"I'm trying baby, I'm trying to meet you there, but I'm not there yet."

Emma continued to sob as I pulled her into my chest.

Who wouldn't want this? What was wrong with me? Marrying a doctor is every mother's dream for their daughter, even if that doctor was another woman, right? The arrangement spoke of horseback lessons and private school for our future children, and shiny cars, and never having to worry if my rent check would clear, but it wasn't my dream. I was a simple girl. I couldn't ignore the fact that Emma had never wanted for anything in her life. She excelled at everything she put her hand to. She was an ace tennis standout in college, and she went into pre-med on a partial tennis scholarship. She got into University of Michigan Ann Arbor after having the highest MCAT score in her class. I struggled to get through my junior college nursing education. Not that I was ashamed or felt that I was in some way beneath her, but I could see it in her once in a while. She didn't know how to struggle. When things didn't bend themselves to her will, including myself, she got mad. I embraced the struggle. I welcomed it and questioned that something wicked was afoot when things came naturally to me. I was always waiting for the other shoe to drop. I had to fight for everything that I had in my life, and I couldn't sit in this open concept knowing that I was with someone who thought that struggling was unfair somehow.

Being on the physician track is a whole fulminant crisis of self on its own. Although there are other ways to approach it, what I had observed in Emma, and what I had seen from a distance in other physicians, is that they had very few real life experiences on their journey to earn their white coat. They were never rebellious, they conformed at all costs, they worked hard to the point of near self-destruction, their memories of wild parties, skinny dipping, and breaking curfew were few and far between, if not entirely non-existent. They were so laser focused on grades, and AP classes, and sciences, they never learned how to fail. Failure comes at potential collapse of identity, of life, when all your life is running on a zero-fail standard. The pressure to succeed, to specialize, to get the perfect match for residency, the perfect fellowship, to never crack under pressure, to never show fear or emotion or weakness, to never, never fail under any circumstances, to endure malicious bullying by upper levels and attendings, people you aspire to be, people you look up to, well, it's enough to drive you insane. Literally.

I used to find Emma cleaning when I'd get home from work. Normal, right? This was not your average surface clean. This was cleaning to the point of 'out, out damn spot,' Lady MacBeth, wear-a-dent-in-the-granite-countertop level cleaning. She had more idiosyncratic repetitive behaviors than I could count. She didn't deny it or try and hide it from me, but if I would try and interrupt her there was hell to pay. She couldn't relax. She was always on the clock. She had a schedule for her days off, and she was driving me crazy.

When I came home one morning and couldn't find her in her usual haunts, I became nervous. I called throughout the house and got no answer. I finally found her in the guest bedroom scrubbing the baseboards with a rag and some hot soapy water. So hot it could scald your hand.

"Emma baby, I was calling you," I said.

She didn't look up or even realize that I was there. I watched her scrub, and dip, and scrub. I could see the striations and sinews of her deltoids strain with every clawing stroke.

I crouched down beside her and touched her shoulder, and she jumped, startled at the disruption.

"Jesus Christ Daniela, can you knock? You scared the shit out of me!' She gasped.

"Emma, honey, I was calling you all through the house. I called you in here, you didn't even hear me."

"Yeah, well I wasn't expecting you home so early, I was just trying to get this done before you got here."

"Sweetheart, I'm not home early. I had to hold over for Katie. Her babysitter was sick, so she had to wait on her mom to get the kids. I'm almost an hour late."

She glanced at her watch and stood up dismissively.

"Oh, well, ok, so you're home now. Ok, I guess I'll head to the gym and get the groceries. What time will you be up? I wanted to go out to the farmer's market this afternoon so we can get some more of that honey you like."

"Emma baby, I want to sleep. I'm not setting my alarm for the damn farmer's market. I have to work tonight. Did you even sleep last night? What time did you get up? You've got nowhere to be. Why not take the day off for once instead of having this whole fucking minute-by-minute itinerary?"

"We can't both just stay in bed all day like you and work three days a week Daniela. This whole place would go to shit with that thinking."

"Excuse me? *How dare you*! I fucking work my ass off Emma! While you sit on deck and write orders, its nurses like me running my ass off to do your dirty work! I run sundown to sunup, and excuse me for wanting to sleep because I actually give a shit about my health and wellbeing! Don't you fucking go and act like I'm not pulling my weight around here!"

"You have no fucking idea what it's like up there Dani! I'm not just sitting in some ivory tower writing orders! Where the fuck are you when I go in and tell a mother her son is dead? Where the fuck are you when I ask a patient's husband if we can make his wife of fifty years a DNR? You always think shit runs downhill and right in your lap, but what you don't see is that it's raining down on me all fucking day! Not a second of my day goes by where I don't feel like every one of my patients could crash and die because they forgot to tell me one of their thirty medication allergies, or that they take Amioderone and I write them for Levoquin? I pray on my way to work every day, '*don't let me fuck up, don't let me fuck up, don't let me fuck up,*' the whole way there, because one oversight, one hesitation, one little thing that I do could kill somebody! You have no idea what you're talking about Dani!"

I stopped and looked at my feet for a moment and waited for her to finish tongue lashing me. She had never exploded like that. She had never voiced to me her fears or frustrations like that. She just locked them up out of view, choosing instead to read me the highlight reel.

"Do you think I do any less?" I asked quietly. "We risk the same thing. Grab for Versed, pick up Vec. Just because we have orders doesn't mean all that risk is only on you. We risk to."

Hot tears began peeling off trails of foundation from her cheeks. Her frustration and fear and just the massive, massive burden of perfectionism she had been carrying her whole life crushed her. I caught her in my arms and we both slid to the floor crying.

"Something's gotta give baby. We're driving each other nuts. We can't keep working like this and stressing out all the time. We're going to put ourselves in one of those hospital beds, and you know nurses make terrible patients." We both laughed and rolled onto our backs and stared up at the ceiling.

We were both so tired. We were both so burned out. This job will eat you alive if you let it. A hospital system will fire a twenty year veteran nurse because a patient says, "*I don't like how she looked at me,*" and they will blame it on her for lack of empathy, and not being in control of her non-verbal communication. I've seen it happen. Every moment, every interaction you are on stage. I once had a patient pull the curtain open while we were coding the man in the bed next door, and he yelled out to us as we were actively doing CPR.

"Yo, I know you're busy, but I asked you for juice five minutes ago, where's my juice bitch? You gonna drag this on long or get me what I asked you for?" If I could have poured his urinal out on his face like I wanted to and told him, "drink this," I would have.

That's the level of entitlement we deal with on a near constant basis. Even in the face of another human being actively losing his life, some people will only think of themselves. While we absolutely fight the good fight for some really deserving individuals, there are those out there looking to work the system, berating us endlessly, running us ragged, assaulting us, sexually harassing us, reporting us for frivolous injunctions like, '*didn't smile and greet me like she's supposed to,*' or '*she told me to wait when she was doing CPR, even though I asked for juice five minutes ago.*' These are the things that steal your joy. These are the things that burn you out and make you want to leave healthcare all together.

Endless charting, less and less time to see patients, constant demands. Twenty-three year olds asking to be put on a bedpan and have you wipe their ass, when they walked themselves in the room just five minutes before. Stuff like that just kills your motivation. Add that to the chronic stress, the constant heightened awareness and state of hypervigilance you have to stay in, plus the hours, the sleep deprivation, the endless parade of human suffering. It's all too much to put yourself last all the fucking time.

After the shock of Emma's proposal had a chance to dissipate, we sat there in the middle of the foyer of this beautiful home and held each other, wiping each other's tears.

"We need a break," Emma finally admitted.

"Agreed."

We emerged about thirty minutes later to our bewildered realtor, holding hands to keep each other from falling. Emma drove back to the office in the realtor's car and I drove back to the hotel in the rental to collect my things and catch the first flight off the West Coast.

CHAPTER ELEVEN

Rarified Air

I didn't want to leave the ED. I had found myself there, and I prided myself on being the "bad ass ED nurse". Ultimately, after two and a half years there, I had lost a piece of myself. It wasn't the breakup that caused me to lose love for the place that made me the nurse that I am today, it was the burnout. I needed a change. I needed to come back to my humanity. Besides the untold toll that working trauma takes on a person, at some point in your career, the ED makes you jaded. It just does. It's the crush of humanity clawing at you twelve hours a day, it's the constant requests, everyone trying to get one over on you, everyone asking what's taking so long and why are they being ignored. You get to where you don't trust anyone. I've taken care of little old ladies addicted to crack, sweet little second grade school teachers with perfed colons after their dom went raw on them with a giant dildo, a seventeen year old found covered in his parents blood when he killed them on a camping trip and was brought in by the cops for medical clearance because they weren't sure if the blood he was covered in was theirs or his. No one is innocent. Eventually you get tired of the drunks, the rapes, the psych, the abuse, and you want to take care of a person that is just plain sick.

I started looking into making a career change.

"It's a natural progression," I rationalized. But despite having now four years of ED and trauma experience under my belt, I didn't know if I was ready for the acuity of ICU, or if I would like the change of pace.

I shadowed in the OR, I checked out the Cath Lab, I looked at NICU, PICU, even PACU, but none of them felt like a fit. When I called up the nurse recruiter for the sixth time, she finally stopped me.

"Listen, Daniela, I see this exact scenario play out multiple times. You've pigeon- holed yourself in the ED, and nothing can live up to it. We would like to help find a place for you, but you've built up this unattainable standard for yourself that no unit will be able to live up to. You've got to think outside the box a little bit. I don't do this much, since it's such a difficult position to fill, but I have an opening in CVICU I think you might be a fit for. These are hands down the sickest patients in the hospital, and I don't offer the position to just anyone because typically the unit only hires experienced nurses who already come with a CVICU background, or at the very least, a surgical ICU background. Barring that, I think you're tough enough to handle the learning period. I'm not going to lie to you or sugar coat this, this is a hard unit, and they don't take kindly to outsiders. I've had new hires walked right back down to my office after their first day because the nurses decided they weren't a good fit. I don't want to see that happen to you, but I feel like if anyone can handle it, you can."

I considered what she said. The unit was completely outside of my comfort zone. Highly specialized, research driven, device heavy, completely surgical. Nothing about it sounded good to me, but the challenge of sticking it out in a place very few could, piqued my interest. I set up a shadow and talked to Sabine about it that night after we got off our shift.

"I don't know. What do you think? Am I crazy for even considering it? It sounds awful. The recruiter told me straight up, 'if they don't like you, they'll walk you right back down to her office to try something else.' I'm looking for something new, but I don't want to work with a bunch of bitches."

"You know, Daniela, just because its different, doesn't mean it's bad. You have no possible way of knowing if you'll like it unless you see it for yourself. Don't let that recruiter intimidate you. You're ready for the next level. Just see what happens."

The next day, I arrived on the unit for my shadow. I was with Martha, a nurse who worked ED at one point in her career, but eventually found herself in CVICU for the last twelve years. Evidently everyone on the unit had been there for a decade or three. The newest nurse they had had been there five years, so, as you can imagine, turnover wasn't a thing they were used to managing with any sort of frequency, and they weren't used to newcomers.

"So, Daniela, do you have a boyfriend? Any kids?" Martha asked me right out the gate, blinking several times after asking her question, while we sat in awkward silence a moment too long for her to feel comfortable.

"No, Martha, actually my girlfriend and I broke up a few weeks ago and she moved out to California. I'm single. No kids yet," I said casually, blinking several times after I laid it out there.

"Breakups are so hard," Martha said, after a beat, and then she blinked again. I figured I'd just open with it. Get it out there, so it wasn't this ever-unfolding secret to be discovered. I wanted to skip the pretense if I was going to make a new start.

"So, why do you want to leave the ED?" She continued.

"I'm looking for something new and challenging. I have been down there the last four years, and I'm ready to see what else is out there before settling in one specialty for the rest of my career." I explained.

Martha blinked again.

"Well, that's exciting," Martha said with forced enthusiasm.

"Thank you. Yes, I'm very excited for the opportunity."

"Well this is definitely going to be a challenge. Remind me again, have you worked ICU before?"

"No, I haven't. I've done Med/Surg and ED/trauma, but no ICU. I know this is going to be a steep learning curve, but I think I'm ready to take it on."

"Well, it certainly is, but it's not impossible. Look at me. Twelve years later and I'm still standing," she smiled. I smiled back, trapping my breath inside my lungs while I did.

"Well, let's show you a little bit of what we do here."

Martha walked me past a few of the seventeen rooms on the unit. There were more numbers on the monitor than I had ever seen. I didn't even know our monitors could be programmed to display so many values, let alone know what they all meant. The enormous rooms seemed cramped with the number of devices each patient was attached to. Vent, CVVH, LVAD, Swan-Ganz catheter, fourteen different drips running into one patient. I had never even seen most of these things, let alone managed them. I didn't even really know what was going where. I had never seen a patient that looked like this, and Martha acted like this was all completely normal.

We toured a few other rooms. ECMO, total artificial heart, a post-electrocution on hypothermia protocol.

I had seen enough. This was it. I was in. I was so fuckin' in. I wanted to one day possess the wherewithal to quickly swap out dialysate and efferent fluid and not panic at which line went to which bag. I wanted to titrate eleven drips at a time and not have to ask the doctor what rate to set it to. I wanted to know this stuff. I wanted to be here.

I met with Nathan the manager after Martha had given me the grand introduction to everything. Nathan seemed easy going and unlike my first manager, Melissa, or anything at all like my manager in the ED who I tried very hard to only meet at my interview. He gave no rousing speech and made me no promises. He only said if I can stick around long enough to really learn this, I'd be counted among the top one percent of nurses as far as clinical knowledge goes. That was all I needed to hear.

The nurse recruiter called me that evening with an offer. Ayanna was home with me when the call came in. I tried to keep a poker face and not let her know how excited I truly was to get out of the ED. She poured us each a glass of prosecco before I got off the phone.

She looked at me, eyes wide, smiling ear to ear.

"Well?!"

"I got it," I finally sighed, as she came around the counter and gave me a joyous dancing hug.

We toasted to new beginnings. I promised to pick up shifts when she was working. She called me a liar. She knew me so well.

*

When I got to the CVICU, I didn't know where to go. I had no badge access to any of the doors, and I couldn't even get onto the unit without asking someone to help me.

I found Lindsay in the break room after one of the techs showed me where it was. She looked even younger than me, but starched and pressed as if she had just walked out of a J. Crew catalogue.

We made our introductions and I quickly realized I didn't have a locker to put my things in, so I crammed in with her until we could figure something out. We went out to get report from Rianne on our two patients.

For the first time in my career, we got report and I had no idea what was said. I couldn't tell you what surgery they had (probably their heart, but I couldn't attest to that in a court of law), I couldn't tell you what meds they were taking, or what we needed to do. There were so many acronyms I was completely lost. Even just looking at the patient, if it weren't for his vital signs and the whoosh of the ventilator, I would think the guy was dead.

For the first day I just shadowed. Unfortunately for me, Lindsay was a quizzer, and there was nothing in life I hated more than a pop quiz. The worst part was, she hadn't taught me anything yet, so I felt completely stupid.

"Do you know what this is? Do you know how this works? If my hemodynamic parameters are this, what would this be?"

"I don't know. I don't know. I don't know" I was like a broken record. Not only were the quizzes brutal, and made me feel like a complete failure, my knowledge deficit was broadly on display in full view of the patient, their families, and the docs and any other nurse in earshot. I was suddenly very aware of every little puff of air escaping from people's nostrils, every eye roll, every stifled smirk. I felt like I was already losing, and it was only my first day. I felt like I had made a huge mistake. Moreover, I felt completely useless. The charting system was completely different than what we used on the floor or in the ED, I didn't know where to start with an assessment, I didn't even know what I didn't know. With that degree of ignorance, it would be unsafe for me to even do something as simple as a bed change. I was completely overwhelmed, and I was starting to have some major doubts about my ability to this job.

By the end of the shift, I was exhausted, and more than a little overwhelmed. I was trying to reign in my frustration, and the sense of impending doom that was percolating deep in my chest.

Ayanna called me to check in after my first day. Not wanting to give away exactly how much I loathed it, I deflected her questions with one-word answers, and proceeded to grill her on her assignment back home in the ED. I wanted to know every patient on her list. What was their chief complaint, what were their presenting signs and symptoms, what were their labs and vitals? Her answers ultimately made it worse, because it was just a reminder of what I had left behind. I loved emergency medicine. I loved the hilarity, and the tragedy, and just being part of the solution. When patients come to the ICU, they already have a diagnosis. They are no longer a mystery, and anything you go poking around for is not well received. But I loved a good mystery. I loved problem solving with the docs and seeing if I couldn't figure it out before they did.

I had one patient that came in from a nursing home with altered mental status. He was hypotensive, and they were starting him as a sepsis workup, but I went up and talked to the doc and said, "ya, know, for a guy who's been in a nursing home for a long time, he sure is tan. Like, JFK tan. Do you think he has Addison's?" And sure as shit, his potassium and cortisol and everything else were way off, and he was having an Addisonian crisis. Totally undiagnosed previously.

That's why I loved it. My voice, my assessment, my thoughts on the matter actually counted for something. I was part of the team. Here I was no one. My opinion was meaningless. No one wanted to hear my thoughts on anything. I was just there to do my vitals, I&Os, and pass meds. I had no clinical collateral. I was just a body with a nursing license. License to shut the hell up was more like it.

The next day, I was a train wreck. My hair was a frizzy poof that refused any attempt at submitting to my will. I had broken out in the middle of the night, and had two large, cystic acne outcroppings front and center on my face, that no attempt to spackle would camouflage. I had slept fitfully. My coffee wasn't working. It was already a bad day and it was only 0605.

I came in to Lindsay's perfectly groomed tresses, dewy skin, and sparkling post- orthodontia smile. To make matters worse, she and the tech, Mindy were fervently planning their triathlon schedules in the middle of the break room. Disgusting.

I went out ahead of them to get report, and the night nurse refused to give it to me, and instead made me wait for Lindsay like a child waiting for her mom. I stood there awkwardly while Lindsay dawdled until the last possible minute. Ultimately, I was glad I waited because I still had no fucking clue what anyone was even talking about.

Time marched forth like this: me, stupid, doesn't know anything, confidence waning, shattering, waking up, doing it all again. I felt like the whipping boy. I'd come in, take my beating, arrive the next day and say, "thank you ma'am, may I have another?"

Unlike my time on the floor as a new nurse, I was like an empty vessel, just waiting to be filled up. I was allowed to be ignorant. I wasn't supposed to have all the answers. I was allowed to be a novice. Even in the ER, the expectation was never that I was supposed to know how to do any of this without being taught. Here, it's like everyone expected me to know the difference between an SVR and an SvO2 the minute I walked onto the unit. They expected me to know what the significance of an elevated PAD or wedge meant. Wave forms were suddenly a thing I was supposed to care about. A patient that to me, looked incredibly concerning, was 'totally expected,' and not worth investigating further. Not only did I know nothing, what I did know was meaningless. In fact, all of my prior experience was viewed as a handicap, being that most of it had to be unlearned in favor of what these nurses considered to be "best practice." I just felt hopelessly lost. And alone too. I found myself missing Emma. I missed being needed and wanted and having someone to discuss a case without feeling like I was being patronized.

My life raft during this time, was that I found that I could retain about five new things a shift. Really, not much more than that. But I clung to those five things as my foundation and tried to build from there every day. As inadequate and slow going as that was, there was a Filipina named Evelyn, who told me, "don't get down on yourself. This all seems like a tangled mess and like nothing has to do with anything else, but eventually, it will all come together. It will be like a little bird alighting on your shoulder, and you'll come to me one day and say, 'Evelyn, the bird has landed!'"

"I hope so," was all that I could say, but I couldn't see it. I was being barraged by so much information at once, it all seemed fragmented, single facts in isolation, nothing interconnected. Eventually, as I neared the end of my orientation, I remember feeling it.

I had a patient with severe right sided heart failure. All of his hemodynamics on his Swan were fucked up. Diastolic dysfunction, screaming high PA pressures and CVP, and suddenly, the little bird, that seemed to be flying about erratically in my mind, got his shit together and that little bastard finally landed. It all made sense. PAD, SVR, MAP, CVP, SvO2, Starling's law, everything, I finally got it! It was a major shift in the universe, and from there, I could finally rebuild.

I poked my head out of my room and found Evelyn and told her.

"Evelyn! It landed! The bird landed!"

"Good!" She laughed. "Of course it did!"

I made it off orientation after that, but truly that was just the first of many hurdles thrown in front of me.

The midlevels that covered on night shift, which was what I hired into, didn't like me. That's the long and short of it. They just didn't like me. They didn't feel like I provided the same level of care as their senior nurses. No shit. I was still learning. But they couldn't be bothered with my learning curve and had absolutely no qualms with ransacking my rooms looking at my exact drip rates, comparing them to my MAR, and tearing me a new asshole if they ever found a discrepancy. It was always one question behind. Any time I'd approach them to ask for clarification, or to report a finding, they'd lob question after question at me, and when I'd tell them I'd get the answer for them, they'd scoff loudly and say, *I'll look for myself.*

I was so irritated, and absolutely exhausted by it. They were hazing me. Waiting for me to mess up. Riding my ass like fucking Seabiscuit, sending me after one thing, then another, then another, then going behind my back and getting a senior nurse to do something I was already in the process of doing, just to make me look incompetent and with the goal of humiliating me. Any time I would ask for something, they would act like I was asking for the moon, like doing me any kind of favor was an insufferable chore. And it's not like I was asking for anything more of them than to simply do their job. I was furious. I had nights when I would get ready for work, and just sit on the stool in the kitchen and stare off into space, and before I knew it twenty minutes had passed. I could practically hear Mami say *come on babygirl, you gotta do this. Do one more for me. Let's get after this thing! This one's gonna be good! I can feel it!* And she'd force me to walk to my car, and stand in the driveway waving to me while I pulled out and begrudgingly drove off to a job I felt like I was drowning in. During that relentless dark period, when I felt like every shift was worse than the last, when I felt like I couldn't make it twelve more hours, her love was there pushing me along, telling me she was proud of me. Were it not for her spirit giving me that nudge out the door, I don't know if I could have survived that first year.

One night, at change of shift, I picked up my assignment from Dustin, an experienced nurse who had probably one of the best heads on his shoulders in the unit. He was actually nice and genuine, and he took exceptionally good care of his patients.

His report on my one patient was that she was now day two post-op S/P CABG x2. Easy peasy. She had been up all day, walked several laps around the unit, and had loads of family in to visit her. She even ate all her lunch and dinner with no problem and was up and sitting in the geri-chair still because she had requested to stay up until she was ready for bed. She was alert and oriented and would use the call light when she was ready to lay down. She was extubated and de-lined yesterday on day one, and all of her numbers looked great before they pulled the Swan. The plan was to get her out to the stepdown unit in the morning. The only thing a little off with her was that she had been drooling copious amounts of oral secretions throughout the day, and they weren't sure why. He thought it was weird, but she was self-suctioning, and was able to swallow to eat and drink just fine. He assured me that despite the drool, she was protecting her airway. He had mentioned it to the team on rounds, but they just said if she kept up, we could try some scopolamine patches or something, but they were otherwise unconcerned.

My other patient was post op day one, and a little sicker, so I went to see him first. When I went to assess my lady, she looked like absolute dog shit. Oral secretions were literally pouring out of her mouth, and she had snoring respirations. She was definitely not protecting her airway. I suctioned her mouth and tried to wake her up, but she was barely responding. I ran out to get the PA Amy who was on that night and was one of my main detractors.

"Hey, Amy, sorry to bother you, but the patient in eight looks awful. She's drooling everywhere and she's not protecting her airway."

"What does that even mean, exactly?" Amy hissed, not even looking away from her computer to acknowledge what I was saying.

"It means," I hesitated, *what the fuck do you think it means bitch?* "it means, she's, um, not protecting it?" I didn't even know what to say.

She finally spun in her desk chair and faced me, to give me the full weight of her reprimand.

"You can't just come to me at 1905 and say, '*this patient's not protecting her airway.*' That literally means nothing to me. Is she hypoxic? Is her sugar low? Give me something! I don't want to hear your stupid opinion on things if you don't have a single piece of objective data to support your nonsense. Get out of here and go do something with yourself."

My heart pounded in my chest. My face was on fire, and tears were stinging in the corner of my eyes. I didn't possess the vocabulary to adequately describe what I was seeing. This lady looked like shit, and she wasn't the patient Dustin described. Not by a long shot. Her GCS was about a five. She looked bad, and every fiber of my being was telling me shit was about to go downhill fast.

I went to get a blood glucose on her. 149. I went and told Amy.

"Ok. And? Did you get an ABG?"

I turned on my heel and slunk back to my room. Numbers. All they cared about were numbers. No one actually wanted to look at a patient.

The ABG was back, and it actually didn't look that bad. I handed it to her.

"Ok. So, she's fine. So, you were wrong. Shocker." She said and went back to checking her email.

I couldn't take her condescension a second longer. I went and got my charge nurse, Bernice.

She had already heard the whole exchange and seemed to be hanging back waiting to see how I handled it.

"Excuse me Bernice, I'm having a bit of a problem in room 6, with Mrs. Landry. She just doesn't look good. The report I got from Dustin doesn't match the patient I got. I told Amy, but she won't come and see her because her numbers all look good, but I just have a bad feeling. She's up in the chair still because she was tired earlier. Can you just give me a hand getting her back to bed?"

"Sure thing darlin'," Bernice cooed, causally.

As soon as Bernice's toes hit the threshold of Mrs. Landry's room, she stopped dead in her tracks.

"She look like dog shit," she said in her deep Jamaican tenor.

"Yeah," I said.

"Let's get her in bed, fast."

I slapped defib pads on her before we moved her just to be safe, and Bernice and I half dragged her and flopped her into bed. As soon as we got her horizontal, she coded.

I couldn't get the side rail down do adequately do compressions, so I hopped on top of her and straddled her to get some force going behind my CPR. The first pump broke probably all of her ribs. Oof. You never fully get used to that.

Amy came barging in.

"What the hell is going on in here? Why didn't anyone get me?" She demanded.

I had swapped out compressions with Denny, the tech, and I looked her straight in the eye and said, "I tried. You were more interested in your email."

She shot daggers from her eyes and ran out to call the surgeon. You could hear him screaming at her through the receiver, which was probably the most satisfying thing I had heard all week.

We eventually got her back into an organized rhythm and floated a Swan, and found that her cardiac index was 0.8. I don't know if you know anything about cardiac index or not, but that's bad. Like, not compatible with life bad.

The surgeon came in from home and we raced her to the OR where she wound up with an open chest on VA ECMO.

Now when I ask Amy to come and see my patients, she actually gets off her ass to see them.

Mrs. Landry was a test. I passed. It took my patient nearly dying, but I passed. That was the thing about this unit that got to me. In the ED, when you come in with some experience, even if it's just a year of med/surg, people trust you. You're a nurse. You passed your boards. This isn't your first day. You were given the benefit of the doubt that you brought some value to the group unless proven otherwise. Up here, in CVICU, the rules changed. Even with five years of nursing experience, countless traumas, countless critically ill patients successfully managed, you were shit until proven otherwise.

*

I may have won the battle for respect on the unit for that shift, but I certainly had not won the war. The coming year would bring a thousand glimmering sparkles of light, followed by vast expanses of darkness. I hated it. But just like a kid hates broccoli, I knew it was good for me in the end.

The incessant jabs and pettiness became easier to avoid, and less biting as time wore on. The only recourse I had was to continue to improve my practice. I learned early on that if you ask too many questions, people assume you don't know much. Asking questions is obviously extremely important, and you should never just act on an assumption or something you're not entirely sure of, but perhaps the greatest lesson I learned, was to ask once I had at least made a good faith effort to find the answer myself first. In time sensitive, critical situations obviously, the cult of public opinion be damned, *ask the fucking question*, but when life and limb are not imminently threatened, see if you can't figure it out before you ask to be handed the answer. Yes, it slows you down, yes, it takes longer, but generally you'll get the right answer the first time, and you'll be less likely to forget it in the long run having done your own leg work.

That being said, the unspoken rules, the flaming hoops to jump through became navigable, and eventually the place grew on me. It took a solid year of loathing every minute of it, but ultimately, I fell in love with the heart. It's just so dang practical. It's just a pump. A pump that is infinitesimally complex, and sensitive to things like cold, heat, dehydration, electrolytes, ischemia, chamber size, muscle strength, infection, electricity, fear, love, excitement, it is our most perfect secret teller. It does so much, so well, but when it goes wrong, God, the whole thing goes wrong. There's a lot we can do in between the good and the bad and the getting it back to good, which is why I like it. I feel useful. I feel like I can actually do something, and it's damn near instant gratification. Your Swan numbers tell you everything. Give pain medicine, HR goes down, give fluid, SVR goes down, give inotrope, CI goes up. It's incredibly rewarding to be able to look up and say, 'I did that.' But, just because we can, does not necessarily mean we should.

I found that out with one particularly gut-wrenching case. We got a young guy as a patient who had viral cardiomyopathy. His heart became so overwhelmed by the infection that it just dilated out and could no longer pump effectively. We placed a balloon pump and once his infection was under control, we took him to the OR for LVAD placement, which he lived with quite well for a few months. When a heart became available for transplant, he was the perfect candidate, and the donor was a perfect match. They took him down to the OR, put him to sleep, and once the donor was prepped, the surgeon went and looked at the donor heart, and gave the ok to start the harvest. While the transplant team took the donor's kidneys, liver, corneas, and skin grafts, our patient was in the adjoining OR suite having his heart removed while he was on bypass. When the surgeon returned to pull the donor heart, he came back and found it barely moving, under resuscitated, and completely non-viable.

The old heart couldn't be replaced, they didn't have another heart on standby, and he couldn't stay on bypass forever. The only option was a total artificial heart, but due to his extremely large body habitus, it wasn't a great option.

After Dr. Sisson went to speak to the family, his mother dropped to her knees and begged through hysterical sobs to try, even though he knew it wasn't going to be a good outcome. He agreed to try.

It was awful. He came up spewing more pulmonary edema than I had ever seen in my life. Liters upon liters of pink, frothy sputum. We were swapping out suction canisters every fifteen minutes. We had the OR send up the big five liter dumpster canisters and within minutes we were filling those too. We ran the total artificial to its absolute max rate to try and generate some kind of cardiac output. It sounded like a freight train standing still, spinning on the track.

We let his mom in to see him. He looked horrendous. We were beyond mass transfusion protocol. He was bleeding, we were losing fluid from pulmonary edema, we could barely maintain any sort of preload. We were just dumping volume into him. His eyes were swollen shut. His hands looked like water balloons. His scrotum looked like a cantaloupe about to burst. His feet were like hams.

I thought I knew what she would do. I thought she would stroke his hair and whisper her goodbyes, knowing full well he was beyond saving. But a mother's love, and denial are powerful drugs.

He never did stabilize. Dr. Sisson tried to explain the gravity of the situation to his mom, but she wasn't ready.

"I don't want to hear one negative word out of your mouth doctor, not one word. You come to me with good news or you don't come to me at all," she admonished. He walked away.

When he came back in the morning, we had limped him through the night with one hundred and sixty-eight units of blood products. Red cells, platelets, FFP, cryo, whatever we could fill his tank with, we gave. We cleaned out the entire blood bank of the trauma center, and the blood bank down the street, and we were pulling from the one across town.

When I was working trauma, I once had a trauma surgeon tell me not to spike a second bag of PRBCs because a patient was "unsalvageable." "Save it for someone who can actually use it," he said before he called time of death.

If there were ever a case of a patient being "unsalvageable," it was this one.

When the surgeon saw him, and the pile of empty blood bags on the floor, and our pitiful hemodynamic numbers, he went down to prep the OR to start ECMO on him.

In the coming weeks we played a very scrupulous game of fluid dynamics. Put enough in the tank to flow through the TAH, and the ECMO circuit, but not so much that it fills up his lungs.

When I say weeks, I mean he lived like that for weeks. Not alive, but not dead either. We circulated, we oxygenated, we perfused, but eventually everyone had to come to the table and acknowledge that despite every intervention we have available, at some point, a patient will declare themselves. His kidneys failed. Start him on CVVH. His eyes were so underperfused they actually died. They literally shriveled up in his skull. They looked like slimy grey jellybeans. So, we sewed his eyes shut since he was too unstable to go to the OR for an enucleation. Eventually his liver failed, and his gut died. That was when he finally declared himself. He screamed it. *No more* he said.

When the day came, we anticipated a knockdown dragout. We had security on standby. We had a wheelchair in the corner ready to scoop her up and take her to the ED if she fainted. But, all of our planning was for naught. She said her goodbye and that was that. No histrionics, no falling out. Just *goodbye son.* And oh Jesus, my heart. As we watched him suffer, we all 'tsk'ed our tongue, but if that was your kid, and you knew there was one more step, one more tube, one more hope, why wouldn't you try? Would you hate yourself more for making them suffer, or would you hate yourself more for not trying? I don't know. We all shake hands with the devil from time to time. It's hard to say in that situation what you'd be willing to agree to. As a nurse, I feel that it's my professional duty to prevent suffering at all cost, but it's all suffering. Getting an IV is suffering. GI distress from antibiotics is suffering, giving birth is suffering, but in the end, you forget the suffering when there is a positive outcome.

The reality is, what I see as only the shell of a man, limping along on every man-made intervention to prolong his perceived suffering, his family will forever see their grandfather, their brother, their beloved husband through all those tubes and wires. Those are just accouterment. They don't know what full scale AV ECMO does. To them, it's just a box at the foot of the bed. Their dad is still right there. Listening. Dreaming. For them, just being this side of the tulips is a meaningful recovery. They'll worry about the million plus dollar medical bill another time. Or they won't worry about it at all. Their concern is in their tomorrows. It's their granddaughter's graduation, their son's wedding, their niece's bat mitzvah.

Ethicists and scholars have debated these issues for decades now that our technology seems to be gaining some ground on the Almighty Himself. Are we tempting fate? Playing God? Contributing to the mounting cost of the healthcare crisis?

Above my pay grade. Don't know, don't care. You got a patient, I'm gonna save their ass (unless they're a DNR. That's a whole other deal).

In the ED, when I was coding a patient, the minute the doc would say, 'does anyone have any further suggestions?' I would never speak up. What kind of quality of life are they coming back to? Why let them *suffer*? But I've seen dozens of patients arrive on our unit looking like something we would have called time of death on in the ED without hesitation, but hypothermia protocol, ECMO, LVADs, RVADs, TAHs, they're game changers. It's hard to call someone "unsalvageable" after seeing them turn around on ECMO, go home, rehab, and then come back and shake our hand a month later to tell your unit thank you for saving their life. It definitely shifted my level of commitment in not giving up. You tell me to fight, I'll fight.

*

In the past year I had learned so much. I was running hemodynamic numbers in my head, calculating out drip rates, fluid losses, ventilator settings, MAPs, SVRs, it was a point I never thought I would arrive at. I had seen so much, done so much, learned so much, but it put me in a bad headspace as an otherwise young woman. I feel like I missed my twenties entirely. When you're on this work treadmill of twelve hour shifts, covering staffing shortages, and just the pressure to maintain a presence on the unit and look like a go-getter, comes at a personal loss. Doing the work of finding yourself away from the trauma and suffering you see every day is difficult. Sickness seems normal. It normalizes stress and tragedy, and if you're not stepping away to discover, *that's not normal*, you can wind up in pretty dire straits.

CHAPTER TWELVE

Acute on Chronic

Being a workaholic is a disease. You're addicted to the success, to the skillset and expertise experience brings you, to the gratification of a marginally fatter paycheck, to the passing accolade of having a colleague say, 'she's a hard worker.' That colleague doesn't know that you missed spending last Christmas with your family, or the five Christmases before that, or that you missed your anniversary, or that your own birthday came and went with no acknowledgement whatsoever.

What's that worth? Who reimburses you the life you are missing out on? Can you write that off as a tax deduction? Once that stuff is gone, you never get it back. We wear our workaholism in healthcare like a badge of honor. We brag about how many hours we worked in a week, or how few hours we slept, or how many IVs or traumas we got. When we leave a unit, or retire, or get fired, nobody even feels the loss by the time the next schedule rolls out. Our job gets posted the minute HR finds out we died. Our hospital will have a vacancy listed before the ink is dry on our obituary.

To stave off the gnawing sense of loss that whittles us away bite by bite, twelve hour shift by twelve hour shift, as we surrender our time, our memories, the genuine emotions that we suppress and laugh away, we develop a thick skin, and a dark as night sense of humor. It's a powerful coping mechanism for dealing with the fact that you care more about the patient laying in that bed than you do for yourself.

Burnout. It's a black hole of apathy, anger, pent up resentment. It is a steeping distain for the bureaucracy, the micro management, the needy fists clawing at you constantly begging for ice chips, pain medications, fresh sheets, a recliner chair for the family member that doesn't like the plastic seat, footie socks, a fruit cup, and another request to speak to the doctor for the third time. It's a backlash to the snarky comments, the lack of interest in the report you give, the meds that didn't get passed on the prior shift, the refusal to meet your gaze, the gossip, the pettiness, the broken promises and broken equipment. It all whips to stiff peaks until you feel like you're being smothered by the thousands upon thousands of tiny grains of sand of irritation that eventually rub your flesh clean off, leaving you raw and exquisitely pained with the addition of even one more grain. The only way to escape burnout is to remove yourself from it.

I took a vacation. I went and talked to my manager Nathan I said exactly that. I was burned out and I needed a vacation. The only non-bereavement time off I had taken in my entire time as a nurse was one PTO day to move out of my old apartment.

I spent three days with Marisol and Tommy and my new niece Emily who I had only met at her christening two years before. I drove another few hours down to Manhattan to see Valentina and meet her boyfriend Kent, a musician and sometimes craft beer brewer trying to upstart a label with some of his buddies in Brooklyn. I felt like a third wheel, but apart from Kent's handlebar mustache, I liked him. I could see why Valentina did too.

When I drove back home after my visit, I felt like I could finally breathe again. I had enough perspective to finally look back through the vignettes that made up the chapters of my life and I saw a plan in place for me. I saw tragedy and triumph, I saw victory and loss, I saw friendships, and lovers, and so many lessons learned. I felt confident in who I had become, and I felt ready to tackle this monster that was CVICU. I felt better about where I was in the learning curve. I was definitely over the hump, but I still had so much to learn. I was finally settling in and making friends for the first time since I got there. Evelyn and I hung out regularly, and I came to love Bernice like the mother I no longer had. I was still in touch with William and Sabine and Ayanna. Our friendship consisted of texting each other nursing memes and promising to get drinks and then never making time to do it, but when we did break out of that crazy place, we were always better for it.

I started dating again. It took me a while, but I finally felt alright putting myself out there.

There was a cop that was guarding a patient prisoner that stayed on our unit for over a month. Her name is Cici. Well, it's actually Cecilia, but she goes by CiCi because it's what her brother Richie called her when he was a toddler and it stuck with her ever since. She was born and raised in the Bronx, so she's a tough cookie by birthright, which makes her kind of a natural pick to be a cop. She's a loud Italian who makes anyone within earshot laugh, including Bernice who doesn't laugh for anyone. And God, does this girl look good in uniform. We're doing good. She actually remembered me from my days down in the ED. She tried to shoot her shot back then and ask me out while I was working a trauma she brought in. The patient was under arrest and she was waiting for us to give med clearance following a DUI which led to a rollover MVC that killed his passenger. I was with Emma at the time and had to decline her kind offer, but I remember her boldness, and that naughty little smile. When she asked me out this time, I accepted without hesitation. She took me to play mini golf, and I did terrible, but we kissed over some frozen custard we grabbed as we were wrapping up our night, and I was pretty much in it from there. We've barely been apart since then. If I'm not staying over at her place she's staying at mine. At this point, I forgot what it's like to rollover in bed and not find her hand to hold.

Cici doesn't necessarily understand all of the medical stuff that I do, but she likes hearing my stories, and I like hearing hers. Our roles are amazingly similar in some aspects. We're both just trying to help people out. We're trying to save the world on some level. Or at least save ourselves in the saving. She understands the weight of tragedy and what it means to be married to your career.

We tried taking it slow at first. But I like her, and I like who I am with her, and we feel better when we're together. I tried to hold back this time around, and not go straight for the deep end, but something in our time together felt familiar, like coming home. Not like this clawing need, but like being held, and safe, and eventually space didn't feel like something I needed. I always felt like my relationships were an escape. A distraction from dealing with my bullshit. I liked my world better when someone was pulling me away from my responsibilities. With Cici, I felt like my bullshit wasn't so shitty. I felt like I made peace with it, and for the first time, I felt like I liked the real world better than how I thought it should be.

I met her family about two months ago, and we've been going over there every Sunday for dinner. Her mom is an awesome cook, and her Italian food is doing a number on my hips but Cici doesn't seem to mind. They're like the perfect family I never had. Being just welcomed in like that, without all the pretense is amazingly comforting. It's like a hug. Her two burly brothers Ricardo and Leo are pretty great too and having that brotherly energy around me feels really nice somehow. I love it here. I hope I can hold onto this one a while.

ABOUT THE AUTHOR

Anna Fares is a Registered Nurse whose career started in New York State and led her to Florida where she is currently practicing as a flight nurse both in civilian helicopter Emergency Medical Services, and as a flight nurse for the United States Air Force Reserves. Anna has been a Registered Nurse since 2009 and has worked in Medical/Surgical, Emergency, Trauma, Cardiovascular Intensive Care, Rapid Response, and Flight specialties. She holds advanced certifications in Emergency and Flight nursing. Anna has a love and passion for nursing and hopes this book inspires others to view nursing as a calling, and encourages new nurses to see the integral role they play in caring for patients. Anna is married to Ali Fares, a career long ED nurse whom she credits with much of the success and stamina she has found in her nursing career. Anna has three children Aaron, Matt, and Lilly who remind her every day why she gets up and does what she does. A lifelong lover of poetry and creative writing, this is Anna's first novel.

Made in the USA
Middletown, DE
08 November 2020

23499523R00146